Finding Grace

Finding Grace

A Novel

AMBER WELLIN

This book is a work of fiction. The names, characters and events in this book are the products of the author's imagination or are used fictitiously. Any similarity to real persons living or dead is coincidental and not intended by the author.

Finding Grace
Published by Amber Wellin

ISBN (paperback): 9781662957673
eISBN: 9781662957680

DEDICATION

To my husband, Clint. This book would not be possible without you. Thank you for encouraging me, believing in me, and pushing me to have faith in myself. You are my greatest blessing. I love you.

ACKNOWLEDGEMENTS

First and foremost, I would like to acknowledge Jesus Christ, my Lord and Savior. I am nothing without His grace and the guidance of the Holy Spirit. Thank you, God, for equipping and blessing me with this opportunity.

I would like to express my deepest gratitude to the friends, family members, and colleagues who served as beta readers. Your feedback and suggestions have helped make this book possible, and I am forever grateful.

I would also like to express a special, heartfelt thank you to my friend and colleague, Amy Mayes. Thank you for not only serving as a beta reader but for also serving as my proofreader. I sincerely value the time and effort you put forth to help my dream come true.

Finally, to all the readers who embark on the journey that is *Finding Grace*, thank you. My prayer is that this book will be as much of a blessing to read as it was for me to write.

But he said to me, "My grace is sufficient for you, for my power is made perfect in weakness." Therefore I will boast all the more gladly of my weaknesses, so that the power of Christ may rest upon me.

—2 Corinthians 12:9 (ESV)

PROLOGUE

Grace lay completely still, the cold ceramic tile cool against her burning skin. She didn't dare open her eyes. Her pulse pounded a frantic, deafening cadence in her chest and in her head. Her right arm was tucked beneath her in an awkward position, but she couldn't make herself move. Not yet. She worked to inhale oxygen into her lungs, but the constricting pain in her ribs made the effort feel like a knife piercing her side. If she cried out, it would only make things worse.

She sucked in a sharp but silent breath at the hot, wet liquid streaming down her face. Her mind worked to process what was happening. Was she bleeding? Her frantic heart somehow pounded even harder. *No. No. No.* An open wound was more difficult to hide, especially on her face. As the wetness reached her lips, she breathed a hesitant sigh of relief. The salty taste confirmed it was only tears. No blood this time.

As she continued to lie motionless, sprawled uncomfortably on the hard floor, her sweat-dampened hair blanketed one side of her face, shielding her from view. The bathroom floor hid the other side. He wouldn't be able to see her tears. Good. He didn't like crying. Tears only served to flare his anger further. Right now, she desperately needed to avoid anything that would make the situation worse.

Keeping her eyes closed, she listened as he paced nearby. Every nerve ending in her body was pulled taut. *Please leave. Please leave. Please leave.* She repeated the silent plea over and over in her mind. Finally, after what seemed like an eternity, she heard his footsteps move toward the door. She heard the click of the door opening and the bang of it slamming shut. She didn't even flinch at the sound. She was accustomed to it. This was her life.

Hesitating only a moment longer, she slowly began the agonizing process of uncurling her body from the awkward position she had landed in. Her back and right side screamed in protest. Pushing herself up from the floor into a sitting position was almost unbearable. The pain stole her breath, and a wave of nausea threatened to overtake her. The room around her spun like a top. She pinched her eyes shut, trying to will the dizziness away. She had to get up. She had to pull herself together. Her girls needed her, and she couldn't let them see her this way. She had managed to shield them so far, and that wasn't about to change now.

Forcing her limbs into cooperation, she slowly rose to her feet. The fierce ache in her side was making it nearly impossible to take the deep breaths she desperately needed. *Breathe, Grace. Breathe.* She coached herself through the pain, focusing on the need to get to her girls.

Turning to the mirror, she gently wiped away the remnants of her tears. Her eyes were red rimmed and puffy, but her face was otherwise free of marks. She wished the same could be said for the rest of her. She didn't dare raise her shirt to look. She already knew she was black and blue.

Raising her arms to comb through her matted hair brought on a fresh wave of pain. She sucked in sharply on reflex, but that only made the searing knife in her side stab deeper. Taking shallow breaths, she made a second attempt to comb out the knots. As the comb slid over a tender spot on her scalp, she tensed. Using her fingertips, she found the painful lump developing on the back of her skull. She must have hit her head when she fell. She needed to get some ice on it, but that wouldn't happen anytime soon. She had dinner to finish and dishes to wash.

Laying the comb aside, she stared into the mirror. She hardly recognized herself anymore. A hollow ache filled her chest as the burning behind her eyes intensified. Taking a shuddering breath, she willed the tears not to start again. This was her life. Her daily existence. She had put herself in this position, and she had to live with it. Relief was not coming. She was on her own.

CHAPTER 1

G race sat in the hospital emergency room staring blankly at the gray wall across from her, tears dampening her cheeks. She couldn't seem to focus on any one thing. It was like being in an overcrowded concert with music blaring while at the same time, she could have heard a pin drop. She knew there was commotion around her, people coming and going. Somewhere in the distance she could hear a siren. Was it an ambulance? Her mind couldn't seem to process the sound. Across the room, she could hear the faint clicking of someone typing on a keyboard. She could hear people talking, but it all seemed indecipherable. Nothing was making sense.

Her gaze briefly wandered the wall she was absentmindedly staring at. Framed portraits of various landscapes filled the space, showcasing serene lakes and majestic mountains. Her mind worked to grasp the peace captured within the photographs. She felt herself exhale a long sigh before sucking in another breath, tasting the sterile environment around her. She drew her eyes away from the wall.

Shifting her gaze to the chairs scattered around the waiting room and the slick, blue material covering them, her mind became fixated on the color. She vaguely remembered reading somewhere that blue was meant to have a calming effect. Looking down at the chair she was sitting in, she ran her hand along the smooth vinyl. Her thoughts grew quiet but only momentarily. She could hear a voice gently saying her name, slowly pulling her back. She felt as if she were in a long, dark tunnel, the faint echo of the voice drawing her out.

"Mrs. Thompson? Mrs. Thompson? I'm so sorry. I know this must be hard for you. Is there anyone I can call?"

Grace turned toward the sound of the gentle voice. Her mind worked to identify the kind-eyed, middle-aged police officer who had driven her to the hospital. Officer Parks. That was his name. She studied him through watery eyes. He wasn't an extremely handsome fellow, but he had the kindest eyes of anyone she had ever met. They were a warm shade of amber that reminded her of one of her favorite horses from when she was a child.

Startled by the sudden recollection from her childhood, she began to regain focus just as Officer Parks repeated his question, "Ma'am, is there someone I can call to come be with you?"

Grace registered the look of concern on his face as he waited for her to respond. He was waiting patiently while she remained frozen in time, unable to speak. Or was it the fact that she didn't know how to answer his question? *Is there someone he can call?*

She had, in a sense, been on her own for so long she wasn't sure what to say. It had been months since she'd spoken to any of her family. Jared did not want her talking to them or seeing them, so she had obliged his requests as much as possible. It was one of the many things she had learned to do in effort to quench the fire that always seemed to be burning just below the surface, ready and waiting to explode at any moment.

But what about friends? No, she wasn't allowed to have any of those either. The only place she ever really went on a regular basis was the grocery store, making sure she always obeyed her husband's demands about not speaking unless spoken to. And she certainly gave her best effort not to speak to anyone without him being present.

She had learned long ago to keep her head down in public to avoid accidentally making eye contact with anyone. She feared some well-intentioned person would attempt to talk with her, and somehow Jared would find out. She was certain most people, including her neighbors and the employees at the grocery store, thought she was more than a little strange. In fact, she had inadvertently overheard such speculation among a few of their neighbors. It had been beautiful weather outside that day, and while Jared was away, she had opened the windows in their home to let in some fresh air and light. She relished those few times she could pretend their home was full of happiness and peace, even if such times were short lived.

At hearing the gossip, she simply shook her head. "Just let them talk," she had whispered to herself. She, after all, knew exactly what she was doing to protect herself and her children.

So many thoughts flooded her mind it seemed as if life were flashing before her eyes. But whose life? Whose life is this? Now that she thought about it, it seemed impossible that it could be hers. To an outside observer, her life would appear rather pleasing – two children, a handsome husband, and a beautiful home. It certainly would appear she had it all. But what the casual observer couldn't see was inside the walls of that beautiful home, especially not behind the closed door of her bedroom.

When Grace first met Jared, he had seemed like a dream come true. Handsome, charming, and so confident he could literally captivate an entire room with his presence. Just over six feet tall with broad shoulders and a dazzling smile, he didn't have to put forth much effort to turn on the charm when needed. His deep, brown eyes and thick, dark hair only added to his allure, easily providing him with a type of Prince Charming facade. A facade that might cause a woman to think he had stepped straight out of a fairy tale, especially a woman with a wounded heart.

But oh, how deceptive those charms had been. Grace had decided long ago that instead of the warmth she once thought was present within the deep hue of his eyes was nothing more than a mask hiding the darkness within his soul. He always knew how to flip that switch whenever he was in public, masking his true form behind the deceptions of charm and confidence. She heard many times over *what an amazing husband you have*, and *how did you get so lucky?* If only they knew. If only.

Grace closed her eyes and rested her head in her hands. She knew Officer Parks was patiently waiting for an answer. Inhaling a fortifying breath, she lifted her head. "Can you take us home, please?"

She looked to where her girls sat playing with Officer Parks' partner, Officer Beckett. He was seated at a tiny table in the children's corner of the ER waiting room, a table he was obviously too large for. There were a few books and toys scattered around. Her girls had him holding one of the baby dolls, pretending to feed it a bottle.

Grace assumed he couldn't be much older than twenty, and right now she was thankful for his playful spirit. His honey-blonde hair was cut short, and he had a welcoming smile and manner that seemed to draw her girls in. He had kept them occupied while Officer Parks tended to her, attempting to help her absorb all the life-altering information she'd just received.

"Ma'am, I'd be glad to take you home if that's what you want. Are you sure there isn't someone I can call?"

Grace shifted her gaze to the worried face of Officer Parks. "Yes, I'd just like to go home," she said, her voice sounding hollow to her own ears. She could feel the exhaustion seeping into her bones.

Officer Parks smiled slightly and nodded. He rose and said something to his partner, who then stood and scooped up little Abby. Anna followed along beside him. As they headed for the door, Grace smiled just a little as she watched her girls. They were giggling with Officer Beckett who had so graciously distracted them from all that was taking place. As she watched, she thought about how different life would now be for the three of them.

During the quiet ride home in the back of the patrol car, both girls asleep on either side of her, anxiousness crept into her thoughts. *How am I going to make funeral arrangements? How am I going to go anywhere?* The fiery crash that had claimed Jared's life had also claimed their only vehicle as a total loss. He had never allowed her to have her own car. Why would he? She was hardly ever allowed, and most of the time wouldn't even dare, go anywhere without him.

For some reason, at the moment, the thought of having no transportation was more concerning than that of having no husband. Then suddenly, inhaling sharply, she froze mid-thought. "I have no husband," she whispered ever so slightly. "I have no husband." Thick tears clouded her vision as her body trembled with the realization. She quickly swiped away the tears, breathing deeply, not allowing the slight tremble to morph into violent sobs.

Looking to her girls, she inhaled another calming breath. These two precious lives she was responsible for had a way of grounding her, bringing her balance in a way nothing else could. With Jared gone, what would life become for them? He was Abby's father and the only father Anna had ever known.

Grace had met Jared when Anna was just six months old. She was still vulnerable and heartbroken over the abandonment she felt when Anna's biological father abruptly left, ending their relationship when he found out she was pregnant. The heartbreak was hard for her to wrap her head around or make sense of because she knew she had never really been in love with him, but that didn't seem to spare her from feeling broken and alone.

Under the circumstances, Jared had seemed like a dream come true when she met him. The confidence and self-assurance she had known most of her life had faded into feelings of shame and guilt over the mistakes she had made. In essence, she felt too damaged to be wanted by anyone.

Chris, Anna's father, had come into her life the summer of her high school graduation. He was from out of state and was spending the summer in her small hometown of Marble Falls, Texas. He and a group of his college friends had leased a vacation home for the season. Grace met him at the local coffee bar where she worked part time and honestly didn't pay him much attention at first. Albeit he was attractive enough with his sun-kissed skin, sandy-blonde hair, and steely blue eyes, but she was accustomed to meeting a variety of new people when she was working during the summer vacation season.

Up to this point in her young life, no man had yet to steal the full attention of Grace Buckner. Confident, full of life, and quick to smile, she had turned down more than a few offers from young, lovesick boys from junior high through high school. Her wavy auburn locks paired with the vibrant green of her eyes often drew attention, and at times, more attention than she had patience to deal with. She had always attempted to be kind in her rejections, but she sometimes became frustrated with the continual refusals a few persistent admirers required before admitting defeat.

Chris, however, was different. She wasn't sure whether she found herself drawn to him because he was quite attractive, more a man than a boy, or because his attention toward her was novel. He wasn't pushy or immature, which was what she had come to expect from the opposite sex.

Then, after a handful of run-ins and short visits at the coffee bar, he asked her for a date. His request was harmless enough, so she gladly accepted. Truth be told, she was beginning to enjoy his attention toward her, but never in a million years would she have predicted what was coming next.

After a few casual dates, she found herself in a compromising situation. Chris had conveniently arranged for them to be alone at his vacation home. Grace thought she was coming over for a party, one she was admittedly excited to attend. After all, she would be lying if she didn't admit that dating Chris, a junior in college, was rather flattering to her ego. Besides, Chris had yet to give her any reason to question his motives.

As for peer pressure, she wasn't concerned about that. If asked to drink or participate in anything else of a questionable nature, Grace had never been one to cave. If Grace Buckner was going to do something, it was because Grace Buckner wanted to do it! It certainly wasn't going to be because someone told her she should.

Nevertheless, in that big empty house with only Chris, she unexpectedly found herself feeling less confident than usual. Having not dated much by choice, she had yet to find herself in a position where her courage and moral fortitude would be put to the test. But now, alone with a man and not a boy, she suddenly felt more unsure of herself than she ever had in her entire life. As she attempted to maintain a confident facade, not wanting to seem like a child to him, she allowed things to happen she would never have imagined herself doing with anyone who wasn't first and foremost her husband.

After that night, Grace found herself meeting up with Chris more and more frequently. While on the inside she was nearly dying from shame and guilt, she had now crossed a line she did not know how to retreat from. Ignoring the voice inside her, refusing to stop and think, she was in too deep. And that's when it happened, less than two months into their so-called relationship, a positive pregnancy test. Shocked, scared, and full of uncertainty, she immediately ran to Chris for help. But much to her surprise and dismay, he instantaneously wanted nothing to do with her. His eyes were cold and emotionless as she told him she now carried his child. To her horror, he asked, *"How do I even know it's mine?"* She had never felt so ashamed and so alone. If ever she could turn back time, this would have been that moment.

She spent the rest of the summer mostly alone, trying to figure out how on earth she had gotten herself in this situation with a man who now wanted nothing to do with her or their unborn child. Chris had conveniently left town of course, and she was too ashamed to seek him out. Although she did have to tell her parents, she certainly didn't have to spread the shame and disappointment she now felt by running after him.

Nine months later, Grace welcomed Annabelle Jane Buckner into the world. Holding that beautiful baby in her arms made the mistakes of her past temporarily fade away. No one could look at this beautiful little miracle and ever call her a mistake. Although circumstances were not as Grace would have planned or truly wanted, she now had new purpose and meaning in her life.

Grace snapped back to the present just as Officer Parks pulled into her driveway. The headlights from the patrol car illuminated the large, two-story house in an eerie light. Grace shook herself mentally as Officer Beckett opened the door for her to step out. She moved slowly toward the front door and unlocked it. As she pushed it open, it felt much heavier than normal, the sturdiness of the solid oak seeming to push back against her. She reached just inside the entryway to turn on the light, the weight of her own body almost becoming too much for her. She stepped aside allowing the two kind officers who were carrying her sleeping girls to pass by.

Officers Parks and Beckett walked quietly in front of her, pausing at the end of the hallway. A slight turn left would lead into the large, open kitchen and a slight turn right would lead into the spacious family room. She motioned to her right and stood silently as the officers gently placed her girls on a large, overstuffed sectional. Officer Parks spoke softly to her as they walked back toward the door, but she couldn't get her brain to respond. She could see his lips moving, but nothing was making sense. It all seemed muffled and out of place.

Overwhelmed and exhausted, she offered a slight smile of thanks as she silently shut the door. She looked around at the dark, quiet house. Everything was just as Jared had wanted it, and everywhere she looked reminded her of him. Every paint color, every piece of furniture, and every decorative touch was designed to please her husband. To her the house looked lifeless and void, much like how she felt on the inside.

Turning to her sleeping girls, she was reminded how very much she was not alone. These two would need her more than ever, and she would somehow find a way to be strong for them. She smiled softly as she watched them sleep, the joy of their little lives filling her heart and bringing some semblance of peace.

Looking at Anna, she was reminded how much of a blessing this child had been and continued to be. Along with her quiet, calm demeanor came Chris's blonde hair and complexion coupled with Grace's hazel-green eyes. Anna also shared the same compassion and depth of emotion as her mother, always feeling and thinking on a deeper level than most. She knew Anna would be deeply affected by this sudden loss, and she hoped her oldest daughter would be brave and optimistic, despite what the future might hold.

Turning to Abby, she gently stroked her youngest daughter's auburn curls. Very different from her sister, Abby was energetic and lively with a tender heart. Her eyes were a warm shade of brown, like her father's, and Grace was convinced her smile could soften nearly any heart. But unlike Jared, Abby's charm was genuine, and her love of laughter was evident, even at this young age. This child loved to smile, and even more so, loved to see those around her smile. For this reason, Grace had always worked diligently to hide her own pain from Abby's innocent eyes.

A sudden shiver coursed through her. The house seemed unusually cold for a mid-summer night. Hugging her arms tightly around herself, she searched for a blanket large enough to cover both girls. As she roamed the dimly lit house, an uneasiness settled in the pit of her stomach. She quickly took a blanket from the bed in a nearby guestroom. Laying it across the girls, she thought about how unnecessarily expensive the thing had been. For Jared, nothing less than the best would do. Another shiver snaked up her spine.

Grace tucked the cover around the girls and lay down opposite them. Before she could even think another thought, her eyes drifted shut, weighed down with the heaviness of the night's events. Unfortunately, this was not the peaceful type of sleep her mind and body so desperately craved. While outwardly her body appeared to shut down, her mind had other ideas. Her sleep was filled with the type of dreams that leave you tossing, turning, and breaking into a cold sweat. These dreams, however, were not based on imaginary fears. As she slept, it seemed her memory was bound and determined to relive every horrible thing Jared had ever said or done to her.

She soon found herself reliving her first date with the attractive, unattached Jared Thompson. It had been so exhilarating at the time knowing he was interested in her despite her recent indiscretions and despite her being a new mother. Left feeling unwanted and unworthy by Chris, she had openly invited Jared's advances far more quickly than many people would ever deem appropriate. Scared to lose the interest of such a handsome, confident man, she had given him whatever he wanted, even if it meant losing herself along the way.

Within a short time, Jared proposed to Grace. Her family and friends were not thrilled with the fast pace of their relationship, but she didn't want to chance letting him slip through her fingers. While she did have some reservations about jumping into another relationship with another man she barely knew, she pushed all concern aside and took the chance to provide what she thought was a future and a family for her and Anna. After all, her hopes for her future had taken a completely different turn the day she found out she was pregnant.

As she continued to toss and turn, her dreams took a much darker path. Her memory began to produce in vivid color every devastating, painful second she had suffered as the wife of Jared Thompson. The verbal and emotional abuse had begun almost immediately following the wedding and continued to evolve with increasing severity and harshness until she no longer felt any self-worth. The physical abuse soon followed.

Grace learned to endure as best as she knew how. When Jared was upset, as he so often seemed to be, she would walk on eggshells, hoping not to make the situation any worse for herself. While the verbal and emotional abuse were devastating enough, it was the physical abuse that left her reeling in pain for days. If she could somehow manage to keep him somewhat satisfied with her, their home, and life in general, she could alleviate some of the wrath that always seemed to come her way.

She continued tossing and turning as her mind hurtled through memories like a movie played in fast forward. Her dreams shifted to the day she found out she was pregnant with Abby. As she sat in the doctor's office with tears spilling into her lap, an immobilizing fear had filled her heart. At only six weeks pregnant, she worried about the baby's survival and the very real possibility of a miscarriage. Would she be able to carry full term knowing that at any moment Jared's anger could be unleashed?

Surprisingly, however, those next seven and half months were the most peaceful months of their marriage. Jared seemed pleased she was pregnant. After all, playing the part of the doting father while they were in public only deepened the facade he created around their life.

Then, after carrying a full-term, healthy baby girl, Abigail Elaine Thompson was born. The past seven or so months of relative peace in their home and marriage had given Grace hope, a hope she had not known since marrying Jared. She had hoped things would be different and had allowed herself to feel true joy at bringing another beautiful, baby girl into the world.

Her hopes, however, were quickly crushed. Only a few days after returning home from the hospital, Jared unleashed all the fury he had been holding in. His laundry wasn't done, the dishes were dirty, Anna's toys were laying in the floor, and Grace couldn't remember what else she took a beating for.

Thankfully, his violence was typically confined to their bedroom. Anna had not witnessed how truly awful things really were for her mother, and Grace assumed Jared would spare Abby as well. This did, however, mean she would always ensure all aggression remained directed at her, no matter the cost.

As her mind remained determined to relive every nightmarish moment of her marriage, she awoke suddenly, drenched in sweat and gasping for breath. Her heart pounded against her ribcage as she worked to slow her breathing. She looked at her girls still sleeping peacefully and pulled herself to her feet. She walked through the dimly lit house into the kitchen. Opening the refrigerator, she closed her eyes and let the cold air waft over her face. She took a glass from the neatly organized cabinet and filled it with water. She drank nearly all of it before taking a breath.

Grace started to place the glass carefully in the dishwasher but paused, deciding against it. Looking at the glass and in rebellion against all of Jared's ridiculous rules, she sat it on the counter. In this one simple action, she felt some strength return to her. Thinking how angry he would have been to find it sitting there, she smiled ever so slightly.

She turned and looked at the clock on the microwave. It read 5:45 am. It was still too early to make any phone calls. Knowing she would not be able to sleep peacefully even if she tried, she opted to make a cup of coffee and stay awake. She knew she had a daunting number of things that would need her attention and didn't even know where to start. Jared had always handled their finances, and she wasn't even sure if he had life insurance.

Once her coffee was ready and she took several slow sips, she decided she had no choice but to enter his private home office, the one room in the house she was never allowed in. A nervous uncertainty coiled in the pit of her stomach, threatening to send her sips of coffee up and out. But she had to do this. She couldn't give in to fear. She had to start the process of sorting things out.

Much as expected, Jared's office was perfectly organized. He had a file for everything. With not much trouble at all, she found paperwork on the car insurance, home insurance, and sure enough, life insurance. As she flipped through the policy, she was stunned to learn he had recently purchased policies for both him and her totaling nearly one million dollars each. She sank into the large desk chair next to her. Why had he so recently done this? Struggling to wrap her mind around it, she thumbed through the pages of each policy.

As she began to think of the many things that needed her attention – planning the funeral, attempting to explain things to her girls, what their lives would become without Jared – the uncertainty that had coiled in her gut snaked its' way into her chest, constricting her breathing. Tears dampened her cheeks. For seven years, she had not had to think of much else other than keeping her husband as happy as humanly possible. As abusive as he was toward her, he was a good provider financially and had never laid a hand on either of the girls. They had wanted for nothing, and he spared no expense to have the finest things money could provide. Albeit this was likely to ensure he maintained the status quo and looked the part of the perfect husband and father, but Grace never once had to worry about money.

Now thinking about it, she wasn't even sure how many or what type of business endeavors Jared was a part of. In fact, she wasn't completely sure what his occupation was. From the beginning of their relationship he had simply said, "I'm in finance. You wouldn't find it all that interesting." Initially, she had been too blind to question him. After being married to him, she was too terrified to question anything.

Grace honestly didn't know if there was anyone she should call to let them know Jared had passed away. She had on rare occasions entertained a few out-of-town business associates at their home for small dinner parties, but she couldn't recall ever hearing any last names and had zero contact information.

And what about the bank? She didn't even know how many or where all of Jared's bank accounts were. Thankfully she was on a joint bank account he had opened for expenses like groceries, but other than that, she was not privy to his other accounts or investments. She could only hope she could find enough paperwork in his desk or in one of his filing cabinets to point her in the right direction.

Just as she was opening yet another drawer filled with papers, she heard a small voice, "Mommy, why are you in daddy's office? He says we can't be in here."

Grace turned to see Abby staring at her from the doorway, still wearing the clothes she had fallen asleep in. She was twisting the bottom of her shirt, just as she always did when she was sleepy. Grace smiled. Abby had gotten that habit from her.

She opened her arms, and Abby immediately took the invitation, crawling into her mother's lap. "It's okay baby, Daddy won't be upset anymore if we're in here."

Grace gently stroked her daughter's hair as she nestled herself under her mother's chin. She held her youngest close, not wanting to tell her just yet that her father would not be coming back. In fact, she wasn't even sure how to tell her.

As she sat there in the chair in the office she had rarely set foot in before today, she quietly held her daughter. The magnitude of what she now faced was setting in more and more. Just as Abby and Anna had always come to her for comfort, she now longed for the comfort of her own mother. With that thought, she picked up the phone. There was no one to stop her, no one to forbid her to call home.

The phone rang only once. "Grace?"

The sound of her mother's voice immediately brought raw, untapped emotions to the surface. As tears clouded her vision and grief constricted her throat, she somehow managed to speak the words she desperately needed to say. "Mom, I need you."

CHAPTER 2

Grace paced nervously as she watched the clock and repeatedly looked out the window. She felt so anxious to see her mother. She knew she would be arriving any moment, and she could hardly contain her anticipation. What would she say to her? How would her mother act toward her? She knew her mother loved her, but it had been so very long since she had seen her in person. She had rarely been allowed to talk to her on the phone let alone visit.

It had only been one day since her early morning call home, telling her mother about the accident and asking for help. Her mother, Jane, had not hesitated for a moment. She had assured her daughter she would be on the first flight out of Austin she could get.

In fact, Jane had called Grace back within minutes of hanging up to tell her she had booked a flight leaving at 8:35 a.m. the next day. Unfortunately, there were not any non-stop flights from Austin to Boise so her mother would have to accept a short layover in Phoenix before traveling the rest of the way. Even still, she would be landing in Boise around 1 p.m. From there, she would pick up her rental car and make the nearly two-and-a-half-hour drive to Grace's.

The clock now read 3:31 p.m. Grace knew her mother would be pulling into her driveway at any moment. She left the front entryway only long enough to check on the girls. Anna was sitting quietly with her tablet and headphones, and Abby had fallen asleep on the couch next to her sister. The day before, she had painstakingly told the girls about their father while also telling them their grandma was coming to visit.

To her wonder, Anna's reaction had been more concern for her mother than sadness over losing the only father she'd ever known. With sorrow drawing at her little brow, she had immediately embraced her mother asking, "Mom, will you be okay?" Grace could feel her heart constricting with grief for her daughter. Anna's reaction, however, should not have come as such a surprise. She was the perfect mixture of compassion and resiliency. Rather than being concerned for herself, Anna's first reaction was always to be strong for those around her. The level of empathy she possessed far surpassed her age and maturity.

Grace felt a new wave of guilt wash over her. She knew Anna, being eight years old, had been much more aware of Jared's behavior than Abby. While Grace had worked diligently to protect both girls and hide the ugly truth from them, not much escaped Anna's notice. Her oldest daughter seemed to have developed an intuitiveness of when it was best not to bother Jared. She had taken on the role of babysitter countless times, attempting to keep Abby from under his feet. Grace knew Anna was not only protecting her baby sister, but she was also trying to protect her mother.

Abby, on the other hand, at just three years old, was not as observant as her older sister. She did not like for anyone or anything to suffer, and thankfully it was less complicated to hide any outward signs of pain from her. She might shed a few tears if she happened to witness one of Jared's verbal outbursts or if she noticed her mother wincing in pain, but she didn't seem to have any real understanding of how bad things really were.

In fact, Abby did not react right away when she learned Grandma Jane was coming to visit because her daddy would not be coming home. Grace could visibly see her little mind attempting to process the information. After a brief period of silence, she finally asked, "So Grandma is coming to our house, but Daddy can't come home anymore because he had an accident?"

Grace had lovingly stroked her youngest daughter's hair as she answered, "Yes baby, your daddy went to be with Jesus, but he loved you so very, very much."

As soon as the words had left her mouth, she felt the sting of guilt and a sickening feeling in the pit of her stomach. She had quite possibly just lied to her youngest child. She could not honestly say whether Jared was with Jesus or not. All she could do was hope that possibly at some moment before his death, *just maybe*, he had made things right with God.

Snapping back to the present, Grace returned to the front entryway window just in time to see her mother pulling in. She was certain her heart skipped a beat at the sight. But despite her excitement and relief knowing her mother was now here, she quietly and with reservation opened the front door and stepped outside. Her mother was stepping out of the car when she caught sight of her standing on the front porch. Not a word was spoken, and as soon as their eyes met, Grace broke down and ran to her.

Suddenly and for the first time in a long time, she allowed herself to feel every raw emotion she'd been keeping bottled inside for far too long. She felt as if her legs were made of jelly, and she could no longer hold her own weight. As she sank to the ground, her mother moved with her, never loosening her arms from around her weeping daughter.

The two women sat in the driveway, Grace weeping uncontrollably and her mother allowing her to do so. It was only when they realized another set of arms were around them that they loosened their grasp of each other. Hugging them both with tears in her eyes was Anna. Jane let go of Grace only enough to envelop her granddaughter with one arm.

Anna buried her face in her grandmother's shoulder and began to sob, "I'm so glad you're here Grandma. I've missed you so much."

Pulling themselves to their feet, Jane held tightly to her daughter and granddaughter. Together, the three Buckner women headed toward the front door, never fully breaking their embrace.

Once inside, Grace awoke Abby. "Abby, Grandma Jane is here," she gently whispered to her sleeping daughter.

Abby sat up, yawning big. She rubbed her eyes, attempting to focus. "Grandma Jane? You're here?" She was still wobbly with sleep.

Jane sat down next to her. "Yes baby, grandma is here."

Abby crawled into her grandmother's lap, giving her a drowsy hug. Anna was sitting beside Jane, leaning into her. She kept one arm around Abby while using her other arm to pull Anna closer. Grace and her mother exchanged glances, their eyes glistening with unshed tears. Despite the tragedy that now brought them together, Grace was practically overflowing with joy at having her mother back in her life.

Moving from the floor to a nearby chair, Grace gazed at her mother, observing the subtle changes since she'd last seen her. She had aged more than Grace expected, her hair having an almost frosted look to it. She also had more noticeable lines throughout her face, etching the corners of her eyes and her mouth. But nonetheless, her mother was as lovely as ever, aging with beauty and poise.

In her fifty-nine years on this earth, Jane Buckner had accomplished many things. She had raised five children, worked in the Texas heat alongside her husband, and loved the Lord and her family with unconditional fervency. Her life and marriage were a testament of hard work and perseverance.

Grace thought back to her childhood. Growing up, she was always told she was the spitting image of her mother. She didn't see it so much when she was younger, but now being a grown woman having been through hell and back, she could clearly see herself in Jane Buckner. Her tenacity and will to survive had come from her, along with a healthy dose of stubbornness and strong will from her father. It had always been her mother's determination that kept their family home running smoothly. She had loved her stubborn, hardheaded husband through the good times and the lean times, quietly resolving they would only get from their marriage whatever they were willing to put in. Her mother truly was the heart of the Buckner family.

Grace sat back in her chair, sighing in contentment. It seemed to her, no matter how old you are, you never stop needing the comfort of your mother. Having now experienced a long overdue release of emotion, she felt hope and a sense of peace returning as she watched her mother so lovingly care for her girls.

Breaking the silence, she enquired about her father. "How's dad?"

Her mother sat up a little, putting Abby down beside her and loosening her arm from around Anna. "Oh, you know your father, he's either yelling at the cows or the horses. But I guess that's what keeps him young. I think he's afraid if he slows down any, age might try to catch up with him," she said, grinning at her daughter.

Grace smiled. "I've really missed you, Mom. More than you know."

"We've missed you and the girls, too, Grace," Jane said, looking intently at her daughter. "It's been hard on us, on the whole family."

Grace's smile faded as she dropped her head. She felt yet another sting of guilt, this time for the hurt her family had experienced because of her, because she chose to marry Jared. She could hardly remember the last time she'd seen or spoken with any of her siblings or her nieces and nephews.

Within a year of marrying Jared, he had abruptly announced they were moving to Kentucky. Grace barely had time to say goodbye to her family before he ushered her off to another part of the country. This seemed to be normal for him, not staying anywhere for very long. He always chose to live in some small town, but it always had to be within a few hours of a major city and airport.

In her seven years of marriage to him, they never stayed in any place longer than a year or two. In fact, living in their current home had been the longest they'd lived anywhere. From Kentucky, they had moved to upstate New York. From New York, they lived briefly in Minnesota. Then from Minnesota, Jared moved them to Idaho. All the while, she couldn't help but sense they were running from something. From what, however, she never knew. Jared always said their moves were business related and asking too many questions was not a risk she was willing to take.

Her family, on the other hand, had always been tight knit. To them it must have seemed like she was turning her back on them all. What could they possibly think of her? Would they forgive her for the choices she'd made? How could she ever find the courage to tell them all the truth? Her mind was racing as she thought of a million things at once.

She thought back to how Jared had lived in her small hometown for only six months when they married. No one really knew much about him or his past, other than he was a successful businessman who all the single ladies found charming and attractive. Grace's family had not been fond of the fast pace of their relationship, and they definitely did not like the fact that Jared seemed to have no past to speak of.

Being nine years her senior and not from Texas originally, Jared seemed to have appeared out of nowhere. Grace's first encounter with him, similar to that of meeting Chris, had been at her favorite coffee spot. He had stopped by to use the free Wi-Fi, and she had helped him decide which drink to order. He said he had just moved to town for business and didn't know anyone yet. And his smile, *oh that smile*, had drawn her in before she even knew what happened.

After their engagement, Jared had been insistent he had no out-of-town friends or relatives he wanted to invite to the wedding. He kept reassuring everyone that his only friends, aside from the acquaintances he'd made since moving to Texas, were business associates. As for family, he was estranged from them and hadn't seen or spoken to them in years. Grace didn't push the envelope about his family because he visibly became agitated whenever the subject was broached.

Grace squeezed her eyes shut and forced herself to take a deep breath, attempting to stop the onslaught of memories. With her mother sitting here now and Jared gone, she would have to be honest about all she had suffered and endured at the hands of her husband. She knew it would cause her mother even more distress, knowing what her daughter had been through, and she also knew her mother would ask why she hadn't reached out for help. It wasn't like a Buckner to let someone push them around. But she knew sharing the truth would be the only way to explain why she had practically cut her entire family out of her life. Only the truth could make things right.

"I've got a lot I need to tell you, Mom." Her voice broke, and she couldn't look her mother in the eye.

Jane immediately grasped this was not a conversation her grand-daughters needed to hear. "It's okay, Grace. We'll talk later. When you're ready." Her smile was warm, but her eyes were sorrowful.

After dinner and lots of snuggles, it was finally time for the girls to go to bed. Grace and Jane tucked them in after bedtime prayers. As exhausted as Grace found herself, she knew this would be a long night. With the girls asleep, now was the time to sit down and share the raw, painful truth about her marriage. She needed to do this, not only for her mother but for herself.

* * *

Grace felt the next morning came far too soon. What little sleep she did get was filled with unpleasant dreams and memories. She had also stayed up far too late sharing the truth with her mother. That process had been agonizing for them both, and it left her feeling completely drained.

Picking up her phone she blinked a few times, willing her eyes to focus. The time read 8:30 a.m. Sitting up ramrod straight, panic stole her breath. Abby never slept late, and she always came into her mother's room when she woke up. Grace flung her body out of bed and dashed down the stairs, calling her girls' names as she went.

Her mother met her at the bottom of the staircase. "Grace, are you okay? What's wrong?"

She tried to gather her thoughts. "I woke up and realized what time it is. Abby always comes in my room when she wakes up. She isn't in there. Where are the girls?"

Jane motioned around the corner, walking back toward the kitchen. Much to Grace's relief, there sat the girls, enjoying juice and pancakes.

"Mommy, Grandma made us pancakes!" Abby squealed as she shoved another bite in her mouth.

"They taste just like yours, Mom," Anna added.

Grace took a deep breath and sank into a chair at the table. Her heart was beating against her ribcage like a bass drum. Her mother quietly set a cup of coffee in front of her and kissed her on the forehead. "I love you, Grace," she whispered.

Once again, that same peace wafted over her just as it had yesterday evening while watching her mother with her girls. She closed her eyes and let it sink in, enjoying the feeling of something that had been missing from her life for too long.

"Are you hungry?" her mother asked.

She opened her eyes. The girls had finished eating and were scurrying off to play. Her mother was putting dirty dishes in the dish-washer. "Yes, actually, I think I am hungry," she answered.

Jane set a plate of pancakes in front of her daughter and then sat down with her own plate. "I was awake this morning when Abby woke up, so I had her come with me to let you sleep. I'm sorry it scared you."

"No, Mom, it's okay. I'm just not used to having any help. Plus, these last few days have been a whirlwind. I still can't believe you're here. I can't believe Jared is gone." She put her fork down and took a few slow sips of her coffee.

"Grace, I know I said it last night, but I can't say it enough. I'm so sorry for what you've been through. I always knew something wasn't right, but I had no idea how bad it really was. But I'm here now, and it's all going to be okay," Jane reassured her daughter, reaching for her hand across the table.

Grace smiled at her mother as tears filled her eyes. She knew she was right. She knew everything would be okay. After all, she had survived hell on earth. She would pick herself up and move on with her life - for her girls, for herself, and for her family. *But where do I start? What if I can't figure it out? What if I can't figure out the finances? And the funeral? What if I can't do this?*

She forced her mind to stop. The constant questions she'd been asking herself since the night of the accident were so overwhelming, creating nothing but anxiety. She was already starting to feel nauseous again, and she'd been awake for less than thirty minutes.

"I don't know where to start, Mom," she said, putting her head in her hands. "Jared controlled everything. I don't know *anything* about his bank accounts or even what bills need to be paid. I don't even know if he has business partners I should call to let them know what happened."

"Take a deep breath, Grace," her mother urged. "We'll figure it out together. And what we don't know or can't figure out, we'll give it to the Lord to worry about."

Grace half smiled. Her mother had always lived out her faith, never doubting the Lord. Even when things didn't make sense to the natural mind, Jane Buckner would practice what she preached. Grace had always admired her mother's unwavering faith and now was no different.

"Let's finish our breakfast, make sure the girls are entertained, and we'll tackle this one task at a time," Jane affirmed. "We know we have to get the funeral arranged. Let's start there."

* * *

Over the next few weeks, Grace followed her mother's lead. They efficiently planned the funeral, took care of life insurance requirements, found additional bank and investment accounts, and put the house up for sale. Although Jared never disclosed much to Grace about their finances, he did have her name on nearly everything. This greatly simplified things for the two women.

As for selling the house, it didn't take any coaxing at all to convince Grace to move back home to Texas. She already knew she would need the support of her family. Although she and the girls were perfectly fine from a financial standpoint, Grace was not fine emotionally. Healing would take time, and she would need to learn how to live again.

In two weeks' time, everything that required immediate attention was taken care of and all else was left in the capable hands of the realtor and probate attorney. It was all happening so fast, but that was a relief to Grace. She was ready to close the chapter on this part of her life and move on.

Shutting and locking the door to her home for the final time, she paused briefly on the front porch, taking in the landscape around her one last time. Although Hailey, Idaho had not been a place she was ever allowed to truly enjoy living, she couldn't help but admire the beauty of creation around her. Under different circumstances, living here with the mountain backdrop and small-town feel would likely have brought with it a serene peacefulness.

Offering one last, saddened smile to her now former home, so much raced through her mind. What did the future hold? What would her life back home in Texas be like? Would her old friends, and even her family, welcome her back into their lives? She would have close to fifteen hundred miles to think it all through.

Grace plopped down in the front seat of her mother's rental car and let out a sigh. She buckled her seat belt and looked over her shoulder toward the backseat. Her girls were already entertaining themselves with their tablets, paying no attention to anything else around them. She had prepared them for the trip by explaining it would take a few days to reach Texas. The girls seemed excited, which was a huge relief to Grace.

Jane backed out of the driveway and headed down the street. Grace looked behind them, and the rented moving truck was following. Her brother, Eli, had flown up to drive the truck to Texas. Jane was worried about Grace emotionally and didn't want her to make the long drive herself. She had tried to argue with her mother that she would be fine driving, but that was a moot point.

But the truth of the matter? Grace really was *not* fine. She still felt like she was walking around in a fog most days, just watching her life pass by. She knew she didn't need to be driving. But she also knew the real reason why she'd argued in favor of driving herself. She didn't want her mother to ask her brother to come.

Grace was nervous about seeing Eli, unsure how he would react to her and what he would say. She hadn't spoken to him in what seemed like years, and she had no idea how he felt about her after all this time. Jane had picked him up at the airport the night before, and Grace had nearly made herself sick waiting for him to get there. Much to her relief, he had jumped out of the car and immediately hugged her so tight she could hardly breathe. He was smiling from ear to ear, holding onto her a little longer than she thought would be normal for him. That was enough to tell her their mother had likely filled him in on the circumstances of her marriage. She felt a twinge of embarrassment knowing he knew, but she also felt relieved she wouldn't have to tell him herself.

Just like Jane, Eli had made himself at home and acted as if nothing had changed. His same playful spirit was there like always, and the girls instantly adored him. He spent the evening playing with Abby and Anna, telling stories about family and friends back home, and showing off pictures of his two girls – six-month-old twins, Makenna and Madalyn.

Grace smiled as she thought about Eli interacting with her girls, and she was thankful he had come. She was also thankful he had continued working with their father on the ranch. Of all her siblings, he was the one who shared the same love for the land and the livestock as their father.

Being her younger brother, she could hardly believe he was a husband and father now. Eli had married his high school sweetheart, Hannah, two years ago. Grace had not been allowed to attend the wedding. Jared said he didn't have time to go and had laughed off the idea of her and the girls going without him. But now she was headed home, and no one was going to stop her.

"So, I was thinking we would drive until the girls can't take being in the car anymore. Or us! Whichever comes first," Jane laughed.

Grace smiled at her mother. "Sure Mom, whatever you think."

"Are you okay, sweetie?"

Grace didn't know how to answer the question. "Yes and no," she said. "I just feel like everything is happening so fast, changing so quickly."

"Oh honey, did I push you too much to get everything settled and move back home?" Concern pinched her mother's brow.

"No, I want it all over and done with. I *want* to go home. I just don't think I know what that means anymore." She gazed out the passenger side window.

"It means you're coming home to your family and friends who've missed you. It means you get to start living life again. It means you're doing exactly what you should be doing for you and for the girls." Jane said firmly. "Besides, it's really the perfect time of year to be making this move. With it being summer, Anna will have some time to adjust before starting at her new school. It will be good for her to start on the first day like everyone else. You know, not have to be the new girl that shows up after everyone else has already made friends. And we can probably find a nice preschool program for Abby. Maybe just a few days a week." She glanced Grace's direction. "But enough with that," she said, waving off her comments and smiling warmly. "We've got plenty of time to figure it all out."

Grace knew her mother was right. It would be good for the girls to spend some time with family before shuttling them off to school. They could get to know their cousins and maybe even make some new friends. Along with Eli, two of Grace's other siblings and their families lived close enough to home for frequent visits – her oldest brother, Andrew and her older sister, Beth.

Andrew, a Texas Game Warden, was able to continue living in Marble Falls with his wife and kids. Beth and her husband had moved to Austin for her husband's law practice, but the drive wasn't far for visits home to the ranch. Her middle brother, Caleb, had started working for the Border Patrol and was now living in New Mexico. He wasn't married yet, always making excuses for staying single.

Caleb had joined the Army straight out of high school, serving overseas in both Iraq and Afghanistan. He joined the Border Patrol after deciding not to re-enlist for a third tour of duty. While he may claim he is too busy for a wife and family, Grace has always suspected his time overseas affected him more than he lets on. Seeing that much devastation and loss would take a toll on anyone mentally and emotionally.

Grace looked at the envelope in her hand. "If you don't mind, swing by the post office so I can mail this before we leave. I need to buy a stamp before I can send it."

"I'm glad you decided to write that letter," Jane said endearingly. "We may not know who this woman is, but if she's somehow family to Jared, she deserves to know he's passed on."

Grace again looked at the envelope. She had addressed it to Clara Thompson in Greenville, Ohio. She had no idea if this woman was related to Jared or not, but she had certainly given it a great deal of thought since finding the name and address in one of Jared's desk drawers. She had often wondered who his family was and if they were anything like him.

There hadn't been much to go on, just a name and address on an otherwise blank index card. She couldn't find anything online for Clara Thompson in Greenville, Ohio either. Her google search didn't turn up any leads, and the woman didn't seem to exist on social media. Honestly, she didn't even know if this letter would reach the intended recipient.

CHAPTER 3

Grace let the hours and miles wash over her, showering her in freedom. She even rested some without having the nightmares that had plagued her since the night of Jared's accident. It seemed the farther they traveled away from Idaho and the closer they were getting to Texas, the more she felt her mind clearing and peace returning.

The girls had withstood more hours of travel over the past two days than either Jane or Grace had anticipated. Now on their third day, they fully expected to reach Marble Falls sometime this evening. And with Eli ready to be home with his wife and daughters, he was not one to complain about the long hours on the road. Grace even felt up to driving some, allowing her mother to take a break. "It's okay, Mom, I promise I'm good to drive. I've rested better on this trip than I have in weeks, maybe even years," she said, rolling her eyes.

"Well, it sure does feel good to stretch my legs out for a while. I don't remember the last time I was in a car this long for this many days. My poor, old back definitely isn't what it used to be," Jane said, gingerly massaging her lower back with one hand.

"You are *not* old, Mom. Even I'm sore. A long soak in a hot bath would feel so good right now."

"I think the hot tub is calling my name when we get home," Jane said, resting her head back and sighing.

"Hot tub? When did you get a hot tub?" Grace exclaimed, wrinkling her forehead.

"Oh, I'm sure a great deal has changed since you were last on the ranch, Grace," her mother said with a wink. "I'm not saying that to be hurtful. I just think you'll be pleasantly surprised with what you find."

She gave her mother a sideways glance, making sure she didn't lose focus on the road. "What is *that* supposed to mean? Should I be preparing myself for something totally unexpected? I think I've had enough of that lately!"

"No, no. Don't be so dramatic. I've tried to keep you up to date on things when we've talked, but it's not the same as being there and seeing things with your own eyes."

Grace tried to recall the few and far between conversations she'd had with her mother over the years since leaving Texas, but it was difficult. She was starting to realize she had somewhat shut out what her mother was always so eager to tell her because it was just too painful. Too painful because she knew she couldn't be a part of any of it, and too painful because she harbored so much guilt and shame over her own choices.

"Mom, I have to be honest. I don't think I remember very much of what you've shared with me since I left. It was always so painful to hear and think about everything I was missing, what the girls were missing."

Grace felt hot tears starting to cloud her vision. *Why am I just realizing this?* She mentally scolded herself, letting her heartache turn to frustration. She took a few deep breaths, working to maintain control and forcing the tears to stop.

"Grace, I'm sorry. I never meant to cause you pain. I just wanted you to feel included, to let you know we all still love you." Jane's voice was edged with concern.

"No, no, please don't be sorry, Mom. It's me. It's *my* choices I'm frustrated with. I have no one to blame but myself."

"You've got to let all that go," Jane said, her tone gentle yet firm. "If you live your whole life full of regret, it will consume you. You have two beautiful girls and a family who loves you. And Grace," Jane paused, "the Lord loves you, too."

That did it. The wall broke loose. Grace quickly pulled to the side of the road, no longer able to control the flood of tears that had been threatening to come. She rested her head against the steering wheel as she sobbed.

Jane gently put her left hand on her daughter's shoulder, using her right to wave Eli away from the window and back to his truck. "It's true, Grace. He's never stopped loving you. And despite what you've been through, He never left you either. I've prayed for you every day, prayed that He would be with you."

It had been so long since Grace truly thought about God or her relationship with Him. While she had prayed frequently over the years, those prayers typically consisted of her asking the Lord to protect her children. She had allowed the guilt and shame she carried to prevent her from believing the Lord would ever do anything for her personally. She felt too unworthy, too damaged. In fact, she sometimes believed she deserved the abuse she had received at the hands of her husband.

How will I ever get passed this? Please help me, Lord! Please forgive me! The purity of her silent pleas to Him were unnerving. She had not asked Him for anything for herself in so long, and she had never asked for His forgiveness for the mistakes she'd made.

A hushed little voice interrupted her thoughts. "Mommy, are you okay?" Abby was sitting up tall in her car seat, leaning forward, trying to see her mother's face.

"It's okay, Abby. Mommy is just sad," Jane said, reaching into the backseat to gently pat her granddaughter on the knee.

"I miss Daddy, too," came Abby's reply, almost a whimper.

Grace dried her eyes and took a few deep breaths. She turned to face her daughter. "I know you miss him, baby. But we will be okay." She gave her daughter a reassuring smile. Then, turning around to gain more composure before pulling back on the highway, she uttered another silent prayer. *Thank you, Lord, that my daughter doesn't know the real reason for my tears.*

As the miles continued to roll by, Grace was determined not to have any more breakdowns on the side of the highway. She could tell her mother was thinking the same thing and was attempting to keep the conversation light and on a more pleasant track.

"Oh, I forgot to tell you, Grace," Jane started, "Noah came home. He's been back on the ranch for about six months now."

"Really? He's back working for dad?" She gave her mother a sideways glance.

"Yes, and we are all so thrilled he's home. You know how much your father and brothers think of him," Jane said, her smile warm.

Grace thought back to when she first met Noah Miller. She had been sixteen, and he was eighteen. Her father had been out of town, gone to a large auction near San Antonio. He had taken her brothers Caleb and Eli with him, and when they came home, Noah was with them. It was immediately obvious he wasn't quite like them. His clothes, haircut, and straw hat made it clear he was Amish. His bronzed skin and strong, lean build were proof he was accustomed to long days of physical labor under the hot Texas sun.

Grace had been curious to learn all about him and what had brought him to her family's ranch but obtaining that information directly from the source had proven more difficult than she'd imagined. Most of what she learned initially came from her mother. Although he was always kind and respectful, Noah remained distant, not engaging much in conversation with her personally.

Over time, she learned he had chosen to leave his family and community near Beeville, Texas when he knew he could not bow his knee and be baptized into the Old Order Church. It wasn't that he lacked faith in God, he just couldn't make a lifelong commitment to live by rules and standards he wasn't completely sure about. Ultimately, he never wanted to make a commitment to the Lord he wasn't sure he could follow through with. Grace respected that.

Her father, Jake, had met Noah at the auction. His knowledge of horses had saved her dad from a bad deal, and that was enough to turn Jake Buckner's head. And after hearing Noah's story, he said it only felt right to offer him a job and a place to stay. At the time, the small bunkhouse they used for ranch hands or guests was sitting empty and was the perfect solution.

Truth be told, Jake Buckner had always had a soft spot in his heart for young people who were trying to find their way in this world, especially when that young person embodied the skills and work ethic of Noah Miller. The whole Buckner family soon learned that not only did Noah work harder than anyone else on the ranch, but he also possessed a gift for working with the horses. His quiet, calm demeanor seemed to overtake even the unruliest of creatures. He made breaking and training look effortless.

Over time, Grace and Noah did become friends. Their love for horses drew them together, and Grace soon considered him her best friend. That's why it hurt so much when he decided to follow Caleb in joining the Army. She felt like she was losing not only a brother but her best friend as well. During her senior year of high school, the two men left. Noah had gotten his GED after coming to live with the Buckners, and he said he felt the same draw as Caleb to serve. He knew that without the brave men and women who put their lives on the line, we wouldn't have the freedoms we do, including his family's right to live their lives as they do.

No one wanted to see either of them go, but not even Jake Buckner himself could argue with their willingness to serve and sacrifice for their country. It was a noble thing they were doing, and the rest of the family would proudly support them. Even though she was heartbroken, Grace had done her best not to let it show.

"Grace, are you okay?" Her mother's voice interrupted her trip down memory lane.

"Huh? Oh, yeah, just thinking." She pushed aside her thoughts of Noah.

"You've been awfully quiet for a while now. Just checking on you." Jane smiled sweetly as she patted her daughter's leg. "We're getting close now. It won't be long until we're home."

Grace felt her pulse quicken, knowing she would soon be home for the first time in years. Anticipation knotted in her stomach as they made their way through Marble Falls and turned onto the county road leading to her family's private lane. Even the girls appeared more alert, excited their long journey was coming to an end.

* * *

Try as he might, Noah could not get his mind to focus on the task at hand. The young filly he was working with in the round pen obviously knew it, too. She was taking full advantage of his distracted state and was being as lazy as she could get away with. Finally conceding his attempt to keep his mind occupied was likely only doing more harm than good, he brought the horse to a halt.

"Sorry, Jingle. We're getting nowhere, and I'm only teaching you bad habits." The young horse seemed to nod in agreement as he unfastened the lunge line from her halter. "We'll try again later, girl." He gave her a quick scratch on the head before exiting the round pen.

He stepped from the stall barn just as an unfamiliar car and a moving truck pulled in by the house. He didn't have to be told who it was. He already knew. This was the reason he couldn't seem to gather his thoughts or stay focused on his work. As the car doors opened, he held his breath, and his heart skipped a beat. *What are you doing? What's wrong with you?* He silently scolded himself.

Noah had not seen Grace in almost nine years, but just knowing she was here now did peculiar things to him. He couldn't help but feel like he did. He had missed her tremendously. And knowing what she'd been through the past seven years caused feelings of pain and anger inside him he'd never experienced before.

As much as he wanted to run to the car and greet her, he didn't know if he should. He wasn't sure how she would receive him after all this time or how much her own life experiences had changed her. He decided it might be best to hang back, give her some time.

* * *

Grace slowly stepped out of the driver's seat, taking in her surroundings. The two-story home she'd grown up in wasn't much changed.

The front porch with its stone columns and wood beams was as inviting as ever. Her mother's landscaping and flower gardens surrounding the house were breathtaking as always. The large oak tree where she'd swung as a little girl was still standing tall and strong, the old rope swing swaying gently in the light breeze.

Her gaze wandered to the wooden fencing surrounding the nearest pasture. Longhorn cattle were quietly grazing, giving no notice to her return home after all these years. Their tails were swishing back and forth, attempting to keep the flies at bay. The sound of a whinny drew her attention to the large stall barn where the horses were kept. She knew they were all safely inside with fans going, shielding them from the hot summer sun. At dusk, they would be let out to roam freely in the pastures and enjoy the coolness of night.

Her gaze landed on the entryway. Leaning against the door frame with his hands in his pockets, looking her direction, stood Noah. Even from this distance and after all the time that had passed, she would recognize him anywhere. That boyish grin she remembered tugged at the corners of his mouth, and his blonde hair, a dark toffee color, was cut shorter than she remembered. She couldn't make out the deep blue of his eyes from this distance, but her memory served her well to remember their sapphire color that always reminded her of the ocean.

She started to smile and offer a wave in his direction but was soon caught up by her family. Almost everyone was present for her arrival, and now they all seemed to be hugging her at once. Abby and Anna had gotten themselves out of the backseat and were shyly remaining tucked near her legs. She stole one more look in Noah's direction, but he had disappeared back into the barn.

Grace gave in to the joy of being with her family again, and the tears began to flow. When her father greeted her, his eyes misted, and he held her close. But true to himself, he quickly choked back his emotions and lifted both of her girls in the air. Jake Buckner was not a small man and lifting Anna and Abby into his arms seemed effortless. The girls smiled and giggled with delight, clinging tightly to the grandfather they barely knew.

As the family migrated toward the house, Grace hung back. "I'll be in in just a minute," she called. Her mother turned and nodded, smiling warmly.

Grace ambled slowly toward the barn, a nervous tingle racing up her spine and kicking her heart rate up. She couldn't quite put her finger on why. The past few weeks had been filled with so many emotions, and she was trying to stop analyzing herself so much. Doing so had about driven her crazy.

Once inside, just being back in this place so familiar with so many cherished memories, a sense of calm flooded her soul. She walked down the long center aisle, noticing the names on stall doors. She was just itching to get back in the saddle and didn't realize until now how much she'd missed it. Or perhaps she knew all along how much she missed it, missed it all, but it was too painful to think about.

She paused, stopping at a stall and eyeing the young horse inside. The name on the door read *Jingle*. She was a magnificent animal, more beautiful than any horse she ever remembered seeing in her father's barn. She was a dark, steel gray with two white socks and two black. Her mane and tail were long, thick, and streaked with silver. Grace was captivated.

"I thought you'd like her."

She turned to see Noah standing a few steps from her, a tender smile drawing up one side of his mouth. Her breath caught, and her voice seemed to have disappeared. Her lips parted but no words came.

She'd always known he was attractive, but now after all this time, she was struck silent gazing at the man standing before her. When they'd parted ways all those years ago, he'd barely been older than a teenager, still a boy in many ways. Now, after all the time apart, there was no question the broad-shouldered man standing before her was no longer a boy in any sense. She suddenly felt vulnerable, awkward, as apprehension tightened inside her chest.

* * *

Noah sensed something was amiss. He started to move toward her, to welcome her home with a hug. But as he reached for her, she withdrew, looking at the floor. He tried not to feel hurt, knowing she'd been through hell. He settled for a verbal greeting, attempting to rid the atmosphere of the awkwardness that had settled between them. "Welcome home, Grace. I'm glad you all made it safe."

She raised her head and met his gaze, uncertainty clouding her beautiful face. "Thank you," she spoke, her voice barely above a whisper. She attempted a smile, but it didn't quite reach her eyes.

Noah could feel the grief constricting his heart. He could almost feel the pain he saw in her eyes. He wanted to hold her and tell her it would all be okay. He longed to see the same sparkle in her eyes his memory had held onto all these years, to see that smile that could light up a room. But for now, he could do only one thing to help her. He would pray.

* * *

Grace left the stall barn feeling defeated and broken. Noah had always been a friend, and now she felt ashamed of her reaction when he reached to touch her. *What has Jared done to me?* She was screaming on the inside as hot tears streamed down her face. Up until this very moment, she hadn't realized the true depth of her wounds. For the first time since leaving Idaho, she felt hopeless.

Suddenly, feeling exhausted and longing for sleep, she trudged toward the house. She didn't want to go inside and face her family, but she knew she had to. She knew they were all waiting for her, including her girls. She would have to be strong for them until the time came when she could retreat to the privacy of her bedroom. Then and only then could she give into the anguish that was threatening to drown her.

* * *

Grace picked up her phone, looking at the time. It read 9:15 a.m. Morning had come. She knew she needed to get out of bed but couldn't seem to do it. She felt like someone had drugged her. Her mind was foggy, and her body was weak. When she finally settled into bed the night before, the peaceful sleep she so desperately needed was nowhere to be found. In its place her nightmares had returned. She tossed, turned, and sweated herself wet. More than once during the night, she had woken up breathing heavy and crying in her sleep. It was miserable.

Now lying here in the light of day, safely at home with her family, she couldn't grasp why the nightmares had returned. It didn't make sense. She had assumed it would all stop once she was back in Texas. Dragging her tired, listless body from the bed, she caught a glimpse of herself in the mirror. What a sight! If she were a drinker, people would assume she'd been on a bender. She sighed heavily and headed toward the bathroom for a shower.

Finally making it downstairs, the house was quiet. She wandered through the large family room and into the dining area. Her childhood home had always been a safe place, full of love and peace. As she entered her mother's spacious kitchen, she allowed her eyes and senses to feast on everything she'd missed tremendously. Large windows facing the southern pastures and stall barn let in brilliant amounts of morning light, the radiant glow flooding to the full height of the ceiling and dancing around the wooden beams. The whole house had her mother's rustic yet sophisticated touch, and the kitchen was no different. Her mother had given the Buckner home a hint of elegance. Nothing too feminine or fancy of course, just enough here and there.

Grace found her mother and grandmother sitting quietly in the breakfast nook, drinking what was likely their second or third cups of coffee. They were gazing out the window, likely watching the men work or the cows meandering through the pasture. She smiled. Her Grandma Elaine, her father's mother, had come to live with them several years ago after the passing of her husband. Always a quiet, gentle soul, her soft white hair was set neatly in a bun on top of her head. As usual, she was wearing one of her simple, hand-sewn dresses, just as Grace remembered.

"Good morning," Grace said as she joined them at the table. Her grandmother quietly patted her hand and smiled while her mother rose to retrieve another cup of coffee.

"I was starting to worry about you. I was thinking I might need to come drag you out of that bed." Jane said, setting the coffee in front of her daughter.

"I'm okay. I just didn't sleep well." She closed her eyes as she raised the mug to her lips, savoring the pleasant aroma. As the hot liquid slid down her throat, the warmth soothed her from the inside out.

"I'm sure it will take a little bit to get settled in," her mother said reassuringly. "You'll be sleeping better soon."

Grace turned her attention outside, looking out the window toward the barn. "Where are the girls?"

"Outside in the barn with your dad and Noah. They were so excited this morning to see the horses. We barely made it through breakfast before they were bursting out the door," Jane chuckled, shaking her head.

"I guess I'll put on some shoes and go check on them," she replied.

"My boots are by the backdoor. Just grab them on your way out," her mother offered, pointing toward the mud room.

Grace left the kitchen and slipped on the boots. As she walked toward the barn, she felt the same nervous feeling she'd felt last night. *What is wrong with you Grace Thompson?* She growled in frustration.

When she entered the barn, she didn't see anyone but could hear Abby's giggles. She followed the sound outside and found the girls with her dad and Noah. Abby was sitting on her grandpa's shoulders, and Anna was seated in the saddle of a horse Noah was leading around.

"Mommy, Mommy, look at Anna!" Abby squealed.

"Mom, this is awesome!" Anna was beaming.

It did Grace's heart good to see her girls so happy. After all they'd been through, she was thankful to see them being so resilient. Instantly, she knew she'd made the right decision to come home to her family. Her girls needed this. *She* needed this.

Her dad came over and gave her shoulder a little squeeze. "Morning sunshine. Wondered if you'd join us sometime today," he teased with a wink.

"Ha, ha. Very funny," Grace replied dryly, rolling her eyes.

"Grandpa Jake is going to show us the baby cows next!" Abby exclaimed as Noah was helping Anna down from the saddle. "Do you want to come too, Mommy?"

Grace smiled at her daughter's enthusiasm. "I don't think so, baby. Maybe next time."

"Okay, Mommy!" Abby called, already headed down the hallway with her sister and grandpa in tow.

Left by themselves, Grace turned her attention to Noah. She at least owed him an apology for her cold reception last night, but she didn't know what explanation to offer. She didn't know how much he knew about her situation or how much she even wanted him to know.

* * *

Noah had to force himself not to look at Grace for fear she'd catch him staring. She was even more beautiful in the morning light than she'd been last night. Her hair was still slightly damp, and she had it pulled up loosely on top of her head, strands falling free and flowing down around her face. The sight of her triggered so many memories. Seeing her like this was just how he'd remembered her all these years.

And now, with her standing in front of him, he was at a loss for words. He didn't want to scare her off, make her withdraw like she had last night, but he also didn't want to stand back and say nothing. *Snap out of it! Say something!* "The horse is still saddled... if you want a go," he stammered, holding the reins up and offering a hesitant smile.

She returned his smile, moving a little closer. "I haven't been on a horse in years."

"Well, there certainly isn't one safer than Doc. I'm sure you remember him." Noah patted the horse's neck.

"I'll get back in the saddle. Just not sure today is that day." She looked at him with an expression he couldn't quite read. Then she looked away, staring at the ground. "Noah, I'm sorry for last night. I don't know why I reacted that way. I..." It was all she could manage before she had to stop, visibly choking back tears.

Seeing her eyes begin to water and hearing the catch in her voice, he felt the same mix of hurt and anger welling up inside him that he'd experienced last night. He hurt because of the pain she was obviously going through, and he was angry at the man who had caused it. "It's okay, Grace. You don't need to apologize. I'm here anytime you need me. I've missed you." As the words came out, he was already kicking himself, certain he'd failed at hiding the emotion in his voice. He didn't dare reach for her.

She looked up, meeting his gaze. "Thank you, Noah. That means a lot."

He could still see the pain in her eyes and the remnants of her tears, but she didn't look away. At least she was looking him in the eye. He would count that as progress.

* * *

As the days passed, Grace continued to struggle. Nearly every night her dreams were riddled with unpleasant memories, and she was feeling mentally, emotionally, and physically exhausted. She wasn't much for conversation lately, and she could see the worry on the faces of her family. She wished she was adjusting as well as her girls seemed to be.

Anna and Abby filled their days with baking and visiting with Grandma Jane and Great Grandma Elaine, riding lessons from Noah or Eli, and cattle checks with Grandpa Jake and his heeler pups, Snap and

Bandit. Neither girl had mentioned much about Jared since arriving in Texas. Grace assumed it was good they were keeping so busy with new adventures and weren't dwelling on the past. *If only I could follow their lead,* she thought to herself.

There had also been a continual stream of guests for dinner nearly every night since they'd arrived. So far Caleb was the only sibling who hadn't yet been able to visit. Even Beth, her husband Alex, and their kids had driven in from Austin more times than Grace assumed was typical. Despite her exhaustion and frustration with herself, she was thankful to be surrounded by her family. Her girls were finally getting to know their aunts, uncles, and cousins. And with Eli working on the ranch, Hannah and the twins were frequent visitors. Anna and Abby were head over heels for Makenna and Madalyn.

One evening after dinner, as Abby was entertaining the twins on the floor in the family room, she piped up, "Mommy, can you have a baby for me to play with?"

The color drained from Grace's face. The entire room went quiet. Everyone sat in awkward silence, unsure how to respond, including Noah. She was terrified to look anyone in the face. Her throat constricted, and she could hardly breathe, let alone speak.

Thankfully, Jane Buckner wasn't one to be easily rattled. "Come here, Abby," she called to her granddaughter, patting her lap for Abby to sit. "Do you remember how your mommy explained what happened to your daddy?"

Abby nodded her head but gave her grandmother a quizzical look. "Yes, but can't she find us a new daddy?"

Everyone was speechless, stunned into silence yet again.

Looking between her mother and grandmother, Abby continued, "I loved my daddy very much, and I miss him. But I want to have babies like Uncle Eli!"

Grace hastily stood and exited the room, not wanting to upset her daughter but knowing she couldn't hold herself together a second longer. It wasn't Abby's fault. Her response was as innocent as could be, only voicing what she understood to be true in her young mind. She had no way of knowing the distress it caused her mother.

Grace rushed through the door and onto the back patio. Once she was beyond the line of sight of her family, she dropped to the top step leading down into the yard, sobbing uncontrollably. She could barely catch her breath. The warm, humid air felt as oppressive as the turmoil inside her.

When she felt the presence of someone next to her, she attempted to regain some control. Dashing at her tears with one hand and taking a breath, she turned to see Noah. He wasn't saying anything, wasn't trying to comfort her, but the look of anguish on his face said it all. Grace couldn't for the life of her figure out why her own personal torment seemed to be causing him pain, too.

They sat in silence for a long while, Noah looking off into the distance and Grace working to quiet her breathing as her tears continued to fall. As much as she was hurting, there was somehow peace in that moment. Neither one of them said a word, and neither one moved.

Grace turned when she heard the door open behind them. Grandma Elaine stepped onto the patio, taking a seat in the swing. She smiled softly in their direction. Turning back to Noah, his eyes met hers. He held her gaze as his eyes searched hers. Then, without saying a word, he stood and walked away into the darkness. Grace continued to watch in the direction he went until she could no longer make out his form.

Picking herself up, she went to sit with her grandmother. Grandma Elaine was gently moving the swing back and forth ever so slightly. She had her hands clasped, resting them on her round middle. When Grace sat down, she took her hand.

"It's a beautiful night isn't it, Gracie?" her grandma spoke, more a comment than a question. She was gazing into the night sky. "Every time I look at the stars, I'm reminded of the Lord's handiwork."

Grace looked up, taking in the fullness of the Texas sky. With not a cloud in sight and nothing to hinder her view, it seemed to continue on endlessly. She sighed heavily, letting her frustration slip away.

"The Lord sure knew what he was doing, placing all those stars up there," Grandma Elaine remarked. "Can you imagine how dark it would be out here without them?"

Grace kept her eyes trained on the sky, resting her head on her grandmother's shoulder. She knew there was a point to all of this, and she would quietly wait until her grandmother was ready to share it. Elaine Buckner was a quiet woman who often didn't have too much to say, so when she did decide to speak, it was best to listen.

"Just like that sky, Gracie, you have a light inside you, too. Now I know you've had some dark days, but you don't have to let that continue. You have a choice. It might not feel like it right now, but you control what you think on. You decide what fills your mind and how it affects you."

Grace sat quietly, listening to the wisdom her grandmother was gently imparting to her broken soul.

"The Lord tells us in His Word we should take every thought captive, submitting it to Christ. Do you know what that tells me? It tells me we have choice in what we think about." Her grandmother shifted, looking directly at her. She lightly cupped her hand around her granddaughter's cheek. "I know you've been through some awful things, and my heart hurts for you more than you know. But Gracie, you have to give it to Him," she said, nodding toward heaven. "His grace is enough."

Grace sat looking into her grandmother's warm, caring eyes. Silent tears trickled down her cheeks. She knew her grandmother was right, and she knew she had a choice whether to keep living or wither and die.

"I'm going to head back inside. Why don't you just sit here and spend a little time with the Lord. You'll be surprised what that might do for you." And with that, Grandma Elaine kissed her on the forehead and left.

Grace pondered everything her grandmother had just spoken, taking it all to heart. She did as her grandmother said and sat right there in that swing, staring into the heavens. Alone with only the stars in the sky and the sounds of the night surrounding her, she did something she should have done a long time ago. She poured her heart out to her Heavenly Father.

CHAPTER 4

G race awoke the next morning bright and early. It wasn't even 7 a.m. yet, but she was up and going. For the first time since arriving home, she slept the whole night without a single disturbing dream or memory. Dressed and ready to face the day, she headed downstairs. Not finding anyone in the kitchen, she enjoyed a quick cup of coffee before heading outdoors. The cooler morning air seemed less weighty than it had the night before. She smiled. Perhaps it wasn't just the air that felt lighter.

She wandered through the stall barn, savoring the peacefulness of this place so familiar, a place as familiar to her as her own skin. The aroma that so many would find off-putting, pine shavings and hay mixed with dust and manure, stirred feelings of tranquility deep within her soul. These were connections to her childhood, a time when life was less complicated.

Feeling something brush against her calf, she looked down to see Bandit looking up at her. He was already flopping onto his back asking for a belly rub. As she reached down to oblige him, Snap snuck up and stole a kiss on her cheek. She laughed and wiped the slobber from her face. Offering each a quick scratch on the head, she continued outside.

Rounding the corner of the barn, she saw her father leaning against a gate, watching Noah work with a horse in the training pen. She smiled. Her dad always had enjoyed watching Noah work, calling him the most gifted trainer this side of Texas. And if her memory served her right, she had too at one time. She leaned against the gate next to her dad. He turned and smiled but didn't say a word. They both stood in silence, watching man and horse work together in perfect harmony. Grace soon found herself captivated.

Noah was working with Jingle, the young filly she'd seen in the barn on her first night home. She was stunningly graceful, the morning light highlighting the silvery hues that streaked her mane and tail. Her muscles flexed and rippled as Noah took her through different training exercises. Grace's initial observation was correct. She couldn't remember a horse more beautiful than this one ever belonging to her father.

She soon found herself watching the rider more than the horse. Noah truly had a gift for doing what he loved. His firm yet gentle methods coupled with his calm, reserved manner made training look like an art form. His strong, lean build suited him well for the job, and Grace noticed it also made him easy to watch, in more ways than she cared to admit.

"She sure is something isn't she?"

Grace startled at the sound of her father's voice. She could feel the heat creeping up her neck, thankful he couldn't read her thoughts. "She's beautiful, Dad," she replied. "I don't remember you ever bringing home a more gorgeous animal."

"Oh, she's not mine, Gracie," Jake responded, a mischievous twinkle in his eye.

She turned her full attention to her dad. "What do you mean she's not yours? Whose is she?"

He motioned toward the training pen. "That young man right there brought her home."

"Really?" She turned back to look at Noah. "He always did have an eye for a good horse."

"Yep," Jake said, starting to walk away. "Brought her home for *you,* Grace," he called over his shoulder. He turned and offered one last knowing grin before heading back toward the barn, shoving his hands in his pockets and whistling as he went.

Grace was left standing there, stunned. *Why would Noah get that horse for me?* Her mind whirled.

"What do you think of her?"

Grace turned to find Noah standing a few steps away, his brows lifted in question and a grin tugging at the corners of his mouth. She found herself temporarily transfixed, unable to answer. His lips, curved into a hopeful grin, were stealing her focus. She could almost feel the heat radiating from his body. His deep, blue eyes were locked on her.

"Well, are you going to tell me?" he quizzed, his grin slipping a little.

Grace blinked. She looked away, yet again feeling the flush of heat pulsing up her neck, thankful Noah also could not read her thoughts! "She's gorgeous," she finally answered. "I've never seen a more beautiful horse."

He smiled broadly now, his eyes dancing. "Glad to hear it. She's something special alright. I sure am enjoying working with her."

Grace moved to run her fingers through Jingle's mane, unintentionally brushing against Noah when she did. She lifted her gaze to his, and this time, it wasn't her who pulled away. His eyes darted to the ground as he stepped backward. She couldn't be sure but thought his face suddenly seemed infused with color.

* * *

Noah attempted a few calming breaths, trying to slow his pulse. He was certain the heat that had risen to his face was obvious. And he was certain by the strange look Grace was giving him that she detected it, too. Why did she have this effect on him? Ever since she had returned home, all he wanted was to hold her, tell her everything was going to be okay. But now, with just one touch, he felt like a teenage kid all over again.

"Can I ask you something?"

Her question drew him from his thoughts. "Sure, anything."

"Did you really get Jingle for me?" She eyed him curiously, waiting for an answer.

Oh Lord, help me out here! He could already feel the heat rising again, and his palms suddenly felt damp. He raised a hand to rub the back of his neck while looking at Jingle, stalling before answering. *Who told her?* Swallowing the lump in his throat, he faced her. Her green eyes sparkled as a playful grin lifted her lips, more like herself than he'd seen her since her return.

"Well, I had planned to tell you myself but apparently someone beat me to it," he answered, shrugging with embarrassment.

Her entire face lit up as her eyes rounded, and her smile grew wide. "Noah, I don't know what to say!"

He felt relief wash over him, uncoiling some of the tension in his shoulders. "That look on your face right now is enough," he responded. And before he knew it, her arms were around him, hugging him tightly.

Noah dropped the reins, knowing the horse wouldn't go anywhere. He slowly, cautiously lifted his arms as he returned her embrace. He felt her relax into him, resting her head against his shoulder, and he savored the moment. But just as quickly as the embrace had begun, it ended. Grace pulled back, looking at him with some unreadable emotion and moisture pooling in her eyes. It wasn't the pain he'd seen before. It was something different. And before he could say a word, she was gone.

* * *

Grace quickly exited the barn, striding toward the house. Despite the less oppressive morning air, she felt warm all over. Too warm. She hurried toward the mud room door, anticipating stepping into the cool, air-conditioned house. She wanted to clear her mind and free herself of whatever had just come over her. *What was that? What is wrong with me?*

In her frustration, she barged through the door, crashing into someone. Without looking up, she started to apologize. But once she raised her head, her words caught in her throat. Her brother Caleb was standing there, grinning from ear to ear. Without a word, she threw herself into his arms.

"Whoa now, Gracie! I'm happy to see you too, but you're about to take us both down!" he chuckled.

She loosened her grip and looked up at her big brother. He was just as she remembered him, albeit more filled out and well-muscled, but handsome as ever with a confident grin and a twinkle in his eye. She would never openly admit it to anyone for fear of hurt feelings, but Caleb had always been her favorite sibling. Only one year older than her, they had always been close growing up.

"When did you get here?" she asked excitedly.

"Just a few minutes ago. Mom said you were in the barn with Noah, so I was headed out there when you about took me out," he teased.

Grace looked away, heat flushing her face for what felt like the millionth time this morning. *What is wrong with you Grace Thompson!* She released an inaudible growl at herself.

"I think I'll go on out and find Noah. Care to join me my dearest sister?" her brother crooned, offering her his arm.

She hesitated. How could she turn down his simple request? But on the other hand, how could she face Noah again after her erratic behavior? She sighed, "Sure. I'll walk to the door with you, but then I'm coming back inside." Her tone was clipped.

Caleb looked puzzled but didn't say anything, at least not until they were outside. He didn't speak until they were out of earshot. "Why don't you want to see Noah? What's going on?"

She groaned inwardly, rolling her eyes. Her brother knew her too well. "Nothing is going on. I've already seen him this morning."

"And you're point *is*...?" Caleb drew out the question, raising his brows. When she didn't answer, he continued. "You and Noah were always best friends. What's changed?"

Grace stopped walking. "A lot has changed, Caleb," she snapped, more than a touch of irritation in her voice.

Caleb turned to face his sister. "Mom told me what you went through, and I'm sorry. If Jared was still alive, he'd be answering to me. Trust me on that." His tone was low and serious, his jaw tight. "But you aren't the only one who's been through hell."

Grace was visibly agitated now, and her tone reflected it. "What is *that* supposed to mean?"

Her brother gently reached for her arms, squeezing lightly, before pulling her in close. He bent just enough to see eye to eye with her. "Noah has been through hell, Grace. Did you stop and think about what he might have gone through in that hellhole we were stationed in?" His tone was clipped with a mixture of empathy and frustration. He looked away, as if looking into the past. "I saw my fair share of stuff over there that could really mess a man up, but I didn't have to live it like he did."

Grace felt her stomach drop. The irritation she'd felt only seconds earlier was quickly swept away by her brother's words. And when he turned his face back to hers, the sadness in his eyes tugged at her heart. "What happened?" she questioned, an uneasiness settling in the pit of her stomach.

"It's not my story to tell. It's his." And with that, Caleb dropped his hands to his sides and continued to the barn without her.

Grace stood frozen. Her mind was reeling. Caleb, unlike Noah, had always been one to share his experiences, good or bad. For him, most of the time, just getting things off his chest was enough. He'd always been that way, not one to bottle things up. He enjoyed laughing and living life too much to hang on to anything that would rob him of doing just that.

But Noah was the opposite. He worked diligently at keeping his emotions in check, not letting his defenses down very often. Grace thought back to when he first came to the ranch all those years ago and how long it had taken for him to open up and become her friend. And now, when he was likely in need of a friend and a listening ear, she hadn't even noticed.

She suddenly felt selfish, wallowing in her own self-pity. She was too wrapped up in her own problems to take notice of anyone else's. Noah had been her best friend, and he deserved better than what she'd given him. He was doing everything he could to welcome her home and be there for her. What had she done for him?

* * *

As the days passed, Grace tried to remain focused on letting go of her past and living in the here and now, suddenly more aware than ever of the many blessings she had to be thankful for. Despite what the last seven years had held, that season of her life was over. And with the nightmares no longer plaguing her, she was finding more of herself each day, learning to live again.

She followed the sound of voices into the kitchen. It seemed her family was always gathered there for one reason or another, and food was usually involved. In the Buckner house, eating wasn't just about good food and full bellies. It had always been a social occasion, a time for friends and family to come together and share a meal. The smell of her mother's homemade cinnamon rolls filled the air, mingling with freshly brewed coffee and her dad's favorite breakfast food – bacon! She closed her eyes and inhaled deeply, letting her senses delight in the aroma.

"Morning, Grace," her mother called. She was standing at the cooktop frying more bacon while Grandma Elaine and Anna sat quietly at the table listening to Abby's endless chatter.

"Hi, Mommy," Abby exclaimed, realizing her mother was there. White icing dripped from her chin, and some was smeared on her nose. Grace grinned and shook her head. Her youngest daughter was obviously enjoying her breakfast.

Grace sat in an empty chair and motioned for Anna to come to her. Her oldest daughter smiled as she came to stand by her mother. Grace wrapped her in a tight hug. The past few weeks had been such a whirlwind, and Grace was concerned she hadn't focused enough on her girls. "How are you this morning, sunshine?" she asked, kissing Anna on the cheek.

Anna grinned and hugged her mother tighter. "I'm happy. You're smiling again, Momma."

Grace felt as if her heart might explode. This beautiful, courageous little girl had her world turned upside down, yet she was more
concerned for her mother than for herself. *I could learn a thing or two
from my eight-year-old,* Grace thought silently.

"We're all going to church, Mommy!" Abby pronounced loudly,
breaking into her thoughts. "Are you coming with us?"

She hadn't even realized it was Sunday. Since being home, she
hadn't paid much attention to what day of the week it was. "Sure, I'd
like that, baby," she replied, smiling at Abby's enthusiasm.

Jane walked to the table. "I'm so glad you're joining us, Grace.
You haven't been since you came home, but I didn't want to push you.
I know you needed some time." Her smile was warm with understand-
ing.

Truth be told, Grace couldn't remember the last time she'd been
to church. Jared had reluctantly allowed her to send the girls to summer
bible school programs at local churches in whatever town they were
living in, but she knew better than to ask to attend herself. He had made
his feelings about organized religion very clear. *Painfully* clear.

"I think you'll like our new pastor, Pastor Daniel. He's a wonderful
man, and we're so thankful he decided to join us," her mother offered
encouragingly.

"When did he move here?" she responded.

"Oh, I'd say about a year ago now. Pastor Tom retired, and Pastor
Daniel came highly recommended. He's probably around your age,
Grace, but his knowledge of the Word far surpasses that. I can't wait
for you to meet him."

Her mother's excitement was contagious. It would be nice to be in
church again, worshipping the Lord. That was just one of the numerous
things she'd missed out on since marrying Jared.

"Is Caleb coming, too?" she asked.

"No, he went to visit Andrew and Tara this morning," Jane replied. "I'm sure he'll go to church with them, but he'll be back later this afternoon."

Just then Noah and her dad entered the kitchen through the mud room. Her dad was dressed in his old jeans and one of his ratty, button-front shirts he liked to wear for morning chores. He'd already kicked his boots off by the door and was now shuffling toward the table in his socks.

"John Jacob Buckner, don't you dare touch any of that food before you shower and clean up!" Her mother stood with her hands on her hips and one eyebrow raised.

Her father froze mid reach for a slice of bacon. He started to say something, likely to argue his case for why he should eat now. But when her mother cocked her head and lowered her brows, her lips pressed into a thin line, he conceded defeat and ascended the stairs to clean up.

Grace had to hold back her laughter. She figured her father was as tough a cow hand that ever lived, but when his wife used his full name with her hands planted firmly on her hips, he would comply with whatever her request. He'd always told her with a wink that a happy wife is a happy life!

Grace had to smile as she thought about her parents' relationship. She was convinced their love and commitment to each other could move heaven and earth if necessary. They'd never been just husband and wife and never would be. They'd always been partners, best friends through it all. She was surprised to find herself hoping she might have that same type of relationship one day. With a sigh, she offered a silent prayer. *Lord, when I'm ready and it's your time, help me find the right someone for me.*

"Girls, come with grandma. Let's finish getting ready for church while we let your momma finish her coffee." Jane scurried the girls from the kitchen, leaving Grace with Noah.

He was standing at the counter pouring himself a cup of coffee. His back was to her, and she was surprised to find him dressed in clean, dark wash jeans with a crisp, cerulean blue button-down shirt. When he turned her direction, she had to force herself to look away.

He sat down and greeted her. "Good morning."

She met his gaze and smiled. "Morning. Are you going to church with us?" she asked, already assuming the answer to be yes.

"Yes ma'am," he replied, slowly sipping his coffee. As he took a bite of cinnamon roll, he groaned in delight. "I sure did miss your mom's cooking while I was gone. You can't beat her cinnamon rolls." He eagerly took another bite. "Reminds me of my *mamm's* cooking."

Grace caught herself giggling. She'd always liked it when he slipped into a little bit of Pennsylvania Dutch. She couldn't help smiling.

"What?" he said, looking up and grinning at her between bites, "What's so funny?"

She smiled again. "Nothing is funny. I just like hearing you use your first language. I always have."

Noah grinned even wider. "Well, if that's what it takes to make you smile, then maybe I should speak in *Deitsch* all the time!" he replied with a wink.

Grace blushed and looked away. She was becoming increasingly aware that being around Noah was causing her to react in ways she didn't understand. He was her friend, a great friend. She needed to try and be the same for him. She stood from the table. "I guess I'd better get ready, too. Enjoy the rest of that cinnamon roll," she said with a playful grin.

"*Jah*, don't you worry, I will," he said, grinning as he popped another bite in his mouth.

As Grace left the kitchen, she couldn't help but smile, preoccupied by her thoughts of Noah. She wasn't quite sure what just happened. Were they flirting? All the grinning and winking sure made it seem that way. But she shook her head. *Stop being silly! He's your friend. Just focus and get yourself ready for church!*

* * *

Noah was rinsing his dirty dishes in the sink when everyone except Grace came back into the kitchen. Abby ran straight to him, twirling in a pretty, pink dress. "Do you like my dress, Noah?" she asked, grinning from ear to ear.

He couldn't help but smile, scooping her up and spinning her around. "I'd say it's one of the prettiest dresses I've ever seen," he replied, winking at Anna who was quietly observing. She rolled her eyes but smiled when she did.

Abby clung tightly to him. "I like you, Noah. I'm glad we came here." She planted a kiss on his cheek before squirming to the floor. He felt his heart melting.

"Hey now, those are my kisses you're giving away young lady!" Jake exclaimed with a pretend scowl.

Abby ran and jumped in his lap. "Oh Grandpa, I've got plenty of kisses for you, too!" She wrapped her little arms around his neck, giving him a big kiss on the cheek when she did. Everyone laughed.

Just then, Grace entered the kitchen. "I'm ready," she announced.

Noah turned at the sound of her voice, and the breath whooshed from his lungs. This woman had the ability to steal his breath and all coherent thoughts in his head simply by entering a room, especially when she looked like that. She was wearing a simple summer dress that flowed loosely around her figure, and her hair was clipped to one side, falling in long waves across her bare shoulder. Her dress was a shade of lavender that reminded him of the wildflowers growing in the fields, and it fit her perfectly, like it was made for her. He couldn't look away if he tried.

"Ahem." Jake cleared his throat.

Noah jerked his attention from Grace and turned, realizing both Jake and Jane were looking right at him. Yet again, he felt the heat rising up his neck. Thankfully, Grace didn't seem to notice. Abby was at her side, chattering away, stealing her attention. He breathed a sigh of relief. *Get a grip!* He seemed to be telling himself that a lot lately!

"Come on girls. Let's get you settled in the truck. We're going to be late if we don't get moving." Jane ushered both girls toward the door. As she passed Noah, she offered him a knowing grin. "Let's go John Jacob," she called over her shoulder. "Help me get these girls buckled in."

Noah watched as Jake grabbed one last cinnamon roll. Elaine shooed her son away from the sweets and toward the door.

When Noah turned, Grace was right beside him. She brushed against him lightly as she passed by, eyeing him over her shoulder. "Are you ready?" she asked.

She didn't wait for an answer as she kept moving toward the door. Her favorite fragrance, Cherry Blossom, floated in the air. It was nearly intoxicating. Remembering that scent, *her* scent, had gotten him through some rough and stressful nights while he was deployed. He wanted to answer her question with a resounding yes! He was ready to follow her anywhere.

CHAPTER 5

G race was immediately drawn to the quaint, country church her parents attended. She remembered coming here as a child. With its tall steeple and old-fashioned stained-glass windows, everything spoke of a time when things were much simpler. She felt like the building itself was welcoming her home, inviting her in.

She wasn't surprised to find the interior little changed as well. Aside from the addition of a large projector screen near the front for displaying song lyrics and scripture, most everything else held a comforting familiarity. Church attendance, however, had obviously grown. There wasn't hardly an empty seat to be had.

She stood with her girls on either side of her. The worship music was beginning, and the song leader was inviting everyone to join in. As the voices of the congregation rose together, worshipping their King, she felt something shifting on the inside, something changing. The song was an old hymn she knew well, *How Great Thou Art*, and as she closed her eyes and lifted her voice, she felt the waves of peace flooding her soul.

For the next hour, Grace sat transfixed, absorbing everything. Her mother had been accurate in her depiction of Pastor Daniel. The man obviously had a calling from the Lord on his life, and it came through in his sermon. His message was on forgiveness, and she felt as if he were speaking directly to her shattered heart. She sat on the edge of her seat as he spoke of forgiving others and of the forgiveness our Lord Jesus freely offers, but what had her heart pounding hard in her chest was when he spoke of how we must accept the forgiveness Jesus offers and not continue to let the mistakes of the past rule the future.

She felt a stirring deep inside as he eloquently spoke of the Lord's grace, quoting 1 John 1:19, *"If we confess our sins, he is faithful and just to forgive us our sins and to cleanse us from all unrighteousness."*

She knew the scripture well. It was one of the many verses she'd memorized as a child. But now, a woman broken by both her own mistakes and those of others, it took on new meaning. She knew she had asked the Lord to forgive her, but what she had not done was accept His forgiveness for the free gift that it was.

As Pastor Daniel continued, Grace remembered her grandmother's heartfelt words of wisdom. Tears came unbidden as the pastor articulately expressed 2 Corinthians 12:9, *"But he said to me, "My grace is sufficient for you, for my power is made perfect in weakness." Therefore I will boast all the more gladly of my weaknesses, so that the power of Christ may rest upon me."* His voice broke with emotion as he described the love and sacrifice of our Lord Jesus.

Nearing the end of his message, he implored the congregation, "Do not hold onto the wrongs you've done or the wrongs others have committed against you. Do not let guilt and shame rule you. Do not let anger and unforgiveness have a foothold in your life. Give it all to the Lord and allow Him to wash you clean. No matter what burdens you carried with you when you walked through those doors this morning, you don't have to leave with them. You can make that choice to give it all to Jesus. Choose to let his precious blood wash you white as snow."

As the worship leader began to sing *Amazing Grace*, Pastor Daniel called for those who would like personal prayer to come forward. Grace nearly leapt from her seat, a fire now burning inside her. But as she started down the aisle, she paused, overcome by the scene in front of her. Already standing up front with his head bowed was Noah. Pastor Daniel had his hand on his shoulder, praying. She moved slowly down the aisle, not wanting to interrupt but also not wanting to ignore the urging she felt in her heart. She stood a few steps back and waited.

Once finished, the two men clasped hands, Pastor Daniel gripping Noah's shoulder with the other. As Noah turned, her breath caught. His eyes were rimmed pink, and his cheeks were stained with tears. He held her gaze only briefly as he passed by.

Grace continued forward, drawn by the still, small voice inside her. She couldn't find the words to speak as a sob threatened to escape her lips. Pastor Daniel's expression was one of understanding as he placed a gentle hand on her shoulder. As he lifted his voice to the Lord on her behalf, she felt the chains of guilt and shame falling away, no longer a hostage in a prison of her own making. She felt the doors of her heart swinging wide open, as if an unbearable weight had been lifted from her chest. Breathing deeply, she was inhaling peace and exhaling pain. In that moment, she felt the love of God filling every broken, fragmented piece of her heart. For the first time in her adult life, she laid it all aside and chose forgiveness.

Attempting to compose herself, she hadn't even realized she'd fallen to her knees. Her sobs coupled with Pastor Daniel's heartfelt petitions to the Lord had overcome her. Now, as he helped her stand, she was standing in freedom. Although weak from the flood of emotion, she felt lighter. For the first time in so many years she knew the Lord had forgiven her, and she had accepted His forgiveness.

As she sat back down in the pew next to her family, her girls hugged her tightly. She glanced at her parents, and even her dad was fighting back the emotion attempting to overtake him. Her mother offered a gentle smile as her eyes misted. At the far end of the row, head bowed and hands clasped, Noah sat leaning on his knees, reverent in prayer as his own tears continued to fall.

* * *

By the time everyone returned to the ranch, Caleb had also returned. He was enacting a dramatic display about wasting away from hunger while waiting on them, being his usual, playful self.

"What's a man got to do to get some food around here? I had no choice but to eat that whole pan of cinnamon rolls you left on the counter so I wouldn't faint from hunger!" He winked at Grace as he put his arm around their mother.

"Caleb Matthew, if you ate that whole pan of leftover rolls, I'm going to have your head!" came Jane's reply.

Grace knew her mother was just playing along, knowing full well Caleb's sole intention was to get a reaction from her.

"But Momma, I'm a growing boy! I have to eat!" Now he was laying it on thick, sounding more like a whiny ten-year-old instead of a grown man, smiling the whole time like the cat who got the canary.

"You just go ahead and keep eating like that, and pretty soon we'll be using that wheelbarrow in the barn to get you around!" Jane responded, flashing a grin. She was giving her son a taste of his own medicine.

Caleb raised a hand to his chest as if taken aback. "Momma, are you calling me... *fat*?" he said, feigning shock as he gulped the last word for dramatic effect.

Jane reached and playfully slapped his arm, no longer holding back her laughter. He pulled his mother close and kissed the top of her head. "I love you, Mom."

"I love you, too," she responded, continuing toward the door with his arm hooked around her shoulders.

When they were almost inside, he spoke again. "But seriously, what's for lunch?"

Now everyone was laughing!

Once inside, Grace realized Noah had not joined them. She looked out the window but didn't see him. "I wonder where Noah is?"

"I'm not sure," her mother replied. "Maybe he went to the bunkhouse or the barn for something. Caleb can go check on him."

As Caleb headed for the door, his dad followed. "I'll come with you. I need to check on a few things."

While the men went in search of Noah, the women set to work getting lunch on the table. Jane had made two pans of lasagna the day before, ready and waiting to be heated in the oven. As they waited on the lasagna to warm, they tossed a salad, set the table, and poured some drinks. Jane also sliced some of her homemade bread and sat it out with the strawberry butter she'd made earlier in the summer.

"Mom, you sure are something, you know that?" Grace complimented.

Jane turned to her daughter. "Thank you," she said, smiling. "But why do you say that?"

Grace gestured toward the table. "Look at all this. You've always gone above and beyond to make our house feel like a home, to make sure it's not just food on the table, but delicious, home-cooked food. You've always been my inspiration for the kind of mother I want to be."

Jane was nearly speechless, visibly touched by the heartfelt words. "I don't know what to say," she responded, a hitch in her voice. "I've always done the best I know how and just hoped it was enough."

Grace gently touched her mother's arm. "It's been *more* than enough. I'm grateful for all you've done. I had an amazing childhood, and I'm grateful for that. And I'm grateful for all you're doing now, for me and the girls. I couldn't have gotten through any of this without you."

Jane reached up, covering her daughter's hand with her own, tears welling in her eyes. "You don't know how glad I am that you're home, Grace. You and the girls."

As the oven timer chimed, Jane released Grace's hand, swiping at her tears before picking up her oven mitts. "It looks like these are hot and bubbly. Will you go see where the men have gotten off to and tell them lunch is on the table?"

"Sure, Mom." Grace headed for the door.

Once outside, she scanned the area around the house, not seeing anyone. Deciding to try the barn, she strode across the driveway. When she got to the large, open door leading inside, she stopped. At the end of the long hallway, she spotted them. Caleb was embracing Noah, and her dad had his hand clasped on Noah's shoulder, much the same way the pastor had at church. Noah's back was to her, but she could clearly see Caleb's face. He was smiling broadly, clapping Noah on the back. Not wanting to interrupt, she silently retreated to the house.

* * *

While everyone else had lunch, Noah spent that time alone in prayer. Although he was thankful to know he always had a place at the Buckner table, he needed this time by himself. Ever since he could remember, he craved those times of solitude when it was just him and the Lord. It gave him time to reflect and offer both his petitions and his thanksgiving. And today especially, he had a great deal to be thankful for.

He had been attending church with the Buckners ever since returning to the ranch, and he had grown to enjoy it. He appreciated the way their church and the pastor kept things simple and focused on the Lord, focusing on the truth of His Word. And he respected Pastor Daniel more all the time, holding him in high regard, thanking God for him. The man had been a great help to him since his return from active duty, and he had also played an essential role in him deciding to take the first step in making peace with his family.

Noah had dealt with a great deal since returning from overseas, facing issues created when he left his Amish life and family to dealing with problems that followed him home from the Middle East. If it weren't for the love and support he received from the Buckners, he wouldn't have come as far as he had in his journey to find peace. His heart continued to swell with gratitude as he pondered all that had happened over the last six months or so. *Thank you, Lord, for being so, so good to me! Even in the midst of all my trials, You have always been there, never forsaking me. Please help me continue to trust Your plan, Your will for my life.*

With his heart lighter than it had been in years, he found himself praying with renewed fervency. How beautiful it was to let the Lord have all of your life, all your hurt and all your pain. And how beautiful it had been for him to witness Grace finding that same freedom for herself. As he remembered the sight of her falling to her knees, surrendering before the Lord, he felt tears dampening his cheeks. *Thank you, Lord, for showing Grace Your love and forgiveness. Thank you for protecting her and her girls, and thank you for bringing them home. Please help me to do what I can to continue to help her, to be the kind of friend she needs.*

As he continued walking and praying, soaking in the beauty of the day, a thought crossed his mind. On the back of a horse was another place where he found peace and clarity to think. Doing what the Lord had gifted him to do always filled him with a sense of appreciation and gratefulness for all he had in his life. And at that moment, it occurred to him what he could do for Grace. He could get her back on a horse, the place she'd always found so much joy before life had taken its toll.

* * *

Grace sat swinging quietly on the back patio. The sun was hot on her skin and the air humid, but she didn't mind. A mild breeze swirled around her, gently tousling her hair. As she watched her girls playing with bubbles in the yard, running and giggling, she smiled. The contentment and peace she felt on the inside was overflowing from her heart. Laying her head back and closing her eyes, she let the warmth of the sun's rays wash over her.

It wasn't until she heard a nicker close by that she opened her eyes. Standing at the edge of the patio with two saddled horses was Noah. He smiled at her from beneath the brim of his cowboy hat, handing a set of reins in her direction. "Care to join me?"

The smile that flickered on his lips made her very aware, yet again, of how strikingly handsome he was. And how his presence continued to have a strange effect on her. Meeting his gaze, she knew she wouldn't be able to tell him no. Even though she hadn't yet ridden since returning home, today seemed to be the day that would change.

Rising to her feet, attempting to stifle a wide smile, she nipped at her bottom lip. "You know I haven't ridden in years," she said, moving toward him. She stopped at the railing, standing just above him. The raised patio left her just slightly higher than him, putting her about eye level with the horses. She reached and gently stroked Jingle's cheek.

Noah shrugged. "No time like the present to change that," he said. That boyish grin that made her heart flutter crooked up one side of his mouth.

Grace couldn't contain her smile. "Let me check with Mom and see if she minds watching the girls."

"Mom doesn't mind at all," came Jane's answer.

Grace turned. Her mother was stepping onto the patio, wiping her hands on a dish towel. "In fact, I'd like to teach these granddaughters of mine how to make Cowboy Cookies."

At the mention of cookies, Anna and Abby came running. "What are Cowboy Cookies?" they asked simultaneously.

"Well, they just happen to be the most delicious cookies ever, filled with chocolate chips and all kinds of goodies!" Jane winked at Grace and Noah as she ushered her granddaughters inside.

Grace gave her mother a grateful smile before turning back to Noah. "Let me change really quick, and I'll be ready!"

Upstairs, she quickly changed into jeans and a t-shirt before heading back downstairs to slip into her boots. When she stepped back outside, Noah was patiently waiting, his cowboy hat dipped low, shading his eyes from the sun. When he raised his head and locked his gaze on her, her heart rate spiked involuntarily. *Stop it, Grace! You're being ridiculous! It's just nerves. Breathe.*

Once in the saddle, she felt surprisingly confident and comfortable. As they meandered through the wide, open pastures, she couldn't stop smiling. She had missed this part of her life more than she'd allowed herself to think. Turning to her right, Noah and Jingle were quietly ambling along beside her.

"So... if you say Jingle is mine, why are you riding her and not me?" she asked, narrowing her eyes, teasing him. She already knew the answer.

Noah looked down at Jingle and patted her neck before answering. "I want to get some more ride time in on her before I trust her with you. She's doing well but could use more time out in the open like we're doing now." He gestured toward Doc, the horse Grace was riding. "And walking alongside a calm, steady horse like Doc who doesn't spook for anything is good for her, helps build her confidence."

Grace smiled, looking from Doc to Jingle. Jingle was more alert than Doc. Her ears remained perked, and she kept her head up, watching her surroundings. Doc, on the other hand, kept his head low and body relaxed as he leisurely sauntered along.

"How old is Doc now?" she asked.

"Your dad said he figures he's around twenty-two."

Grace patted the old horse's neck. He'd been around for as long as she could remember. He stood about fifteen hands tall and was sorrel in color, a white blaze running down his face. He was your typical, average quarter horse to look at, but she knew he'd always been trustworthy, a good kid-broke horse. And he'd lived a darn good life on the Buckner ranch.

"You think he's got a little pep left in his step?" she asked, giving Noah a mischievous grin.

Noah furrowed his brow. "*Why...?*" he asked, drawing out the word. "*Grace...* what are you thinking?" His tone held an edge of warning.

She didn't answer. Instead, she gave Doc a gentle squeeze with her legs as she pushed the reins forward. He responded to her cues, raising his head and quickening his pace into a canter. As she continued to urge him on, they were soon galloping across the pasture, the wind whipping by. Grace felt a rush of exhilaration. A wide smile spread across her face as she tingled with excitement. Bending slightly at the waist, she leaned forward toward Doc's outstretched neck, letting him run. The world around them seemed to blur as they raced past.

Finally easing up, sitting back in the saddle and pulling gently on the reins, she turned to see Noah and Jingle not far behind. The smile on her face quickly faded as she realized that unlike Doc, Jingle was not slowing her pace. With eyes wide, she watched helplessly as Noah fought to maintain control of his horse. Jingle was throwing her head, pushing hard against the bit. As they bolted past, Grace could see the alarmed look on Noah's face as he attempted to calm Jingle, firmly and repeatedly commanding her to stop. "Whoa! Whoa, girl! Whoa!"

As Noah continued his struggle with the horse, sitting back in the saddle with all his weight, Jingle slowed her pace only to lunge forward again before bucking hard. Grace watched in alarm, helpless to do anything. Jingle continued to buck, fighting against Noah as he worked to pull her head around to her side, an attempt to get her back under control. Just as Grace thought he'd won the battle, Jingle lunged forward, bucked hard, and unseated her rider. Noah was pitched in the air, reminding Grace of someone tossing a ragdoll. He hit the ground hard, landing flat on his back. His body rippled with the force of the blow.

Grace jumped off Doc, racing toward Noah on foot. She could hardly breathe, her heart pounding. She slid to her knees beside him, her entire body vibrating with panic. "Noah! Noah! Please be okay!" she pleaded.

He was gasping for breath, wincing in pain, his eyes closed against the bright sun above. Her eyes darted back and forth, looking him over, expecting to see an exposed broken bone from the fall he'd just taken. Her gaze rested on his abdomen. His shirt was bunched up, exposing angry scars starting just above his right hip that continued up his side, wrapping around onto his back. She traced the path of the scars with her eyes, stopping when she could no longer see what remained hidden by his shirt.

* * *

Noah opened his eyes, squinting against the sun. Grace was hovering over him. The wind had been knocked out of him, and his back was aching. He raised himself to his elbows, looking at her. Her eyes were darting frantically over him, her gaze wandering between his face and his midsection. Her eyes were wide, her mouth slightly agape. A look of distress was etched across her beautiful face.

Looking down, following her eyes, he noticed his shirt wasn't fully covering him, exposing his scars. He quickly tugged his shirt down, grimacing in pain. He took slow, deliberate breaths, attempting to ease the discomfort and fill his lungs with oxygen. He closed his eyes again, focusing on his breathing. He didn't want to speak, knowing he might say something he'd regret. He couldn't remember ever feeling this aggravated with Grace. She should have known better than to take off like that with him riding a young horse still in training. And now he was suffering on the ground, feeling the pain physically but also because his pride was hurt. He couldn't recall the last time he'd been thrown by a horse.

To make matters worse, she'd seen his scars. That meant she'd be asking questions, and he would have no choice but to tell her the truth. What had started off as one of the most incredible days he'd had in recent memory was now taking a turn for the worse.

He still had his eyes closed when Grace's gentle voice broke in. "Noah, are you okay? I'm so sorry."

Opening his eyes, he forced himself to sit all the way up. He ignored her question, looking around. "Where's Jingle?"

She turned and motioned toward a large tree near the fence line. Several yards from them, near the tree, Jingle stood calmly. *Oh, now you're calm!* He rolled his eyes and shook his head, pushing himself off the ground. Grace reached for his arm to assist, helping him stand. Normally her touch would send a rush of heat coursing through him, but right now, still irritated and in pain, he barely noticed. If anything, he wanted to give her a piece of his mind!

Taking a few more deep breaths, he started walking toward Jingle, snatching his hat off the ground as he went. Grace had released his arm and was standing frozen in her spot. When he realized she wasn't following him, he turned and looked over his shoulder. He was only a few feet from her and as he turned, his anger dissolved. Tears were streaming down her cheeks, and the look of anguish on her face ripped at his insides. Either she was crying because she could tell he was upset with her, or she was crying because she knew he was in pain. Regardless of which, he felt responsible.

Walking back to her, he instinctively reached, pulling her into his arms. "Grace, it's okay. I'll be fine. Probably just sore for a few days." He could feel her body shudder against him with each sob.

"I'm so sorry, Noah. I wasn't thinking. I just wasn't thinking."

Sighing heavily, he pulled away from her just enough to see her face. "Really, it's okay. I promise I'll be fine." He cupped her cheek with one hand, gently wiping away her tears with his thumb. The sorrow he saw in her expression tugged at his heart. She closed her eyes, nestling her face into his touch. He felt that familiar rush of warmth as he gazed at her, savoring the feeling of her closeness.

When she opened her eyes, meeting his gaze, his breath hitched. The sorrow was gone, replaced by a look he wasn't quite sure how to read. He couldn't recall her ever looking at him like that. As if beyond his control, he found himself closing what little distance was left between them, an invisible magnet drawing him to her. He heard her suck in a breath as his own breathing seemed to halt. His gaze dropped to her slightly parted lips as his heart hammered in his chest.

Just as he felt he'd lost all self-control, mere inches remaining between them, a loud whinny jerked him back to reality. Turning toward the sound, Jingle was now trotting in their direction. At the same time, Doc replied with a nicker of his own. Taking a breath and stepping back, Noah dropped his arms from around Grace. When he turned again to face her, her cheeks blushed pink as she shifted her focus to the ground.

Giving his attention to the horse, he started toward Jingle. She was now slowly sauntering along as if nothing had happened. He reached for the reins once she was within arm's reach. He stood and stared at her for a long minute, shaking his head. *Thanks a lot! First you pitch me off, and now you've ruined whatever was just happening with Grace!* Now it was the horse he'd like to give a piece of his mind!

Grace had already collected Doc, and as he met up with her side by side, they headed back in the direction of the barn. "I think I'd better walk. Not sure I'm up to riding at the moment," he said, rubbing his lower back with one hand.

"Sure. I'll walk with you. I still feel responsible," she said quietly, her gaze remaining focused on the ground.

Noah sighed heavily. "I told you I'll be okay. Just sore. Don't beat yourself up over it."

They plodded along in silence. His mind was racing with what had almost happened, and he wondered if she was thinking about the same thing. If he let himself think about that, the soreness in his back didn't seem nearly as pressing an issue.

"Noah?" Grace broke the silence, her tone filled with uncertainty.

"Yeah?"

"Can I ask you a question?"

"Sure..." he replied hesitantly, unsure where this was headed.

When she didn't respond, he looked at her. Her brow was creased, her lips pressed into a tight line. She seemed to be pondering what to say or maybe how to say it.

"I saw your scars. Did that happen when you were in the Army?"

Noah stopped walking. He took a deep breath and sighed. He hated the story that came with the scars. Every time he showered or dressed, he was reminded of it. And he hated to tell Grace this particular story. She'd been through enough without having to know what happened to him.

While he tried to think of how to answer, she seemed to detect his reluctance. "It's okay, you don't have to tell me if you don't want to."

When he turned her direction, that same look of anguish had once again hijacked her beautiful face. He knew he had to tell her. If he didn't, she would just continue to worry about him. Sighing heavily yet again, he responded, "It's a long story, Grace. Can I tell you about it another time?" This really wasn't a good time to share what he would have to say.

"Sure," she answered, offering a half-hearted smile. She didn't say anymore.

CHAPTER 6

As the days passed, Grace's relationship with Noah took an awkward turn. They hadn't spoken much since the incident in the pasture, and he hadn't asked her to go riding again since. Any interaction between them seemed to have dwindled to nothing more than a few shared looks here and there. In some ways, she felt like he was avoiding her. Maybe she was avoiding him, too.

She also found herself attempting to avoid thinking about him. Her mind was clouded with so much uncertainty, and it caused a coil of doubt to lodge in her chest. Maybe she had misread what happened, assumed too much. Maybe he had no intention of kissing her. And why would she want him to? He had always been such a good friend, and why would she want that to change? She wasn't sure she could trust her own judgment when it came to her feelings, considering all she'd been through.

While riding with her brother one evening, roaming quietly across the peaceful landscape, she found her mind gravitating to the very subject she had been trying so hard to avoid. *Am I drawn to Noah because I know he cares about me?* When she thought about it, it saddened her to the very core to know the only two men she'd shared her heart with likely never really loved her at all. She didn't know what it was like to be loved the way a man *should* love a woman, to be treasured and respected, protected even. A tear trickled down her cheek.

"You okay, Gracie?" Caleb's question pulled her back to the present.

Quickly swiping away the lone tear, she answered, "Yeah, I'm okay. Just thinking." She offered him a slight smile.

Caleb grinned and returned his attention to the horizon. A beautiful sunset loomed before them, filling the sky with shades of amber and gold. "Man, I'm sure gonna miss this when I head back home," he remarked, sighing heavily.

"I wish you didn't have to go." She looked at him, melancholy overtaking her at the thought of him leaving.

He sighed again before responding. "I know, but I've about used up all my vacation time. I'll try to get over this way more often now that you're here," he said with a smile. "I've missed you, Gracie Mae."

"I've missed you, too. Thanks for coming home to see me," she said, smiling at her big brother.

Caleb was facing the horizon again when he spoke. "At least you're here with family. *And* Noah," he added, winking in her direction.

Grace shifted uncomfortably in her saddle. "We're just friends, Caleb. He's always been a good friend to me, and I want to be that for him, too. He deserves that."

Caleb shook his head and chuckled. "Oh Gracie Mae, what am I going to do with you?"

She scrutinized her brother, her brows furrowed. "What's that supposed to mean?"

He chuckled again but said nothing. He simply turned Lena, the bay mare he was riding, home toward the barn.

Grace sat perplexed, staring after her brother. She didn't know what he was getting at, and she didn't have the energy necessary to figure it out. She'd practically exhausted herself the past several days thinking about questions she couldn't answer.

Once back at the barn, Grace unsaddled Doc and started to brush him down. Caleb was doing the same with Lena. Together they fed and watered all the horses before heading in for the night. They were just about to the house when they met their father walking toward them.

"Well kids, I've made an executive decision!" Jake's voice rang with enthusiasm. "Since it's almost time for you to head back to work, Caleb, and since Anna is starting school next week," he said, turning to Grace, "I've decided tomorrow we're all taking the day and spending it at the lake. I've already called the rest of the family, and everyone is coming!"

Caleb and Grace exchanged a look as their father continued explaining his plan. "We'll take our boat and jet skis, and we'll rent another boat, too. That way we'll have enough room for everyone to be out on the water together. I've got it all taken care of. We're leaving at 9 a.m. sharp." He clasped his hands together in a show of accomplishment.

Jake Buckner held his head high as he beamed with pride, obviously pleased with the plans he'd made to celebrate the rapidly nearing end of summer. Grace couldn't help but smile. Maybe a day at the lake was exactly what she needed to clear her mind. But then she thought of Noah. Would he be coming, too?

"Uh, dad?" she called after her father who was already walking back toward the house. She shot a quick glance at her brother. *Why am I asking this in front of him?* She rolled her eyes at the thought and continued anyway. "Is Noah coming?"

Caleb darted his eyes in her direction, a broad smile spreading across his face. She quickly cut him a sharp look.

"Of course he's coming," came her father's reply. "He's family, isn't he?" His last comment was more a statement than a question.

As their dad continued toward the house, Grace cut her brother another look. Not saying a word, he broke out in loud laughter. Shaking his head and still chuckling, he left her standing in the driveway. She wasn't about to try and explain herself to him anyway. In her opinion, he could think whatever he wanted. And although she, for some reason, suddenly felt like a nervous teenager, she pushed it aside. Her sole motivation was to put an end to this ridiculous awkwardness that had settled between her and Noah. She longed to have her best friend back. That was all it was. Or so she kept telling herself.

* * *

Early the next morning at the assigned time, everyone was loaded up and ready to go. The weather was perfect for the day - hot and humid, just what a person needed to appreciate the coolness of the water. A brilliant August sun shone overhead, and there wasn't a cloud in the sky. A warm breeze was gently rustling the trees.

Once at the lake and settled on the water, Grace relaxed into the tranquility of the day. She was watching her girls jump off the pontoon boat, landing near the waiting arms of the men floating nearby. She hadn't noticed until today just how much both Anna and Abby had taken a shine to Noah. They were repeatedly climbing back up on the boat, calling his name to catch them before jumping in again. And without fail, he did exactly that. Over and over again, never seeming annoyed or bothered.

She smiled slightly, her heart hopeful for her girls' future but also filled with grief for their past. She couldn't ever remember a time when Jared would have done such a thing. He would never have stopped working long enough to have a day full of nothing but play. And although he was a good provider for the girls' material needs, he offered little to nothing in the department of providing for their emotional needs.

Grace noticed one of the jet skis sitting idle, anchored to the side of the boat. She remembered her goal, desiring to alleviate some of the awkwardness that had settled between her and her best friend. Sucking in a breath and blowing it out to calm her nerves, she walked to the edge of the boat. Noah was catching Abby for the umpteenth time. Water erupted into a volcano of spray as she hit the water. She quickly popped back up, squealing with delight. Grace watched as Noah pulled her to him, laughing along with her. Anna was clutching his shoulders from behind, one arm dangling across his chest, a wide smile filling her face.

Grace felt her heart swell as she clutched a hand to her chest. When Noah's eyes met hers, a flood of warmth pulsed through her. His broad smile was enough to tell her he was enjoying this as much as her girls. And for some unexplainable reason, she had to blink back unexpected tears. She motioned toward the Jet Ski, and he nodded in agreement. She felt her heart flutter as he swam toward her. *Calm down, Grace! You're supposed to be fixing this, not making it worse!*

* * *

Noah climbed on the Jet Ski with Grace. His pulse was pounding a little harder than he'd prefer. He hadn't been this close to her since that day in the pasture, and things had been strained between them ever since. As he scooted in close behind her, he was thankful for the space the life jackets created between them. He didn't want this to turn into another awkward episode of what ifs.

She turned slightly toward him. "Do you want to go first?"

The playfulness of her tone coupled with the closeness of her body muddled his thoughts. For some reason, he couldn't comprehend what she was saying. "Huh?"

She dangled the key at him. "Driving. Do you want to go first?"

"Oh... uh... no. You go ahead." He figured he shouldn't be driving anything right now if he couldn't even think straight! He rolled his eyes and tried to clear his mind.

Grace clipped the key to her life jacket, plugged it in, and pushed start. She slowly maneuvered away from the boat and the swimmers in the water. Abby and Anna waved as they were bobbing up and down next to their Uncle Caleb.

Once they were in open water, she turned her head toward him, a cunning grin teasing on her lips as her eyes danced with mischief. "You better find something to hang on to."

Noah looked down at the seat. He didn't see anything that would give him enough grip to hold on. There was a small strap, but he doubted he'd be able to maintain any balance with that. "Umm... what exactly am I supposed to hold on to?"

A giggle tripped from her lips. He couldn't see her face but could hear the smile in her voice. "Me."

Noah swallowed hard as he somewhat reluctantly pulled himself closer to her, putting his arms around her waist. "Is this... okay?"

"Yep," she replied, still facing forward.

He attempted to keep a little distance between them but that proved difficult to do. Both because he *wanted* to be close to her but also because of how he was forced to sit to hold on. And when she took off, the small bubble of space he tried to maintain quickly evaporated.

As they raced across the water, Noah couldn't help but laugh with every wave they hit. The water sprayed his face, and the wind was whipping, almost stinging his skin. Grace seemed adept at handling the watercraft, and he was having the time of his life! He'd been on a jet ski only a few other times before now.

As Grace slowed, coming to a stop out in the open water, she shut down the motor and turned to him with a wide grin. "You're turn! Trade me places."

He furrowed his brow. "Uh... okay. How are we supposed to do that?"

She grinned again. "I'll scoot to one side, and you scoot to the other."

Noah didn't feel so sure about this. As soon as Grace started to shift, he felt the Jet Ski wobble. He wasn't scared of the water, but he also didn't plan on falling off in the middle of the lake. "Uh... are you sure about this?" he asked, while carefully trying to slip past her.

"Oh, come on, what's the worst that could..."

Her words trailed off as the watercraft bobbled and lurched hard to the right. Before he knew it, they both were in the water. Noah quickly popped back up to the surface, pulled up by his life jacket. He wiped his face and blinked several times, attempting to clear his vision. When he looked at Grace, still blinking water from his eyes, she burst out laughing. "I'm so sorry," she said between chuckles. "I didn't think you'd dump us over!"

"*Me*? How is this *my* fault?" he replied, raising his brows.

"*You* were supposed to balance us while I slid by you. You outweigh me!" she exclaimed.

"Oh, so you're calling me fat now! I see how it is!" He continued to grin, teasing her.

"No! Trust me Noah, there is nothing fat about you!" Her face colored at her words, and she looked away.

He grinned wryly. *So, she* has *noticed.*

Still not meeting his eyes, Grace swam to the back of the Jet Ski, pulling down the small step. "Here, you get on first, and I'll climb up behind you."

He swam to her, raised one foot to the step, and pulled himself effortlessly from the water. Once he was balanced, he reached his hand for hers, also pulling her effortlessly on behind him. She scooted in close, unhooking the key from her life jacket and reaching around to latch it to his. When he turned slightly to look at her, her face was only inches from his. She blushed again and looked away.

"You're all set," she said. "Start it up!"

Noah followed her instructions, and in no time, they were back racing across the water. Grace kept her arms around him, gripping the front of his life jacket. Her nearness combined with the speed at which they were traveling had his adrenaline pumping overtime!

After a while, he reluctantly headed back to the boat. As soon as they anchored and climbed aboard, Jane had lunch ready to go. He hadn't realized until now how hungry he was. His stomach seemed to growl on command at the thought.

"Come help yourselves!" Jane called.

Noah was fixing himself a plate when Abby tugged on his hand. "Noah, can I sit with you?"

She smiled up at him, her deep brown eyes melting his heart. "Of course, you can! Here," he said, "put whatever you want on my plate, and we'll share."

When he sat down, she plopped down in his lap. She grinned at him with each bite she took. Caleb and Anna sat down on either side of him. When Caleb leaned forward, eyeing both of his nieces, he flashed a knowing grin but didn't say a word.

* * *

Grace stood next to her mother as she ate. Her heart swelled with gratitude as she watched her girls with Noah. Yet again he was entertaining them and didn't seem to mind one bit.

"Those two sure seem taken with him," Jane said softly, nodding subtly in their direction.

"Yeah, I guess they are. I don't think I realized how much until today," she replied.

"It's sweet to watch him with them. He'll be a good father someday."

Grace gave her mother a scrutinizing look. Jane smiled, leaning in close to her daughter. "I suspect he'll be a fine husband as well."

"Mom, please!" Grace beseeched in a hushed tone, scanning to see if anyone heard her mother's offhand comment. "We are just friends! Besides, Jared has only been gone a few months. I'm not ready for anything like that."

"Oh Grace, is it wrong for a mother to want her daughter to be happy?" Jane implored. "You might be surprised what the Lord has in store for you if you'd be open to it."

Grace didn't offer a reply as her mother gently squeezed her arm before turning away. Giving her attention to the scene in front of her, she soon became lost in her own thoughts. Wasn't it too soon for her to think about having a relationship with anyone? She'd only been a widow for a few months. Wasn't it improper for her to even consider such a thing? Or was her mother right? Did she deserve to be happy?

Her marriage, after all, had been anything but happy. In fact, was there ever a time she truly loved Jared or that he loved her?

She froze. That's when it hit her. Not only had she never been in a pure, loving relationship with a man, she also didn't know what it was to love a man in that way. As she thought back to Chris, she'd always known it wasn't really love that had brought them together. And with Jared, if she was being honest, she had settled for him out of desperation and brokenness. At that point in her life, she was an emotionally battered woman craving acceptance and someone to be a father for Anna. And for her, at the time, Jared had been the answer to both of those desires. Little did she know that she would go from being emotionally battered to physically battered as well. She had been so blind.

* * *

After their day at the lake, Noah and Grace seemed to settle back into their normal routine of friendship. For the most part, the awkward uneasiness between them had dissipated. They went riding together almost every day, often taking the girls with them. Noah was teaching Anna and Abby how to ride, and Grace was amazed at his patience and understanding, even with Abby.

School had started for Anna, and Abby was attending a half-day preschool program four days a week. Grace found herself with lots of free time, and she quickly settled into a pattern of helping her mother in the kitchen while also taking part in the daily chores around the ranch. When she was younger, she always preferred being outside with the men all day. But now, a grown woman and mother, she appreciated the time she was able to spend inside with her own mother.

Jane Buckner had been preparing and cooking three meals a day for as long as Grace could remember. She always said if her husband was going to provide for their family financially, then the least she could do was provide him with home-cooked food on the table. Her mother always joked that the way to a man's heart was through his stomach.

What had always caught Grace's attention, however, was the loving way her father always appreciated her mother. As gruff and tough as he could be at times, he'd never been anything but gentle and kind toward his wife. In fact, the way he still looked at her after all these years warmed Grace's heart.

One day as Grace sat at the kitchen table enjoying a mid-morning cup of coffee, Jane burst in excitedly from the mudroom, "Look what finally came in the mail!" She held up a small cardboard box and pulled out a plastic bag containing an unidentifiable substance.

"What is *that*?" Grace questioned, her nose wrinkling.

"It's my friendship bread starter from Katie Ann. She told me in her last letter she'd be sending it." Jane set the bag on the counter, lifting a small index card from the box.

Grace was confused. "Who is Katie Ann? And what is friendship bread?"

Jane turned to her daughter, a look of surprise on her face. "Oh Grace, I'm sorry. I thought you knew I've been writing back and forth with Noah's mother."

Grace felt her eyes grow wide with shock. "When did this happen? How do you even know her?"

Jane sat down across from her daughter, looking a little confused. "Well, I don't really *know* her, as in person, but we've been writing back and forth for several months now. Didn't Noah tell you?"

Grace harrumphed. "Obviously not! What am I missing here?"

Jane rubbed her forehead. "I thought he would have told you." She paused, almost as if unsure whether to continue.

"Well, I guess you'd better tell me since he *apparently* isn't going to." She couldn't hide the irritation in her voice.

Her mother eyed her with uncertainty for a moment before continuing. "Soon after he came home from deployment, he went to see his parents. He wanted to make peace with them and explain the choices he'd made." Her eyes took on a far-off look, almost as if gazing into the past. "His time overseas... it... it affected him. Very deeply," she said. She turned her gaze back to Grace. "It changed his thinking about a lot of things, put a lot in perspective. And one of those things was his relationship with his family. He didn't want to continue being separated from them. He wanted them to be a part of his life, to try and understand the decisions he'd made."

Grace sat staring at her mother, confused and irritated. *This is huge! Why didn't Noah tell me?*

Jane reached for her hand. "Grace, I'm sorry. Don't be mad at him. I'm sure he was going to tell you. He was probably just waiting for the right time. I'm sure he was only thinking of you and everything you've been dealing with."

She thought about that. It was true she'd come home with a whole host of her own problems, but why hadn't he told her by now? They'd grown close again, and she felt like she had her best friend back. She couldn't help but feel a little betrayed and disappointed in him.

Grace turned back to her mother, narrowing her eyes. "Do his scars have something to do with it?"

Jane pulled her hand back and sat up straight. She sighed. "Has he told you what happened?"

She shook her head, still watching her mother.

"Well then, I'm sorry, but I can't tell you. That's his place, not mine."

Feeling her frustration rising, she retorted, "That's *exactly* what Caleb told me! Why won't someone just tell me what happened?" She pushed back from the table.

Jane looked at her daughter intently. "Talk to him, Grace." She patted her hand and rose from her seat.

Grace looked at the clock. It was almost ten, and Abby would need to be picked up at eleven from preschool. She tapped her fingers on the table impatiently, trying to decide if she should go find Noah now or wait until later. But the more she thought about it, the more she didn't want to wait.

She'd just stepped outside and was crossing the driveway toward the barn when she noticed an unfamiliar car coming up the lane. She paused, watching as it pulled in near the front door of her parents' home. When a woman wearing a modest blue dress and a white head covering stepped from the backseat of the vehicle, Grace immediately knew she was Amish. Hearing footsteps behind her, she turned to see Noah coming out of the barn. He paused, looking at the woman. He looked back to Grace, a questioning look on his face, before continuing toward the stranger.

Assuming the woman was some relation to him, Grace moved back toward the house. She could hear him greeting the stranger in *Deitsch* and couldn't understand a word he was saying. The woman, however, now wore a relieved expression, answering Noah in the same language. She wondered if this woman might be his mother, Katie Ann.

The more she watched the interaction between them, however, it became obvious they had never met before today. She also noticed they were both stealing glances in her direction as they talked. She still couldn't make out a word they were saying, but she did hear her name being spoken. Curiosity piqued her interest.

Noah took one more, long look her direction, meeting her stare. The tautness of his jaw combined with the vagueness of his expression caused anxiety to ripple through her. He seemed unsure, concern etching his features. As he moved her direction, the unknown woman trailed just behind him. Grace moved slowly toward them.

Stopping in front of her, Noah cupped the back of his neck with one hand, a telltale sign he was feeling uncertain. The woman smiled nervously, her face flushed. Grace furrowed her brow, looking between the two of them.

Noah finally spoke. "Grace, this is Clara Thompson," he said. His jaw grew tight as his eyes searched hers. When she didn't respond, he continued. "Grace," he paused briefly, "this is Jared's mother."

Grace inhaled sharply, drawing a hand to her mouth as her jaw dropped. She couldn't speak. She just stared as her mind raced. How could this woman be Jared's mother? She was clearly Amish. This must be some of Noah's family. Or at least someone from his community. It has to be. Doesn't it? Her mind whirled!

She flinched, startled when Noah touched her arm. "Grace," he said softly, "are you alright?"

She turned to face him, her eyes wide. Closing her gaping mouth, she mentally shook herself and turned back to the woman. "I'm sorry. I just wasn't... wasn't expecting this." She still felt at a loss for words.

Clara smiled sweetly. "It is okay, Grace. I am certain my coming is a shock to you. And I am certain you did not expect me to be Amish."

She studied the woman. Although her eyes were a lighter brown than Jared's, the shape and set were identical. And her mouth, the way her top lip arched into a perfect cupid's bow, instantly reminded Grace of him. She sucked in another breath.

Clara seemed to notice she was being scrutinized, repeatedly glancing at the ground as her cheeks blushed a rosy pink. Unlike Jared, the woman standing before her seemed reserved and unsure of herself. She looked like she might turn and flee at any moment. Grace decided she needed to pull herself together.

"Clara, I have to be honest. When I wrote that letter, I didn't know who you were or if it would even reach you," she said. "But I'm glad you've come." She offered her unexpected visitor a welcoming smile.

At that, Clara seemed to relax a little, as if she'd been holding her breath. "*Danki*, I mean thank you," she said, her voice heavy with emotion. She smiled, relief showing on her face. "I appreciate you writing to me and letting me know about my son. I suppose you have many questions."

Before she could respond, Noah spoke up. "Why don't you two go on inside. I'll be heading back to the barn." He turned to Clara, offering her one more reassuring smile as he tipped the brim of his cowboy hat. Grace could see the gratefulness in her eyes. Noah turned and started for the barn, leaving the two women alone.

"Let's go inside where we can sit and talk," Grace invited.

Clara nodded with a hesitant smile.

Once inside, she found her mother in the kitchen and made the introductions. Much to her surprise, her mother hardly flinched or missed a beat. She welcomed Clara with open arms, almost as if she'd been expecting her. "Please, have a seat, Clara," Jane said. "Can I get you a cup of coffee?"

"*Danki*. That would be nice. It has been a long two days of travel to get here," she said with a sigh.

"Were you unable to get a flight?" Grace asked.

"Oh, we do not fly. It is not our way," she answered.

Grace raised her brows. "Oh, I had forgotten about that. I think I remember Noah mentioning that at some point."

Clara gave her a quizzical look. "I could tell by speaking with him that he is familiar with our language. Did he grow up near an Amish community?"

Before she could answer, her mother joined them at the table, setting a fresh cup of coffee in front of Clara. "He actually grew up Amish," Jane answered.

Clara's eyes grew round with surprise. "Oh?"

"He came here when he was eighteen, and he's been a part of our family ever since," Jane stated. "It's a long story, but don't worry, he's made peace with his family. They get along quite nicely now."

Grace silently swallowed her bitterness that he had yet to tell her any of this himself. Now was not the time to focus on that.

"Oh," Clara responded, still looking puzzled, "He had not yet joined the church when he left?"

Jane smiled. "That's correct."

She nodded her head, seeming to understand. She took a slow sip of coffee before speaking again. "I am sorry I did not write before coming. I know this is a surprise to you. I sat down many times to return your letter, Grace. But each time, I could not do it. I could not put on paper the words that must be said."

Grace noticed Clara's eyes were misting, and her voice was beginning to break. She gently placed a hand on hers. "It's okay. Really. I'm glad my letter reached you, and I'm glad you've come."

Clara took a deep breath. "I cannot imagine the questions you must have or what you must think of me," she sniffled.

"Well, I'd be lying if I didn't admit this is unexpected. Jared never mentioned you. I never knew anything about any of his family."

Clara's eyes continued to fill with tears. "If you will allow me, I would like to get to know you, Grace. Hopefully I can fill in some of the missing pieces for you. And if it is okay," she looked nervously between Grace and Jane, "I would like to meet my granddaughter you spoke of in your letter."

Grace smiled. "Of course. You will absolutely meet Abby. And you will also meet Anna. She is not Jared's biological daughter, but he was the only father she's known."

Clara pulled a tissue from her apron and dabbed at her eyes. "*Danki*, Grace. You do not know how much this means to me."

Jane interjected. "Clara, where are you staying while you're here?"

"I have booked a room in town. I will only be able to stay for a few days, and then I will have to return to Ohio."

Jane shook her head. "No need for that room in town. You will stay right here with us. We have plenty of room."

Clara started to object but Jane raised a hand. "And before you even think of protesting, I won't take no for an answer," she spoke very matter of fact. "You are Abby's grandmother as well as me, and that makes you family."

Clara's eyes again swelled with tears. She seemed at a loss for words, but her expression clearly conveyed her gratitude.

"Grace," Jane spoke up again, "why don't I go pick up Abby while you stay here with Clara? You two can chat a little before we get back."

"Thanks, Mom," Grace replied. "That's probably a good idea." She knew she had a great deal she wanted to ask Clara, and Clara likely had a great deal she wanted to know as well. Grace just wasn't sure where to start or how much to share. Did Clara know the truth about her son? Did she know what kind of man he really was?

CHAPTER 7

Over the next few days, Grace and Clara spent every waking second of each day together. Grace was amazed that this kind, gentle woman was Jared's mother. She didn't seem to have a cruel bone in her body. If anything, she was the complete opposite of her son.

Abby had very quickly taken to her grandmother, and Clara treated Anna like her own as well. When the girls were home, their time spent together was full of activities making up for lost time. The girls had enthusiastically shown Clara all around the ranch, and Clara was eagerly sharing some of her heritage with them.

Noah even sat with them in the evenings. He and Clara exchanged stories, and everyone listened with enjoyment. Grace appreciated learning more about them both, but she still found herself frustrated with him. She still wanted to have a talk with him, and she couldn't figure out why it was bothering her so much.

During school hours, Clara did her best to fill Grace in on her complicated past. Much to her dismay, she learned that Jared hadn't fallen far from the proverbial apple tree, so-to-speak. Clara had tearfully shared with Grace the circumstances of her marriage to Jared's father, Allen Thompson. She had met him when she was just seventeen and wasn't yet baptized in her Old Order church. She was admittedly drawn to the outside world, and Allen represented her way out. She ran away and married him, barely even knowing him. He was twenty-five at the time.

All too late, Clara discovered what an abusive, controlling man Allen really was. While listening to her heartbreaking story, Grace decided Jared's father had been even more cruel than Jared himself. Unlike Jared, Allen was not a good provider for his family. Along with anger problems, he also had a drinking problem and struggled to hold a job. Clara and Jared were often left in need.

Also, unlike his son, Allen's abuse had not been solely directed toward his wife. Jared had suffered right alongside his mother. This was eye opening for Grace, and despite all he'd done to her, she felt her chest squeeze with sorrow at the revelation. At the hands of his father, Jared's childhood had been a living nightmare.

Clara also shared that Jared had been a highly intelligent child. He always worked hard in school and had been determined to make something of himself. He would frequently tell her he was going to get a good job when he grew up so he could take them both far away from the abuse they'd always known. However, as time went on, Allen became sick. He was diagnosed with pancreatic cancer. Clara, having been raised that a woman should care for her husband no matter what, stood by his side.

Jared, on the other hand, became more and more resentful and filled with anger. He couldn't understand why his mother would stay and care for such a man, even if he was sick and dying. As soon as he graduated from high school, he packed his bags and left. Clara never saw him again.

At first, he would occasionally call or write. He was attending college, and she was proud of him for that. But as time passed, their communication became less and less. When Allen passed away, Clara told her son she was returning to her Amish community. All communication ceased. She sent her new address to his last known address, but she never got a reply.

Grace reeled with all the new information she was learning. So much of what she experienced during her trouble-laden marriage suddenly made sense. It didn't make it right by any means, but she now knew why Jared had become such a monster. He was only doing what had been done to him. As an adult, he wanted constant control of every aspect of his life, something he never had as a child.

With reservation, Grace shared her story with Clara. It was extremely painful for them both, and for a long time after, they sat and cried. Clara repeatedly apologized for her son's behavior, and Grace repeatedly told her it wasn't her fault. She also shared how she had given it all to the Lord and was determined not to let her past dictate her future. Clara seemed to find peace in knowing that.

All too soon Clara's short visit was coming to an end, and the day came for her to leave. "*Danki* for opening your home to me," she said, hugging Jane. "I hope I was not too much trouble."

"Nonsense," Jake spoke up. "You are welcome here anytime."

Clara smiled. "And you are all welcome to visit me as well."

"*Mammi* Clara," Abby said in her sweet, little voice, "can I come visit you some day at your house?"

She beamed, placing a hand over her heart. Abby was using the word she had taught her for grandma. "Of course you can," she replied, looking to Grace for approval.

Grace nodded as her heart swelled. *Thank you, Lord, for bringing this wonderful woman into our lives,* she silently prayed.

* * *

Later that day, after Clara had gone, Noah found Grace sitting alone on the back patio. She seemed lost in thought but smiled when he sank down beside her. "You okay?" he asked softly.

She sighed heavily before answering. "Yes and no. These past few days with Clara have been wonderful, but it's also been emotionally exhausting." She rubbed her forehead. "It's forced me to think about a lot of things."

Noah wasn't sure what all Clara had shared with Grace during their private conversations, and he didn't want to pry. But at the same time, he wanted to be supportive, a shoulder to cry on if needed. "I've been told I'm a pretty good listener if you want to talk," he offered, gently nudging her shoulder with his.

She didn't offer a response other than a slight smile that barely drew up the corners of her mouth. She still seemed lost in her own thoughts. He sat and waited, giving her all the time she needed.

"Jared was abused as a child," she said abruptly. "His father was abusive to him and Clara."

When she turned to look at Noah, her eyes glistened with unshed tears. She blinked her eyes shut, loosening the tears to trickle down her cheeks. He took her hand in his and waited, not saying a word. Using his thumb, he gently rubbed small, comforting circles over the smooth skin of her hand.

"He was so mean to me, Noah. You can't even imagine how awful it was. He took every ounce of self-worth I had left and stripped it away." Her voice broke with every word she spoke, and her hands trembled.

Noah felt anger, hot and searing, welling up inside him. He felt an overwhelming desire to protect her with every ounce of strength he had. He wanted to tell her just that but instead silently squeezed her hand, reminding both himself and her that was all in the past. This was the here and now, and he would never allow anyone to hurt her ever again.

After taking a few slow breaths, she started again. "Despite all that, despite everything he did to me, I feel sorry for him. I can't explain it. I know it makes no sense," she said, shaking her head. "But knowing what I do now, I just can't help it."

Grace looked at Noah, tears still streaming down her face. He gently reached to swipe them away, and she let her eyes drift shut at his touch.

Neither one of them spoke for a long while. Noah slipped his arm around her shoulders, and she rested her head against him. As they sat in silence, he prayed. *Father God, please continue to heal Grace's heart. Help her to see herself as You see her, as I see her. And please guide me as I continue to be her friend. Help me know what I should and shouldn't do. I love her more than she could possibly know.*

Her voice interrupted his silent requests to the Lord. "Noah?" Her tone was questioning.

"Yeah?" he answered.

She sat up, and he dropped his arm from around her. She looked at him, her brow creased. "Why didn't you tell me you went to see your family when you came home?"

He knew her well enough to know her voice held just a touch of hurt. She'd obviously found out from someone else that he had visited his parents, and now she was disappointed he hadn't shared that with her himself.

He sighed. "I'm sorry if I hurt your feelings by not telling you. You've had so much to deal with, and I didn't want to add anything else to your plate. But it's my mistake. I should have said something before now."

Her expression didn't change much. If anything, she seemed more irritated at him.

"I get that, Noah. But we're friends. Best friends. I always want you to know you can talk to me. It's not just a one-way street," she snapped, an edge to her tone.

He sighed again, rubbing his forehead. Apparently, she wasn't letting him off the hook so easily. "Grace, I'm really sorry. I didn't do it to hurt you. You know that. I care about you."

He searched her eyes, silently willing her to see the truth of what he was saying. He didn't like her being upset with him. He didn't like the feeling it created in the pit of his stomach.

Her expression finally softened. "Will you tell me about it?"

"Sure," he replied softly. "I'd love to share that with my best friend." He gently bumped her shoulder with his and grinned.

For the next hour or so, Noah shared about his family. Grace listened intently, only interjecting a few questions here and there. She was genuinely interested in all he had to say. As he shared both the good and the bad, he could tell she was feeling every emotion right along with him. She'd always been the type to feel things on a deeper level than most, and he was glad to see that side of her returning, no longer lying dormant under a mountain of inner turmoil.

He could tell it was hard on her to hear about the argument he'd had with his parents all those years ago when he told them he wouldn't be joining their church. His mother, Katie Ann, had been inconsolable, and she had pleaded and pleaded with him to reconsider. His father, Sol, had turned three shades of red and would not even look him in the eye. He simply told him to either be baptized or leave. And when Noah stood firm in his decision, his father walked out, not saying another word.

At the time, Noah had felt like a boulder settled onto his chest with the weight of knowing his father's decision for him to leave would stand unless he complied with the ultimatum that was issued. Leaving his family was the hardest thing he'd ever done. Being the oldest of six siblings, it had pained him beyond words to know he wouldn't see any of his sisters or his brother grow up.

Noah again told Grace how thankful he was for her family. He knew if Jake Buckner hadn't taken him under his wing all those years ago, and if Grace and her siblings hadn't been so accepting of him, he wouldn't be the man he is today. And he certainly wouldn't have had the courage to return home and face his father. Jake and Jane, along with Caleb, had encouraged him every step of the way.

He shared with Grace how shocked his parents had been to see him standing on their doorstep after so much time had passed. And to his surprise, they welcomed him with open arms. Apparently, he was not the only one who experienced heart-altering changes during their years apart.

He explained how Bishop Zook, the man who had presided over their district while he was living there, was a very strict, by-the-book kind of man. He expected parents to have nothing to do with any of their children who chose not to join the church, an unofficial shunning of sorts. Such punishments were meant to bring the so-called "wayward soul" back into the flock. But for Noah, it was just one of the reasons he could not join their church. He just couldn't accept that such actions honor the merciful, loving God he'd come to know.

He went on to explain that while he was home visiting his family, he learned Bishop Zook had passed on. He was able to meet the new bishop, Bishop Beiler, a man whose heart seemed tender to both the things and people of God. Noah proclaimed him to be one of the kindest, gentlest souls he'd ever met. He seemed to be taking the needs of his community to heart, desiring to do what was best for all and what would truly please God most.

Thankfully, Bishop Beiler encouraged Noah's family to have a relationship with him. Noah shared with the bishop how his strong faith and relationship with God were the only things he'd taken with him when left. He never turned his back on the Lord, and he never wanted to turn his back on his family.

The bishop's words to his parents were still fresh in his mind. "Sol, Katie Ann, *kinner* are a gift from *Gott*. I encourage you to have a relationship with your *sohn*. You have my blessing."

Turning to Grace, Noah smiled and said, "So that's the story. Thanks to God and Bishop Beiler, I'm welcome at my parents' home anytime."

He noticed her eyes were still slightly watery as she sighed heavily. It meant more than he could express that his life, his family, could mean that much to her. He was thankful he'd finally taken the time to share this with her, and his only regret was that he hadn't done it sooner.

"Noah, can I ask you a favor? And you can say no if it's not appropriate."

Her words caught him off guard. What could she possibly ask him that wouldn't be appropriate? His mind was speculating even as he answered. "Of course. What is it?"

"I'd like to meet your parents," she said, her gaze warm with sincerity.

He was caught by surprise. He would love for her to meet his parents, his whole family actually, but he never really considered it an option. But now, with both of their circumstances far different than ever before, it was a real possibility. Grinning broadly, he replied, "I would like that, and I think they would, too."

Grace beamed at him, her eyes twinkling. "Really?"

He nodded his head yes, still grinning. She leaned her head against his shoulder again, releasing another heavy sigh. Noah remained still, enjoying the feeling of her closeness. He knew his family would love her as much as he did. He was certain of it.

But that's when it hit him. His family would make assumptions about his relationship with Grace, and primarily those assumptions would include marriage. The excitement he was feeling was now mixed with a bit of apprehension. He would have to ensure they understood Grace was just his friend, nothing more. If he ever wanted his relationship with her to become more than that, he needed this visit with his family to go smoothly.

CHAPTER 8

G race could hardly sit still. She was working overtime to calm her nerves, attempting not to squirm too much in her seat. She turned toward Noah. He sat perfectly calm, one hand on the wheel and his other arm resting on the console between them. He looked away from the road only briefly, just long enough to give her a confident smile. She wondered if he could tell how nervous she was. She was feeling very anxious about meeting his family. She found herself hoping they would like her, but she couldn't exactly figure out why it mattered so much.

She looked down at the dress she was wearing, hoping it was suitable. She'd chosen this dress because of the modest neckline and longer length, falling just below her knees. She also hoped the pale green color wasn't inappropriate. Most of her summer dresses were brighter, more vibrant colors.

She'd chosen not to wear a stitch of makeup for the day, and she had attempted to pin her hair up in the back. Her wavy locks, however, had a mind of their own and several strands were already coming loose, drifting down around her face. She was attempting to put them back in place when Noah spoke. "Grace, I told you not to worry about how you look. My family is not expecting you to look Amish," he said with a chuckle. "They don't even expect it from me. Besides, you look beautiful."

She felt her face heat at his words. She quickly turned away, embarrassed by the redness in her cheeks. Even the simplest of compliments from him seemed to leave her blushing. She was looking out the passenger side window when she spoke. "Are we getting close?"

"Yep," he replied. "Just a few more minutes."

She turned back to face him. He grinned and winked at her, his blue eyes sparkling. She blushed again and returned her gaze back to the window. Noah drove carefully as they passed a few buggies on the road. She felt her pulse quicken, wondering if any of them belonged to his family.

They turned down a long lane leading to a large, two-story home. The white clapboard house appeared freshly painted and was surrounded by an abundance of flowers, dotting the perimeter of the home in every color of the rainbow. It reminded Grace of her mother's flower gardens. Behind the home, she could see a large barn and another outbuilding sitting to the side of it, both painted red and in pristine condition. She already knew Noah's father had a blacksmith shop. He was a farrier and also took in welding work. She assumed the smaller building was his shop.

Noah parked his truck in the driveway at the backside of the house. He turned to Grace and attempted to offer a reassuring smile. She thought he, too, looked slightly nervous.

"Are you ready?" he asked.

She nodded her head, feeling too nervous to speak.

Noah hopped out and walked around to her side. She waited for him to open her door. She had learned long ago not to attempt opening any door for herself when he was around. He told her numerous times it was only right for a man to open the door for a lady. And although some might find such thinking old fashioned and out of place, she found it noble and chivalrous.

* * *

Noah pulled open the truck door, and Grace stepped out. A faint smile tugged at her lips. He wouldn't be surprised if she could hear his heart beating against his chest because his pulse was pounding in his ears. He'd spoken to his parents two weeks ago telling them they were coming and to explain that Grace was just a friend. He'd also called again yesterday, reminding them they were coming. Noah knew, however, that his mother would likely see right through him and read him like a book! That thought alone was enough to make his palms sweaty.

As they moved toward the backdoor of his parents' home, he had to catch himself. He almost reached to take Grace's hand. He knew if he walked in holding her hand his family would immediately assume there was more to the story than he was telling. He clenched and unclenched his fist a couple times, trying to calm his nerves.

Noah knocked on the door before walking in, Grace trailing close behind him. His father was sitting at the kitchen table with a newspaper. He looked up, grinning broadly when he saw them.

"*Hallo, Daed,*" Noah said, greeting him in *Deitsch*.

Sol stood and walked toward them. "*Guder mariye, sohn!*" he exclaimed, clasping Noah's hand.

Noah turned to Grace. "*Daed,* this is Grace Thompson. Grace, this is my father, Solomon Miller. Everyone calls him Sol."

Grace smiled. "Nice to meet you."

Sol also smiled and nodded. "Welcome, Grace," he replied in English.

Noah could tell Grace was nervous, and that made him even more anxious himself. He turned back to his father, his pulse still thrumming. "Where's *Mamm*?"

Before his father could answer, she came around the corner. His mother hurried to hug him, her face beaming. "*Ach, mei sohn,* it is so *gut* to see you!" she exclaimed.

Once she released him, he turned to Grace. "*Mamm,* this is Grace Thompson. Grace, this is my mother, Katie Ann."

"It is wonderful to meet you, Grace. We are so glad you are here," she welcomed in English.

"Thank you," Grace said, offering a shy smile.

Noah felt himself breathe a sigh of relief, relaxing a little now that the introductions were mostly over. His youngest brother, Levi, had to be around somewhere, but he wasn't nervous about introducing Grace to him. Before he could even ask where he was, his mother ushered them all to the table to sit for coffee and pie. He grinned as he watched her interact with Grace. It felt surreal to have them together in the same room. Maybe he should pinch himself to make certain this was real! He chuckled at the thought.

For the next hour, Noah, Grace, and his parents talked and ate. His mother kept the coffee cups filled and their stomachs full. What had started out as just pie had grown to become quite an array of food. Everyone was getting along wonderfully, and he was relieved to see Grace had relaxed. The vibrancy of her smile and soft laughter warmed his heart. He was thankful she was finally getting to know his family.

He was still smiling, lost in thought, when his father caught his eye. Grace and Katie Ann were caught up in a conversation of their own and didn't notice Sol grinning slyly at his son. He offered a knowing smile with an approving nod. Noah immediately felt his neck and face flush with heat. He thought his mother would be the first to see right through him, but apparently his father had beat her to it.

* * *

Grace washed and dried her hands. She had not thought to ask Noah if his family had indoor plumbing or not, and she was extremely relieved to find out they did. She breathed a sigh of relief, thankful for the cool, running water.

She was amazed at the cleanliness of Sol and Katie Ann's home. She was quite certain she'd never seen a house more spic and span than this one. And despite the lack of certain modern conveniences, she found the house charming and inviting. It almost felt as if a tangible peace filled the entire home.

Katie Ann's kitchen, however, is what Grace was the most surprised by. It was much more spacious than she imagined, with ample counter space and a large dining table that could easily seat several guests. The kitchen appliances ran on propane, eliminating the need for electricity. It differed so little in appearance from a typical kitchen you'd see in an average American home. The smell of cinnamon and other spices hung heavy in the air, and yet again she was reminded of her own parents' home.

Katie Ann herself appeared younger than Jane Buckner. The hair that shown from under her prayer covering was the same dark blonde color as Noah's. Fine lines appeared around her eyes and mouth but were only noticeable when she smiled. Her eyes were a beautiful shade of hazel flecked with specks of gold. She was a rather petite woman, and Grace could hardly believe she'd given birth to six children.

Sol, like his wife, also appeared to be younger than Grace's parents. His dark hair and beard were ever so slightly peppered with gray. He was a tall man with broad shoulders, similar in height and stature to Noah. Grace knew immediately upon meeting him where Noah had gotten his striking eye color. Sol's eyes were the same intense blue as that of his oldest son.

Noah stood when Grace returned to the kitchen. "Ready?"

She nodded, and they headed toward the door. Noah wanted to show her around while Katie Ann finished preparing dinner. Grace wasn't sure how she could eat another bite anytime soon!

As they were walking toward the barn, a buggy pulled in, stopping a few feet from them. They paused, waiting for the driver to climb down.

"Hallo, bruder!" Noah called in *Deitsch*.

The young man walked toward them, tipping his straw hat back slightly on his head. He was grinning from ear to ear.

"Grace," Noah spoke again, this time in English, "this is my brother Levi. Levi, this is Grace."

Levi nodded a greeting in her direction, continuing to grin. As she watched him, she was taken with how much he looked like a younger version of Noah. From his hair color to the bright blue of his eyes, he was nearly the spitting image of his older brother.

Noah must have noticed her studying his brother. He spoke up, chuckling as he did. "It's kind of crazy how much we look alike isn't it?"

Grace looked at him. He was grinning, his blue eyes shining down at her. "Yeah, I suppose so. But there's no doubt he's your brother!" she replied, smiling at them both.

Noah turned back to Levi. "I'm going to show Grace around while *Mamm* is fixing dinner. Do you want to join us?"

Levi grinned, an amused smile quirking his lips. He looked from Grace to his brother. "*Nee,* I have chores."

"*Jah*, see you at dinner then." Noah replied.

Grace watched as Levi headed toward his father's blacksmith shop. She had already observed Sol going inside. "Does Levi work with your dad?"

"*Jah,* I mean yes," he answered. "He's learning."

Grace smiled. She still liked hearing Noah speak his first language. "Is it just Levi who works with him?"

"No, my sister Rebecca's husband, Samuel, also works with him."

Grace thought for a moment. She was trying to remember the names of all Noah's sisters. Aside from Levi, the rest of his siblings were girls. She knew all four sisters were already married, the youngest one being nineteen and married less than a year. "Refresh my memory on your sisters' names again?" she asked, slightly embarrassed for not remembering.

"Sure," he said with a grin. "Rebecca is the oldest, just one year younger than me. She and Samuel live just across the pasture there," he said, motioning toward a two story, white house within walking distance. "Samuel was an apprentice under my dad when I left. He and Rebecca were courting and planning to get married. They have three kids." Noah titled his head and raised his eyes to one corner, thinking. "Let's see. After Rebecca, there is Susanna, then Mary, and last is Rachel. Rachel just married Daniel Lapp last October."

"Do they all have children?" Grace inquired.

"No, not Rachel. At least not yet," he said with a grin.

Grace suddenly felt nervous, wondering how many of his family members she would be meeting today. "Uh... will I be meeting *all* of your family today?" she asked, her face scrunched.

Noah chuckled. "No, I don't think so. *Mamm* didn't mention it."

She let out the breath she was holding, relief washing over her.

Noah looked at his watch. "Come on, I want to show you something. We've got about an hour or so before dinner."

As they crossed the pasture field toward a tree line in the distance, he took her hand in his, intertwining her fingers with his own. When she looked at him, he smiled tenderly. The feeling of his hand gently clutching hers caused her stomach to flip as she felt her cheeks color yet again.

* * *

Noah led Grace across the field, hoping none of his family were spying on them. It was slightly risky to take her hand, but he just couldn't help himself. He was growing more and more comfortable with her, and it was becoming increasingly difficult to exercise the restraint he'd always shown with her. It was hard not to stop this instant and pull her into his arms. His heart hammered against his ribcage at the thought.

Giving himself a mental headshake, he refocused his attention. He wanted to show her one of his favorite spots in the world. Just beyond the tree line in front of them lay a small opening leading to a serene, little creek. The slow trickle of water over the smooth rocks and the sunlight dancing overhead always made him feel at peace. He had come here often over the years to think and pray, always feeling close to God in this spot.

As they emerged from the narrow path into the clearing, he was yet again drawn in by the tranquility of this place. The water still flowed clear and cold, and the sun's rays were just barely peeking through the trees above. It was just as he remembered it.

He turned to Grace, grinning, and led her to the water's edge.

"Wow," she said in a hushed tone. "This place is beautiful."

Noah released her hand and sat down on the cool ground. She followed suit and sat beside him, tucking her legs beneath her dress. The calming sound of the slowly trickling water was almost hypnotic.

Grace spoke softly, "I can see why you love it here."

When he looked at her, the sunlight was cascading across her auburn hair, highlighting deep hues of red. Several strands had come loose again and were swirling about in the gentle breeze. Her green eyes sparkled as she held his gaze. She looked beautiful beyond words, and he drank her in. She turned away, blushing, as the curve of a smile played on her lips.

He gave himself another mental headshake, remembering why he'd brought her here. Turning his gaze to the water, he spoke. "There is a reason I brought you here, other than it being one of my favorite places."

Grace looked his way with a puzzled expression, a line appearing between her brows. She sat silent, waiting for him to explain.

Noah sighed heavily. "I promised I would tell you about my scars. I don't like the story that goes with them, but if I'm going to tell you, I want to do it here."

She raised her brows, her eyes growing round. "Noah, you don't have to tell me. It's okay."

"No, I want to tell you. I don't ever want you to think I'm keeping anything from you again." He furrowed his brow, rubbing his forehead with his fingertips.

Grace didn't say anymore. She sat and waited patiently until he was ready. He sighed heavily one more time, looking out across the water, attempting to let it soothe his soul. He was already feeling the rush of emotion that always came with the memories.

"I was stationed in Afghanistan. My unit was responsible for checking for IEDs and other hazards along the roads. There was a little village nearby that was part of our patrol route. The people who lived there were basically trapped in the middle of a war zone, and most of them appreciated us being there. They were mostly families with young children who had nowhere else to go."

Closing his eyes briefly, he took a cleansing breath. "Your mom was always good about sending care packages from home. She put cookies, candy, things like that in them. Each time I knew we were going into the village, I'd make sure I had some candy in my pocket. You know, just a little something to bring a smile to a kid's face who didn't really have much to smile about."

Noah looked at the ground. He could already feel the painful tightening inside his chest as bile rose in his throat, threatening to steal his ability to speak. He swallowed hard, attempting to force it back down.

"On a day that seemed no different than any other day," he continued haltingly, "I was doing what I always did. Most of the kids in the village knew I carried candy in my pocket, and they came running anytime they saw me." His eyes clouded. "I had a group of maybe four or five kids around me, waiting for me to pull out the candy. They were all smiling, laughing." He paused, the memories nearly drowning him like flood waters breaking over a dam.

"That's when it happened." His voice broke as the images that were seared into his memory forever came rushing back, so vivid as if he were there at this moment. "A suicide bomber came around the corner. By the time I saw him, it was too late. I tried to use my body to shield as many of them as possible, but I couldn't get to them all. I just couldn't get to them."

Tears were stinging his eyes as his throat constricted. He kept swallowing, attempting to get the lump of grief now lodged in his throat to go down. "I tried Grace! I tried! But two of the kids didn't make it. I couldn't help them. I crawled to them, but they were already gone. They didn't stand a chance."

Noah leaned his head back and closed his eyes, trying to will the tears to stop. "I blamed myself. Every single day I told myself I killed them. If I hadn't been there, they would still be alive. It was all I could think about. Anytime I closed my eyes I could see it, playing over and over in my mind. I couldn't get past it." He paused again, looking heavenward. "But then God finally got through to me. I gave it all to Him and chose to stop blaming myself. Pastor Daniel helped me realize that's what I needed to do, along with your parents and Caleb. I couldn't keep holding on to it like I was. It was eating me up inside."

When he finally turned toward Grace, she rose to her knees and reached for him, gently placing her hands on either side of his face. Her eyes searched his with urgency, but she said nothing. He surrendered a sad smile, turning his eyes downward, a little embarrassed he'd lost control and cried like that. Before he could say or do anything, she pulled herself to him, kissing him with a gentle force that took his breath away. The world seemed to stop as time stood still, the feel of her lips pressed to his more than his mind could comprehend. A rush of heat roared through his veins, flooding his entire body with warmth.

But just as suddenly and unexpectedly as it began, it was ending. Grace pushed herself back from him, her eyes wide and cheeks flushed. She didn't say a word and hurriedly stood, sucking in a sharp breath as she did. She brought a hand to her mouth, her fingertips resting on her lips.

Noah sat frozen in his spot on the ground. He knew his eyes were wide, mouth gaping. He was at a loss for words. Gathering his wits, he slowly stood and stepped toward her. But just as he found his voice, Levi appeared in the clearing. Based on the rosiness of his cheeks and his downturned eyes, Noah was certain his little brother had just witnessed that kiss. When he looked at Grace, her eyes were also focused downward, and her face bloomed a brilliant red.

"What is it, Levi?" Noah spoke, his tone harsher than intended.

Levi didn't look up. "*Mamm* says dinner is ready," he replied, turning abruptly and disappearing back through the clearing.

Noah turned back to Grace. Before he could say anything, she hurriedly started moving in the direction Levi had just gone. He knew it would only embarrass her further if he called after her, so he remained silent. He followed behind her, his mind racing.

* * *

Grace did her best all through dinner to maintain her composure, pretending nothing had happened. She tried to stay focused on the conversation around the table while also attempting to avoid eye contact with Noah. She was certain Levi had witnessed her temporary loss of self-control. His cheeks blushed pink each time he looked her way, and he was trying to stifle a smile all through the meal. She was mortified!

Grace kept replaying it over and over in her head. Why had she let herself do that? Had she lost her mind! Noah was her best friend, and now she was terrified she'd just destroyed their friendship. Her thoughts and emotions had been all over the place since returning to Texas, and she feared this incident was just another casualty of her instability. *I thought I was doing better. What was that? What on earth was I thinking!* She groaned inwardly.

She tried to force a stop to the onslaught of questions and anxiety flooding her mind. She didn't want this to ruin the rest of the day. She had wanted to come here and meet Noah's family, and he was kind enough to bring her. And now, what had she gone and done other than disrupt everything! She felt herself shrinking on the inside from embarrassment.

But no matter how hard she tried, questions continued to fill her thoughts. *What is Noah thinking? Is he upset with me? Does he feel as confused as I do?* Her mind raced. And the more she thought about it, the clearer it became that she knew only one thing for certain. He did not kiss her back. Not really anyway. That thought alone left her feeling humiliated, and she desperately wanted to run away and hide.

Grace was relieved when the meal finally ended. The men retreated from the house, and she was left alone in the kitchen with Katie Ann. She took a deep breath, thankful it was just the two of them. "That was delicious," she spoke, attempting to drown out her own thoughts.

Katie Ann blushed. *"Danki."*

It wasn't long before Grace found herself talking easily with Noah's mother. Katie Ann shared how much she was enjoying writing back and forth with Jane and how they had exchanged many recipes. She told Grace how appreciative she was that her family took Noah in when he needed someone most and how thankful she was for all they'd done. Grace blushed when Katie Ann went on to mention her only desire now was for her son to marry and give her more grandchildren.

Changing the subject, Grace began to tell Katie Ann about her girls. She was mildly concerned the indiscretions of her past might bubble to the surface because of their conversation, but Katie Ann never once questioned her. Grace wondered if Noah had already filled his mother in before their visit today. She felt a twinge of embarrassment. If Katie Ann did know more than she was letting on, she was hiding it well.

"Will you stay living with your father and mother?" Katie Ann asked in perfect English.

Grace paused. She wasn't sure how to answer. She hadn't really given it much thought. "For now, I suppose so. I honestly haven't thought about it."

Katie Ann smiled sweetly. "I am certain they are glad to have you."

Grace returned her smile. "I know I'm thankful for them, for all they've done for me and my girls. The girls seem happy, and that means a lot considering all they've..." she let her voice trail away, darting a concerned look toward Katie Ann. She hadn't intended to broach this subject and was now mentally kicking herself.

Katie Ann turned and smiled sweetly again. She placed a gentle hand on Grace's arm and spoke softly. "It is okay, Grace. I know you have been through much."

Grace felt an overwhelming mix of relief and humiliation. She hated that Noah's mother knew of her past, and she had no way of knowing just how much she really knew. At the same time, however, she felt grateful for the kindness and compassion she saw on her face.

Katie Ann changed the subject to one much more lighthearted, and Grace was thankful. She soon found herself once again enjoying the company of Noah's mother.

* * *

Noah looked on as Sol and Levi busied themselves in the shop. All the sights and smells were familiar to him, triggering memories from the past. He'd grown up watching his father and working alongside him. He knew if he hadn't left, this is exactly what he'd still be doing. He had learned from the best.

Noah was fiddling with some tools when Sol spoke. "Grace is the woman you spoke of before, *jah*?"

Noah turned to face him. "*Jah*, I suppose I told you about her."

Sol was inspecting a busted buggy wheel and didn't look up as he continued. "She is special, *jah*?"

Noah expected this line of questioning from his mother, but he was caught off guard with it coming from his father. "*Jah*, she is. She is a *gut* friend," he responded.

He heard his brother snicker. Turning to him, he narrowed his eyes. "Do you have something to say little *bruder*?" He knew his tone conveyed the irritation he was feeling.

Levi looked up from where he was working. He was grinning like the cat who got the canary. "From what I saw, she is more than just a *gut* friend!"

Noah cut his brother a sharp look. Levi continued to grin broadly but said nothing more.

Sol divided a look between his sons before settling his gaze on Noah. "What is your *bruder* speaking of?"

Noah flopped down on a nearby stool, momentarily resting his head in his hands. He wasn't sure what to say. When he looked up, he ran his fingers through his hair, scratching his head. "I don't know, *Daed*. I'm not sure *what* exactly happened."

Levi burst out laughing. "If you do *not* know what that was, that explains why you are not married!"

Noah lurched from the stool where he was sitting. Levi retreated backwards but continued laughing.

Sol raised a hand for his sons to stop, muttering something to Levi. Noah couldn't quite hear what was said, but his brother exited the shop. Sol came and stood by him, resting a hand on his shoulder. "*Sohn*, is this something you want to talk about?"

Noah sighed heavily, rolling his eyes. He threw his hands up. "I don't know what to say. My relationship with Grace is... complicated."

Sol chuckled. "When a *maedel* is involved, most a*re* complicated," he said with a shake of his head. He studied his son for a moment, and his tone grew more serious. "What are your feelings for her?"

Noah gave him a forlorn look. "I love her." As the words escaped his lips, his breath left in whoosh. It was the first time he'd allowed himself to say it out loud. Until now, he had never fully confessed his feelings for Grace to anyone.

Sol furrowed his brow. "It wonders me, have you not spoke of this with Grace?"

Noah sighed yet again, shaking his head.

"Talk to her *mei sohn*." Sol offered, clapping him on the back. And with that, he walked away. The conversation was over.

* * *

Grace nervously twirled a loose strand of hair around one finger. She feared this would be a long, awkward ride home. She knew she needed to say something to clear the air, to get them talking, but she couldn't seem to find the words. She continued to play different scenarios in her mind, but nothing seemed adequate for the situation.

Finally, twenty minutes into their drive, Noah spoke. "Grace, we need to talk about this."

She felt a rush of both relief and trepidation course through her. She desperately tried to think of how to respond, what to say that could salvage their friendship. "Noah, I am so, so sorry! I don't know what came over me! I don't know why I... why I did that." She cast her gaze downward, embarrassed all over again.

"Grace, it's okay." His voice was soft, gentle. He sighed heavily, shifting his weight in his seat. "Actually, there's something..."

She interrupted him before he could finish. "No, please don't say anything," she pleaded. "Can we just pretend this never happened? I don't want it to ruin our friendship. Please Noah, please tell me we can forget about it!"

She knew she sounded desperate, practically begging, but she didn't care. She was wrought with panic at the thought of what her momentary lapse in judgement might do to their relationship. The thought of losing him was more than she could bear. *What have I done! Please God, help me fix this! I can't lose him!* Her heart hammered hard inside her chest.

Grace watched him. His jaw worked, but he didn't respond. That only magnified the feeling of dread twisting her stomach into knots. His expression almost looked pained, and he was hesitating far too long. He opened his mouth to speak but clamped it back shut, his lips pursing into a tight line.

Grace tried to be patient, but she was growing more alarmed by the second. "Noah, *please,* say something!" She knew her voice was shaking.

As she continued to watch him, waiting, the blood roared inside her ears. Noah ran a hand through his hair, stopping to rub the back of his neck. He was looking at the road, and she couldn't fully make out his expression but could tell his brow was creased, his jaw tight.

He finally spoke. "If that's what you want Grace, then that's what we'll do." His expression didn't ease as he stared straight ahead.

Relief flooded through her, almost making her lightheaded. She let out the breath she'd been holding, closing her eyes as she exhaled. But for some reason, a reason she couldn't identify, she didn't feel at peace.

The relief she was feeling was mixed with something else, something she was unsure of. She turned her face to the passenger side window as a silent tear trickled down her cheek.

* * *

Noah could feel his heart shattering like glass as a deep, penetrating ache settled in his chest. Grace wanted to pretend she had never kissed him, and that was what he would do. He loved her that much. But it didn't change the fact that it pained him beyond words to know she thought of her actions as a mistake. If anything, he was hoping this would be an open door for him to talk to her about how he felt, how he'd felt since he was eighteen and she was sixteen.

He tried to offer her a reassuring smile, but he knew it fell flat, looking as forced as it felt. He could see the worry etching her face, and he saw the tear trickle down her cheek. As much as it was going to grieve him to be around her now, he would do his best to deal with it. If he could have her in his life only as a friend, then that's what he would take. He knew what it was like to live without her, and he didn't ever want to do that again.

As the hours and miles rolled by, Noah remained lost in his own thoughts. He occasionally stole glances at Grace, but she too seemed lost in thought. For most of the drive, she sat with her body turned away from him, staring out her window. Like it or not, their relationship had now taken a very awkward turn, and he wasn't sure either of them could fix it.

He couldn't help but feel rejected. Before he could share the one thing he'd wanted to tell her for far too long, she had shut him down, pleading with him to forget the kiss ever happened. That, of course, was impossible. How could he possibly forget the one thing he'd dreamed about since he first met her? She, however, didn't even want to discuss it. He'd loved her silently for so long. Would the time ever be right to tell her? And that's when a thought hit him like a ton of bricks, stealing his breath. *What if she falls in love with someone else?*

Noah suddenly felt a flurry of emotion rising to the surface, hot and unpleasant. The thought of her with someone else was something he hadn't considered before now. His stomach instantly soured at the thought. She had been with Chris and Jared while he was overseas, but that was all in the past. Since her return home, he had allowed himself to dream she might choose him. He had even allowed himself to hope they were moving in that direction.

But now, as he considered for the first time that it might not be him she chose, he knew one thing for certain. As much as he loved her, he could not stand by and watch her give her heart to another man, a man who couldn't possibly love her the way she deserved. That would be too much to bear. If it came to that, he would have to say goodbye. His heart could only take so much.

CHAPTER 9

Grace moved slowly toward the stall barn. A warm October sun shone overhead, and the air hung heavy with humidity. Despite the several weeks that had passed since her trip with Noah to visit his family, she still felt herself growing nervous each time he was around. She could tell he wasn't himself either. They both seemed to be trying, but nothing was as it had been. She constantly found herself regretting her actions.

She knew what it was like to live with regret, and she was desperately trying to get passed it. This time, however, everything felt different than ever before. Her thoughts seemed to be wrapped up in a strange ball of emotions. Embarrassment, anxiousness, frustration, and the list went on. And somewhere just below the surface, she was dealing with a mix of loneliness and rejection over the whole situation. She was missing her best friend and couldn't help but wonder if she would ever have him back again.

She saw Noah daily, but that seemed to only compound her feelings of unease and isolation from him, strange as that might sound. He frequently joined her family for meals as usual, and he was still working with the girls on their riding lessons. But as far as her interaction with him, it all seemed to have taken a more formal tone, almost superficial. It reminded her of when he first came to the ranch all those years ago and had kept her at arm's length.

She decided she was going to have to try harder to fix things between them. She felt responsible for this mess, and she couldn't be angry with anyone other than herself. Sucking in a fortifying breath and furrowing her brow, she continued toward the barn, determined to push her thoughts and feelings aside.

Grace noticed an unfamiliar truck parked near the entrance. It was sleek, black, and looked expensive. Really expensive! She studied it for a moment before continuing on. She could hear sounds coming from out back, so she picked up her pace. She quickly made her way down the long aisle and passed the stalls, pausing only long enough to give both Doc and Jingle a quick scratch on the neck. Emerging from the barn, she could see her brother Eli standing back from the training pen. He was watching something. She edged up beside him, following his gaze.

Noah was in the pen on the back of a beautiful, jet-black horse. The horse's long mane and tail glistened in the sun. Every muscle in his body was tensed on high alert, and he did not look happy. His ears were pinned, and his tail was twitching. He was prancing around, tossing his head. Noah, however, looked the picture of calm.

Grace watched for a moment before another movement caught her eye. Near the gate of the training pen stood a woman. Her long blonde hair was pulled into a low ponytail that left wavy curls cascading down her back, and her expression was one of eagerness as she watched Noah. She was wearing skintight jeans and had on an equally tight bright, pink top. From the view Grace had, she could tell it was low cut, *very* low cut. She narrowed her eyes, studying the woman. "Who is *that*?" she choked out.

Eli turned to her, a playful smirk on his face. "*That,* my dear sister, is Mavis Downey."

She eyed him curiously. "*Downy?* Like the fabric softener?"

Eli chuckled. "Sort of, I guess."

Grace only narrowed her eyes more. "Why is she here?"

Eli raised his brows and nodded his head toward the training pen. "That's her horse. Apparently, the big fella has developed an attitude problem, and Noah is trying to fix it."

Grace looked back to where the woman had been standing, but she was gone. She was now in the training pen, and Noah was walking the horse toward her. When he hopped from the saddle, Mavis walked right up to him. She was leaning into him, or at least that's how it looked to Grace. She could tell Noah was talking to her but couldn't make out what he was saying. Mavis cackled and tossed her head, causing her long, blonde ponytail to flounce about.

"How did she find Noah?" Grace asked, turning to her brother.

"I don't really know *how* she found him," he replied. "You'll have to ask him about that. But what I *do* know is that her father is loaded! Money is no object for that woman," he said.

As Eli walked away, Grace turned back to the scene in front of her. Mavis reached to touch Noah's arm, her perfectly manicured fingers trailing down his bicep. Grace felt her jaw tighten, her teeth clench. She decided on the spot she did not like Mavis Downey.

Not. One. Bit.

* * *

Noah worked to avert his eyes from Mavis. The woman was practically falling out of her shirt! To make matters worse, she seemed insistent on touching him. Repeatedly. He was trying very hard to be professional, but she was getting on his last nerve. He took a breath, reminding himself she was a client. If he wanted his business to grow, he could use the referral of a woman like Mavis Downey. He'd just have to suffer through her incessant attempts to throw herself at him. He half wondered if she would take her horse and leave if she knew her blatant flirting was getting her nowhere. He would just have to deal with her until he could prove his skills as a trainer.

"It's only been a few days, but I believe I'm making progress with him," he stated, looking at the horse and not Mavis. "I'll keep putting time in on him every day. You're welcome to check back as often as you like." He almost cringed as he said that last part. He knew good and well she would be checking in plenty without any extra encouragement.

Mavis batted her long lashes and nipped her lip flirtatiously, all the while eyeing him like he was a prime cut of beef she couldn't wait to devour. "I'm pleased with what I see. I'm sure you'll have Jax straightened out in no time. I just hope not *too* soon," she crooned, moving closer to him and resting her hand on his chest.

Noah's Adam's apple bobbed as he attempted to avert his eyes again. Mavis really was a beautiful woman, just far too forward for him. She clearly knew she was attractive and gave every effort to accentuate her features. The problem was she was accentuating all the *wrong* features, and he found little to respect about that.

"I promise I'll get him back to you as soon as he's ready. I won't keep him any longer than necessary."

Mavis batted her long lashes again as a playful giggle tripped from her lips. She leaned in, speaking in a breathy whisper. "I told you, Noah, money is not a problem. You keep Jax as long as you want." She fixed her gaze on his mouth and held steady until the awkwardness of the moment forced his gaze to the ground. Noah uncomfortably cleared his throat. The collar of his shirt suddenly felt tight. He resisted the urge to tug at it.

Sighing heavily, Mavis turned on her heel, swaggering back toward the gate.

Noah let out the breath he was holding. *This woman is going to drive me nuts! No wonder her horse is crazy!*

* * *

Grace kept her arms crossed and eyes narrowed. Her fingertips were digging into her skin with enough force to turn her knuckles white. Mavis Downey was sauntering toward her, a sly smile on her overly done face. As she passed, she didn't say a word. She just flipped her long ponytail with one hand, casting a condescending glance in Grace's direction.

Grace turned, watching her leave. She planted her hands firmly on her hips. She could feel her teeth grinding together with enough force to crack a tooth. She definitely did not like Mavis Downey.

Not. One. Bit.

When she finally peeled her piercing glare from the direction Mavis had gone, Noah was standing in front of her. Her hands remained planted firmly on her hips as she eyed him with suspicion. When he offered a hesitant smile, she cocked her head to one side and clenched her jaw. "What is *her* problem?" she barked, motioning over her shoulder.

His brow creased. He looked puzzled. "What do you mean? What did she say?"

Grace kept her eyes focused on him. "She didn't say a thing. Not a word!"

Noah cocked his head, eyeing her curiously. "Did you speak to her?"

"No," she harrumphed, crossing her arms over her chest.

He chuckled. "If she didn't speak to you and you didn't speak to her, then what's the problem?"

Grace could feel the heat rise to her face. Her blood was boiling! "Nothing, Noah! I guess *nothing*!" she screeched at him, throwing her hands up.

He looked even more puzzled and didn't seem to know what to say. Grace could feel her fists clenching at her sides. For some unexplainable reason, she had a sudden urge to punch something. And if she didn't walk away this minute, she might just punch Noah himself!

* * *

Noah watched Grace storm away. He was at a loss for words. What on earth had just happened? She had yelled at him, and he didn't have the faintest idea why. Based on her line of questioning, it had something to do with Mavis. He rubbed the back of his neck with one hand.

He was still lost in thought when Eli approached. "You want me to put Jax up for you?" he asked.

"Yeah, sure. Thanks," he answered, still looking in the direction Grace had gone only moments earlier. Eli's chuckle caught his attention. "What's so funny?" he asked, furrowing his brow.

Eli shook his head, still chuckling. "I don't think my sister cares for your newest client none too much," he said, grinning.

Noah furrowed his brow even deeper, cocking his head to one side. "Why? What makes you say that?"

Eli raised his brows and smiled. "Based on the look she was giving Mavis when you two were in the pen together and seeing as how she just bit your head off like that, I'd say it's safe to say Mavis Downey is not her favorite person!"

Noah was still confused. What was he missing? Was there something he didn't know about? "Did something happen between Grace and Mavis?" he asked.

Eli tossed his head back and laughed out loud before slapping a hand on Noah's back. Leaning in, he lowered his voice, "I don't think it's what happened between Grace and Mavis that's the issue. I think it's what happened between *you* and Mavis that has Grace all riled up."

Noah's eyes grew round. It had not occurred to him that Mavis's flirtatious behavior might prompt a reaction from Grace. Considering recent events, he had convinced himself she did not and likely never would see him as anything other than a friend.

"I don't know, Eli. She's made it pretty clear we're just friends. I don't think she sees me that way." He recoiled slightly as his own words felt like a punch to the gut. No matter what he tried to tell himself, it still hurt to think she might never return his feelings.

Eli chuckled again. "Noah, I'm her brother. I'm pretty sure I know my sister. And what I just witnessed? Well, that isn't how you act when you want to be *just friends* with someone," he said, using air quotes. Eli clapped him firmly on the back again before walking off to take care of Jax.

Noah was left to his own thoughts. Was he misreading Grace? Did she care for him more than she let on? Was she jealous to see someone else flirting with him? He rubbed his chin, reevaluating the situation. As much as he found Mavis Downey's behavior irritating, maybe her presence could benefit him. If Grace's motivation for not liking Mavis really was because of him, he might be able to test Eli's theory. He would have to be more observant the next time the two women encountered each other.

* * *

Grace entered the house through the mudroom, unintentionally slamming the door as she did. Her pulse was still thrumming with irritation, and she felt very cross with Noah. *Is he blind to what that woman is doing? Can he not tell she's throwing herself at him?* Or worse yet, *does he enjoy it? Maybe he's attracted to her...* She audibly growled.

"What on earth!" Jane exclaimed.

Grace turned. She hadn't even noticed her mother standing there. Jane had an oven mitt on one hand, and the kitchen smelled of freshly baked bread. She could see two loaves cooling on the counter, steam rising toward the ceiling.

"Sorry. I didn't mean to slam the door so hard."

"Oh, I see. So, you *did* mean to slam it then?" Jane questioned, one eyebrow arched upward.

Grace rolled her eyes, not at her mother but at her own behavior.

"Want to talk about it?" Jane asked, removing her oven mitt.

Grace plopped down on a chair. Her mother sat down next to her. "Now tell me, what has you so upset?"

Grace rested her head in her hands for a moment before answering, letting out an exasperated sigh. "Have you met Mavis Downey?" Saying her name left a foul taste on Grace's tongue.

"No, not officially. Noah is working with her horse, isn't he?"

Grace groaned. "Yes."

When she didn't say anymore, Jane probed further. "And...?" she said, drawing out the word. "Is there a problem?"

Grace sat up straight, her resolve stiffening as she did. "Aside from the fact that she dresses like a tramp and throws herself at Noah, I suppose not, Mother!" Her tone was sharper than she intended.

"Grace Thompson!" her mother exclaimed, her tone incredulous. "We do not pass judgement in this household, and I would appreciate you holding your tongue with a little more decorum! Do you even know this woman?"

Grace again rested her head in her hands. "No," she sighed, "I don't *know* her. I just know what I saw."

"Well then," Jane responded, "what does it matter to you how this woman chooses to conduct herself?"

"Because Noah can do better than *her*!" she exclaimed, throwing a hand in the air. "He deserves better than that! He deserves someone... someone who... appreciates him for who he is. Not someone who looks at him like a piece of meat!" Grace pinched her eyes shut and shook her head, pursing her lips into a tight line.

Jane sat back, folding her arms loosely across her chest, a slight grin edging at the corners of her mouth. "Someone like who, Grace? Someone like *you* perhaps?"

Grace snapped her eyes in her mother's direction. She felt her face grow flushed. "That's not what I meant!" she bellowed. "I didn't mean... I just... I... I don't want..." She knew she was stammering. Her words seemed stuck, unwilling to come out.

Jane leaned forward, touching her daughter lightly on the hand. She was still grinning, but her eyes were warm with understanding. "It's okay, Grace. You'll figure this out in your own time," she said, gently patting her hand before standing and exiting the kitchen.

Grace was left alone with her thoughts. She sat with her shoulders drooped, her hands laying loosely in her lap. She realized her mouth was gaping and quickly closed it. She furrowed her brow. "What exactly am I supposed to figure out?" she growled to herself.

She stood from the chair where she was sitting and gave herself a mental shake. So many things had her baffled lately, and she wasn't sure she needed to add yet another piece to the puzzle. She was working hard to find herself again, to figure out what this new life held for her and her girls. What else could her mother be expecting her to figure out?

And what about Noah? What part did he play? Couldn't she just be concerned for her friend? Was there any more to the story than that?

* * *

It was a beautiful Saturday morning. Noah rode relaxed. Jax was much less tense than he had been when he first arrived at the ranch. The horse had come a long way in a month's time and was ready to go home. While Noah had never determined what had sparked the horse's sudden negative behavior to begin with, whatever it was didn't seem to be an issue any longer.

He was loping Jax around the training pen, taking him through a few exercises before Mavis arrived. He smiled when he saw Grace standing at the fence. She had her arms folded across the top rail and was resting her chin on her hands. Nearly without fail, she made her presence known anytime Mavis was around. A cool November breeze rustled the treetops and was tousling her long auburn hair. He liked it when she left it loose, flowing down her back.

When he rode over to her, she smiled up at him, her pale green eyes sparkling in the morning light. Over the course of the past few weeks, he found himself beginning to believe there might be some truth to Eli's theory. Grace definitely bristled anytime he interacted with Mavis, and she obviously was not fond of the woman. He couldn't remember a time when Grace had given such a cold reception to anyone.

At times, he wondered if he should tell her there was nothing to fear with Mavis, that he held absolutely no interest in her beyond a professional relationship. He wasn't sure, however, if he should open that conversational door. He didn't want to open himself up to more rejection, and he didn't want to disrupt the progress they were making. They were growing closer again, and a great deal of the awkwardness between them had dissipated.

"Morning sunshine," he crooned, grinning down at her.

"Morning," she replied, still smiling.

Noah stepped down from the saddle and secured Jax to the top rail of the fence. Grace reached and touched the now gentle giant, scratching his neck. The horse leaned into her touch. Noah chuckled to himself. *I'd do the same thing big fella if I had the chance!*

"When will Mavis be here?"

Her question drew him back from his musing. "Anytime now. I told her to come early. I want to get her and Jax settled and on their way before I get started on anything else for the day."

Grace snickered. "Don't you *like* the flashy ways of *Miss Mavis Downey?*" Her tone was riddled with sarcasm.

Before he could answer, Mavis rounded the corner only a few feet from them. He darted a look at Grace, and her face blushed red. He knew she had to be wondering if Mavis overheard her comment. However, when he looked at Mavis, she appeared oblivious. She seemed as confident and cheerful as ever.

"Good morning, Miss Downey," he greeted her.

Mavis walked right up to him, resting her hand on his chest. "I've told you, Noah, call me Mavis," she said, her eyes sultry.

Noah shot a look toward Grace. Her face was still infused with red but for different reasons now. She narrowed her eyes, studying Mavis. And as usual, Mavis was pretending not to notice her.

"Uh, Mavis, you remember Grace?" he said, taking a step back.

"Of course," she replied, not even glancing in Grace's direction.

Noah could have cut the tension in the air with a knife! When he looked back toward Grace, her eyes were shooting daggers. He decided to get the show on the road before things turned ugly!

Swallowing uncomfortably, he turned his attention to Mavis. "Let me get Jax unsaddled, and he's ready to go."

Mavis moved closer again, nipping at her bottom lip in her signature flirtatious manner. "Do you mind riding him one more time just for me? I can't seem to get enough of watching you work." She eyed him through lowered lashes.

Oh, great! I have to get out of this, he thought. "I just finished working with him. I think it's best if you take him home and start working with him yourself."

She gave a disappointed pout. "If you say so," she sighed. "I guess I'll just have to find another horse to bring you," she said, an indulgent smirk lining her lips.

Noah worked swiftly to unsaddle Jax and led him to the waiting truck and trailer. Grace hadn't yet said a word, but she followed along behind them. He loaded Jax and latched the trailer door shut. He turned to Mavis but kept his distance. "I appreciate your business, and I appreciate any referrals you care to send my way. It's been a pleasure working with Jax."

He was just about to extend his hand when Mavis caught him off guard. Before he could say or do anything, she grabbed a handful of his shirtfront and pulled him toward her, kissing him firmly on the mouth. He froze, her lips sealed to his.

Mavis broke the kiss and pulled back only slightly, loosening her grasp on his shirt. She brushed her lips against his ear as she whispered, "Call me." Now and only now, she shot Grace a cunning glare, her lips curved into a sly smile. Without saying another word, she released him fully and got in her truck and drove away.

Noah closed his gaping mouth and turned to Grace. His heart hammered hard inside his chest, and he could feel a flush of heat running up his neck. He gulped when he met her eyes. "Grace, I promise I don't know why she did that! I've tried to make it clear to her that I'm not interested," he said, his voice ringing with desperation.

Grace didn't say a word. Her eyes were still shooting daggers, but now they were directed at him. She opened her mouth and started to speak but closed it tightly, pursing her lips in a tight line. She glared at him in silence before turning abruptly and walking away.

Noah opted not to go after her. He knew she would need some time to cool down, time to sort through her thoughts. He rubbed the back of his neck and sighed loudly as he watched her walk away.

Apparently, Mavis had heard her comment after all.

* * *

Grace moved briskly toward the house. Hot tears were clouding her vision, and she wanted to be alone. She couldn't make sense of the turmoil inside her. When Mavis kissed Noah, she felt something snap inside her. She wanted to grab the woman by her hair and pull her off him! The more she thought about it, however, the more aggravated she became with Noah himself. He didn't exactly pull back or push Mavis away. He just stood there, letting her kiss him! Or so it seemed to Grace. And to make matters worse, he said nothing to the woman after she'd done it!

Grace wanted to believe him when he said all he wanted with Mavis was a professional relationship, but she found it hard to believe he wasn't the least bit flattered by her attention. Grace couldn't deny Mavis was beautiful. She wore too much makeup, and her clothes were way too tight and often revealing, but she did have a gorgeous figure that would make most women jealous. Like it or not, she had to admit Mavis Downey was a head turner.

Grace sank into the swing on the back patio. It was a place of solace for her. She often brought her coffee here in the mornings, enjoying the first rays of light sweeping across the pastures. It made her feel close to God watching a new day unfold, and it drew her into quiet times of prayer.

A gentle breeze was still rustling the trees, and the warm sun shone overhead. She gently kicked the swing into motion and closed her eyes. *Lord, what am I doing? I can't make sense of what I'm feeling. Why am I so upset about Mavis? I know Noah doesn't really care for her. I believe him. But why is it bothering me so much? Please help me figure this out.*

The sound of the door opening ended her silent prayer. She turned to see her girls bounding outside. "Momma, Momma, it's time to go ride with Noah!" Abby squealed.

"Are you coming, Mom?" Anna asked.

She looked at her girls and smiled. The joy they were finding here on the ranch reminded her of her own childhood and a time when things were much simpler. Sighing, she answered, "No, I don't think I'm coming today, but I'm sure Uncle Eli will ride with you if you ask."

Anna, being ever observant, furrowed her brow at her mother. Abby, on the other hand, grinned from ear to ear. "Let's go find him, Anna!" she exclaimed to her sister.

Abby bounded off the porch, and Anna slowly turned to follow her. Looking back at her mother, she asked, "Are you okay, Mom?"

Grace smiled. "Yes, I'm fine. Go have fun."

Anna seemed hesitant but followed after her sister anyway. Grace watched until both girls were out of sight. She hated not joining them, but she wasn't ready to face Noah just yet. At this point, she had no idea what to say to him. If he asked her why she was so upset, what would she say?

She leaned her head back and closed her eyes, kicking the swing back into motion again. This time, however, instead of peacefully praying, the scene of Mavis kissing Noah kept playing in her head over and over again. She could clearly see those full, pink lips plastered to his, and she could see Noah just standing there, doing nothing. It seemed to be stuck on repeat in her brain.

After a few mental replays, that's when it hit her. She straightened as realization steeled her spine. She was hurt by what happened. Not because Mavis kissed Noah but because Noah had done nothing about it. He hadn't reacted at all. No indication one way or the other. And as much as she hated to admit it, that's exactly what he had done with her. When she kissed him, he'd done nothing. He didn't kiss her back, and he didn't pull away. He didn't even say anything when it was over. Just like with Mavis.

Grace felt hot tears stinging her eyes. *Am I no different than Mavis Downey to him?* Her tears spilled over, pouring down her cheeks in a river of heat. She huffed and wiped at her eyes as she stood from the swing, pacing the patio. *Why does any of this matter? Noah is just my friend. That's all. Suck it up, Grace!*

Inhaling a fortifying breath and blowing it out, she decided going for a ride might be exactly what she needed after all. It always helped her relax and feel at peace, two things she desperately craved at the moment. She wanted to be alone, though. She needed some time to sort things out.

* * *

Noah latched Doc's stall door and turned to Abby. Anna had her hand out for Doc to take her carrot, and Abby was waiting to be picked up. She wasn't quite tall enough to hand Doc his treat on her own. When he lifted her, she reached out, handing the horse an apple. Doc gently took it from her, his soft lips brushing against her hand. She immediately started giggling. "His lips tickle!" she squealed. "Can I feed him another one?"

Her big brown eyes melted his heart every time. "Sure," he said, unable to tell her no.

"Me too?" Anna asked.

When he looked at her, she was grinning as her green eyes sparkled. He knew he wouldn't be able to tell her no either. Every time he looked at her, he could see Grace through and through. Although the shade of her hair and the hue of her skin differed greatly from her mother's, they shared the same bright eyes and smile.

"I have an idea," he said. "Instead of feeding Doc too many treats, why don't we share with the other horses?"

Both girls adamantly agreed, and Noah handed out a few more carrots and apples. He followed them from stall to stall. When they came to Jingle's, he stopped in his tracks. Her stall was empty. "Just a minute. Wait right here," he instructed the girls.

He trekked outside to look around, checking the training pen, the round pen, and anywhere else he could think of. He was headed back inside the barn when Eli walked up. "Did you move Jingle?" Noah quizzed.

"No, why?" Eli replied.

"Her stall is empty. I thought maybe you moved her."

Eli looked around. "No, I haven't had her out today. And I don't think my dad would have done anything with her. He's never messed with her before."

Noah took off his hat and ran a hand through his hair. He scratched his head, trying to think.

"Noah?" came a little voice beside him.

He turned to see Abby tugging on his shirt. "What is it, Abby?"

"I think Momma took Jingle. I saw her ride in there." She pointed to the pasture opposite the barn.

Noah bent down to her level. "When? When did you see your momma do that?" He was trying to hide the alarm in his voice.

"When you were helping Anna," she answered. "Is Momma okay?" Her little voice suddenly sounded worried.

Noah stood and scooped her up. "Of course she is. But I'll go find her just to make sure," he said, planting a kiss on her forehead.

"Do you want me to go?" Eli asked.

Noah turned and handed him Abby. "No, my horse is still saddled. I'll go."

"Come on girls," Eli coaxed. "Hannah should be here by now with the twins. Let's go see your cousins."

Abby's face lit up, but Anna continued watching Noah. Her brow was creased with worry. "Will you find her?" she asked.

Noah smiled down at her reassuringly. "Of course I will. Don't worry."

As Eli headed toward the house with the girls in tow, Noah led his horse to the pasture where Abby said she saw Grace. Once he was through the gate, he shoved his hat further down on his head, flung himself in the saddle and took off. He didn't want to worry the girls, but he was more than a little concerned. While Jingle had come a long way with him, he still hadn't trusted her with anyone else yet, especially not in an open pasture.

He breathed a sigh of relief when he spotted Grace. Both her and Jingle appeared no worse for the wear. They were slowly meandering toward him. He pulled up, slowing to a trot. As he came to a stop in front of them, he hopped from the saddle. "What are you doing?" he barked, far more agitation in his voice than he intended.

Grace glared at him. "What does it *look* like I'm doing?" she replied, her tone equally sharp. Her eyes blazed with fire.

He sighed heavily, attempting to keep his frustration in check this time. "Why did you take Jingle, Grace? What if she acted up? You were out here all alone."

"I *know* how to ride, Noah. Besides, she's been fine." Her tone was clipped. She didn't attempt to hide her frustration as he had done.

He pushed his cowboy hat back and rubbed his forehead between his fingers. He started to speak, but Grace nudged Jingle, attempting to pass him by. He reached for the reins. "Grace, stop. We need to talk about some things."

He could see her jaw tense as she looked off into the distance. She stepped down from the saddle, pulling the reins from his hand. "We have nothing to talk about," she said curtly, walking on past him.

"Grace, please," he pleaded. "We *do* need to talk. If you're upset with me because of Mavis, then I'm sorry. I didn't ask or *want* her to do that!"

She didn't respond but stopped walking, her back remaining to him. He moved closer to her. "Please look at me. I'm trying to fix this." He spoke gently, heeding the tension and uneasiness sparking in the air around them.

She finally turned toward him, tears streaking her face. She wouldn't meet his gaze with her own. "I'll be fine. Just leave me alone."

"Grace," he said softly, reaching to touch her arm, "please talk to me. I don't ever want to be the reason you cry. I can't fix it if I don't know what I did."

"You did *nothing*, Noah! *Nothing* at all!" she said sharply before turning away from him again.

"Is this because I didn't stop Mavis or say anything when she kissed me? Because if it is, I'm sorry! I'm not exactly used to women up and kissing me out of the blue!" he retorted, throwing his hands up in surrender.

"Trust me. I know," she said, her head hanging low. Her voice sounded small, unsure. She started to walk again.

Noah reached for her arm, turning her around. "Grace, please. What could I have done differently?"

She met his gaze, her green eyes blazing. Something more than anger fueled her fire. What was it? What was hidden in that piercing stare? He furrowed his brow, studying her.

"*Something*, Noah! You could have done *something*! Anything!" she bellowed. "Even if it wasn't what you wanted, you could have at least said something!"

He was taken aback by the intensity of her volume coupled with her sharp tone. His mind was racing, trying to piece it all together. "Is this really about Mavis? About one kiss? A kiss I didn't even want!"

Grace turned away, her shoulders slumping. He couldn't help but think she looked ashamed, hurt maybe. "What's this really about?" He gently touched her arm again, but she still wouldn't look at him.

"I'm sorry, Noah," she said, her shoulders shuddering. "I'm sorry I kissed you and ruined our friendship. I made a mistake. I'm so sorry!"

His mouth gaped in disbelief. "Is that what you think, Grace? What you've been thinking all along?"

She turned to face him. "I'm so sorry," she muttered through her tears, her voice barely above a whisper. "I wish I could take it back."

He now recognized the emotion flashing in her eyes. Regret. She was ashamed and hurt. A deep, penetrating pang of understanding settled inside his chest. When she hurt, he hurt.

She started to turn away again, but he stopped her, gently but firmly gripping both of her arms. "Grace, you've got it all wrong. I didn't say anything and haven't said anything because you said you wanted to forget about it. You said to let it go, so I did."

He pulled her closer to him, gently raising her chin so he could see her face. She tried to lower her eyes as an appealing blush tinted her cheeks. "Grace," he said softly, "please don't be embarrassed. It's not at all what you think." He moved to cup her face with both hands, his thumbs gently swiping away her tears.

She started to speak. "Noah, I..," but before she could finish, he dipped his head and firmly yet tenderly brought his lips to hers. A rush of heat flooded his veins as all rational thought seeped from his mind. When she didn't pull away, he wrapped his arms around her waist, drawing her even closer. He wanted to leave no doubt in her mind about how he felt. He never again wanted her to view kissing him as a mistake.

* * *

Grace felt herself relax into Noah, his embrace gentle yet filled with strength, the same as his kiss. A warm, languid feeling seeped through her entire body, rendering her lightheaded and slightly off-balance. She gripped Noah's shirt at his shoulders, anchoring herself to him. The world around them seemed to fade to nothing, her entire focus centered on the feel of his lips on hers.

When Noah slowly drew away, his mouth remaining only a whisper from hers, she could feel his intake of breath. Her own breathing felt ragged in her chest. She was sure she had momentarily stopped breathing, almost certain her heart had stopped beating. As she gazed up at him, his eyes were deeper, bluer than ever before. An almost electric feeling hung in the air between them.

Grace could feel all her carefully crafted restraint slipping away. The walls she'd built to protect her heart were collapsing. She had never felt this way before, never been kissed like that. In his arms, she had melted, and her defenses crumbled.

Suddenly and unexpectedly, she felt vulnerable, powerless. Her mind whirled, trying to make sense of it all. Without invitation, fear was creeping in. She could feel the panic rising as her throat constricted. Her pulse drummed a wild cadence in her ears. Stepping back and sucking in a breath, she started to speak but no words would come.

Noah must have sensed something was amiss, letting his arms fall from around her. His expression grew tense as his eyes searched hers.

Grace stood silent, no words coming. She didn't know what to say. She couldn't explain what had happened when he kissed her because she couldn't make sense of it herself. Emotions she was unfamiliar with coupled with memories of her past left her feeling scared and unsure. A silent battle took hold in her mind, one voice telling her to run and one telling her to stay.

"I... I don't know... what to say," she stammered, still feeling breathless. Tears were involuntarily pooling in her eyes. No words seemed adequate for the moment. She wanted to tell him everything going through her mind, but she didn't even know where to start.

"It's okay, you don't have to say anything," he responded, his voice low and comforting. His eyes searched hers again as a furrow appeared between his brows. He smiled softly, but the action didn't quite reach his eyes.

"I told you, Grace. I never want to be the reason you cry."

CHAPTER 10

Grace walked slowly, leading Jingle toward the barn. Noah walked silently beside her. As she stole glances in his direction, she wondered if they'd now crossed a line from which there was no return. She couldn't help but grow warm thinking of his kiss, absentmindedly brushing the fingertips of one hand across her lips. A flush of heat filled her to the very core, creeping up her neck and flooding her cheeks with color.

But the fear. The fear held her back. She couldn't get past the panic that had gripped her and threatened to overtake her entirely. She felt so angry and frustrated with herself. She obviously hadn't made as much progress toward moving on as she had believed.

And what about her friendship with Noah? What would happen now? She was beyond thankful to have him back in her life, and she didn't want to lose him. With them sailing in uncharted waters, she wasn't sure how they would navigate forward from here. If she allowed herself to feel anything more than friendship for him, what would happen if things didn't work out? She wasn't sure that was a risk she was willing to take, with his heart or her own.

They were almost to the barn when Grace heard heavy footsteps approaching from behind. Her father was trudging in their direction. His cowboy hat sat low on his brow, and his mouth was set into a firm line. Grace could see the tension is his stride as he approached, causing her to halt in her tracks.

"Grace, you have a visitor," he said tersely.

She wrinkled her brow in hesitation. "Who is it?"

Jake's expression softened only slightly as he gazed at her. "I think its best you go see for yourself."

She looked at Noah. He looked just as confused as she felt.

"I'll take Jingle," he said. "You go on to the house."

"I'll help," Jake said, reaching for her horse.

Grace relinquished the reins to her father, and he and Noah continued toward the barn. She, however, still couldn't make herself take a step. She stared at the backs of the retreating men before turning her gaze toward the house. Her father's strange behavior had her feeling more than a little uneasy. What, or better yet *who*, would cause such a reaction from Jake Buckner?

Finally moving toward the house, she saw Eli and Hannah preparing to leave, Anna and Abby in tow. "What's going on?" she asked, her tone laced with apprehension.

When Eli turned to face her, his expression mirrored that of their father. "Mom asked us to take the girls for a while. We'll bring them back later."

Grace felt her anxiety level rise about ten notches as she stared at her brother. She was about to inquire further when Hannah touched her arm. "Grace, I think its best if you go on in. The girls will be fine with us for a while."

Grace simply nodded her head, more uncertain than ever what awaited her in the house. Why wasn't anyone telling her who was inside?

Mustering up her courage, she walked toward the front door. As she pushed open the heavy, wooden door, her heart pounded. Her mother rose from where she was sitting. Jane Buckner, like everyone else, had a look of great concern etched across her face. She said nothing, but as her gaze shifted, Grace followed her eyes. Looking to her left, she inhaled sharply, disbelief coursing through her. She froze in her spot, unable to move as a small gasp escaped her lips.

Chris.

Jane walked over to her daughter, closing the door behind her. Chris rose from his seat at the same time and smiled sheepishly. "Hello, Grace."

She nearly jumped out of her skin when her mother touched her arm. "I'm going to leave you two alone. I'll be on the back patio with Grandma Elaine if you need me."

Grace didn't respond as she continued staring in disbelief. Out of the corner of her eye, she saw her mother exit the room.

Chris spoke again, drawing her out of her temporary state of shock. "I'm sure this is quite a surprise to you," he said, smiling sheepishly again.

She narrowed her eyes, studying him. Her surprise was quickly replaced by years of pent-up anger towards the man now standing in front her. Walking over to him, she raised her hand and slapped him soundly across the face! His head jolted sideways from the force, and her hand stung sharply.

Chris reached up and rubbed his cheek, the imprint of her hand emblazoned on his face. "I suppose I deserved that," he said.

Grace froze in her spot as misgiving sent a shiver up her spine. She drew in a harsh breath, overcome by her reaction to him. She almost recoiled in fear, having struck him. She felt her hands begin to tremble.

Taking in another breath, she willed her mind and body to let go of the fear. *This is not Jared. He will not hurt you.* She kept repeating those two phrases over and over in her head.

After a few moments of taking deep, deliberate breaths, Grace felt the tension coiling in her chest lessening. She dropped onto the couch and temporarily rested her head in her hands. When she did look up, she eyed Chris warily. "What do you want, Chris? Why are you here?"

"I came to talk. I came to tell you I'm sorry," he answered, moving slightly closer to her again. "Grace... I'm so very sorry." His voice was thick with emotion.

She let out a groan of frustration, sitting back and crossing her arms over her chest. "It wasn't just me you *abandoned*, Chris. You abandoned your own child. Your own flesh and blood!" Her volume rose in irritation.

He slumped back into the chair where he'd been sitting, running his hands through his sandy blonde hair. He looked up, his pale blue eyes pleading with her. "I know, Grace. I've made a lot of terrible mistakes in my life, and abandoning you and our unborn child was the absolute worst mistake of all. I came here to tell you that, to tell you how it's haunted me since the day I left."

Grace sighed loudly and unfolded her arms. She rubbed at her forehead with one hand before speaking again. "What do you want?" she asked, her tone not as harsh as before. "Did you come all this way just to ask my forgiveness?"

Chris moved to the edge of his chair, his countenance seemingly lifted by her calmer demeanor. "Yes, partly. I hope you can somehow find it in your heart to forgive me," he pleaded. "But I also hope you will allow me to have a relationship with our daughter, Grace."

She sat up ramrod straight, feeling as if someone had just poured molten steel down her spine. "What makes you think *you* deserve a relationship with *my* daughter?" she said, the volume of her voice rising again.

Chris sighed. "I don't deserve anything, Grace. I know that. But I do think Anna deserves to know her father. Or at least the chance to choose whether or not she wants a relationship with me."

"She's a child, Chris!" Grace responded, her own voice now thick with emotion. "You chose to leave her once already! How could I possibly trust you not to do it again? I know what it feels like to be abandoned, and I *will not* put my daughter through that!" Her voice broke as her eyes welled with tears, and she again rested her head in her hands.

Chris rose and moved toward the couch. He cautiously sat next to her, speaking softly. "Grace, I'm so sorry. I was so selfish back then, only thinking of myself. I was terrified to be a father, and I ran away. But I know there's no excuse for what I did. I will regret that decision for the rest of my life, regret all these lost years."

When she looked up at him, tears were spilling from his eyes, streaking his face. He suddenly appeared vulnerable, almost desperate. He looked like a man marred by life, haunted by the torment of his own decisions. And despite all the pain his actions had caused in her life, she couldn't help but feel sorry for him. Closing her eyes, she offered a silent plea to the Lord. *Why is this man back in my life, Lord, after all these years? What should I do? Can I trust him enough to let him have a relationship with Anna? Please help me know what to do. And please help me forgive him. I know that's what You want of me. I can't do this without You.*

Turning to Chris, she questioned him. "How did you know where to find me after all this time?"

"I know a few people around here, and everyone knows your family. Word reached me you were back in Texas." He paused and sighed heavily before continuing. "I know about your husband, how you lost him. I'm sorry, Grace."

She narrowed her eyes at him again. "Is that the only reason you came? Because of..." she paused. "Because of what you heard?"

"No! No! That's not it at all!" he answered emphatically, his palms facing out in surrender. "I've been trying to find the courage to face you for a long time."

"Why now, Chris? Why after all this time?"

He ran his hands through his hair before rubbing his forehead. A long silence lingered as she waited for him to answer.

"I told you I've made a lot of mistakes in my life. Mistakes that have hurt the people I love." He turned to face her, sighing heavily again. "Anna has half siblings, two sisters and a brother. The girls, Laney and Cassie, are from my first marriage, and my son, Kyle, is from my second marriage."

He paused again, his shoulders slumping. He appeared weighted down by an intense heaviness, clearly bearing a burden of his own making. It was apparent to Grace there was more to the story, so she patiently waited for him to continue.

"It's not just you and Anna I've failed. I have two failed marriages and children I'm barely allowed to see. To say my ex-wives are not fond of me might be an understatement."

"What does any of that have to do with me? With Anna?" she questioned.

Again, Chris sighed heavily before continuing. He looked away, not meeting her eyes this time. "My family encouraged me to get help. I seem to have a pattern of hurting anyone and everyone who cares about me, and I never realized the toll it was taking. I've always run away from my problems rather than facing them. So, much to my own surprise, I've been seeing a therapist." Turning to face her again, he continued, "My eyes have been opened to so many things, Grace. My life has been one failed relationship after another, and I'm doing my best to move past that. But I can't move forward until I've at least attempted to do right by you and Anna." He reached and touched her hand cautiously. "Will you at least give me a chance, Grace? A chance to prove myself to you and our daughter?"

She slowly withdrew her hand from his, her forehead creasing in uncertainty. "What exactly are you asking of me?"

"I just want the opportunity to be a part of Anna's life. I know that's asking a lot after what I've done, but that's what I'm hoping for."

Grace rubbed her forehead again. "I don't know, Chris. I'm not sure I'm willing to take that risk."

"Please, Grace," he pleaded, reaching for her hand again. "Just give me a chance. This can be totally on your terms. I'll do whatever you say if it means I can see Anna."

She didn't recoil her hand this time. She sat staring at the broken man beside her, realizing he was no longer the confident, swaggering young man who'd taken advantage of her all those years ago. No, the man sitting here now seemed anything but sure of himself. And as they sat in silence, Grace again found herself for the second time in one day facing a situation she was anything but sure how to navigate.

* * *

Jake silently helped Noah get the horses unsaddled, brushed down, and back in their stalls. Noah kept looking his direction, but Jake either didn't notice or was pretending not to. Noah finally spoke, weary from the silence. "What's going on, Jake? Who's in the house with Grace?"

Jake removed his hat, slapping it against his thigh. He didn't look at Noah when he answered. "Chris," was all he said, his tone clipped.

Immediately Noah bristled at hearing the name. "What?! What is he doing here?" he barked, moving toward Jake, stopping directly in front of him.

Jake pinched his forehead between his fingers before setting his hat back on his head. "I don't know. I didn't hang around long enough to find out. When he said who he was, just looking at him made me angrier than I've been in a good, long while! I left him with Jane and Eli while I came to find Grace. I didn't trust myself around him."

Noah looked anxiously toward the house, every muscle stiffening in agitation. If he didn't practice self-control this very minute, he'd burst through that door and tear into Chris! Despite being taught most of his life that violence was never the answer, he'd wanted to have a word or two with that man ever since he found out how he abandoned Grace after getting her pregnant.

"Shouldn't we be in there with her?" he asked Jake, his voice gruff. "I don't like the idea of him alone in there with Grace and Jane."

"Slow down there, son. I don't like this one bit more than you, but you know as well as I do, we'd best steer clear unless Grace gives the greenlight for us to be there."

Noah growled. He knew Jake was right. "Shouldn't we at least be near the house in case she needs us?"

Jake nodded. "We can do that."

Noah followed Jake to the back patio. Elaine was quietly rocking in her chair, and Jane was sitting at the table, a book in her hand. Both women looked up as the men approached.

"Thank goodness you two are here," Jane said with a sigh. "I think I've read the same two pages of this book ten times over! I was trying to keep my mind busy, but I can't seem to concentrate."

Jake sat down in the chair next to his wife, taking her hand in his as he did. "It'll be okay. Grace is a strong woman. She can handle this."

Noah studied Jake. His words said one thing, but his body language conveyed a different message. He was clearly trying to offer his wife some comfort, but it was obvious to Noah that Jake Buckner was worried. Noah felt the same way and paced the patio, frequently looking through the windows, hoping to catch a glimpse of either Grace or her surprise visitor.

"Noah, dear," Elaine spoke, "come sit with me," she said, patting the chair next to hers. As always, her face appeared the picture of calm as she smiled sweetly at him.

Noah respectfully obliged and sat down. He nervously kicked his rocking chair into motion, his mind focused on who was in the house.

Elaine reached and patted his arm. "You need to breathe, dear. Everything is going to be just fine," she said with another sweet smile. "None of this is a surprise to the Lord. He always has a plan if we trust Him."

Noah sighed. He knew she was right. Instead of worrying over what he couldn't see or hear, he should he praying and trusting God. "You're right," he responded. "Worrying doesn't change a thing."

Elaine leaned nearer and patted his arm again, speaking softly, "No, it most certainly doesn't. *But...* prayer does." She smiled warmly and returned to her rocking.

Noah knew her well enough to know she was praying this very moment. He silently joined her, asking the Lord to watch over Grace.

* * *

Grace watched Chris drive away. He'd certainly given her a mountain of information and decisions to think over and weigh out. Her greatest concern in all of this would always be, first and foremost, the well-being of her oldest daughter. Anna always felt things on a deeper level, just like her mother. Grace would have to carefully consider how Chris's return would impact her, both the good and the bad.

And now, for the sake of her daughter, she would force herself to spend time with him. That thought alone made her stomach churn. She had reluctantly agreed to his request to spend some time with him first before making any decisions about what would happen with Anna. He'd clearly sensed her hesitation and was willing to do almost anything to win her approval. He'd nearly begged her for even the slightest chance.

Grace heard boots crunching gravel and turned to see Noah. He was slowly approaching, his hands in his pockets and his expression tense. As she eyed him warily, she fought the urge to turn and walk away. Today had definitely had its' fill of surprises, and she wasn't sure she wanted to face him right now. She still wasn't sure what was happening with him or how to handle it. She turned back toward the long lane just as Chris was pulling onto the main road.

"You okay?" Noah asked, stopping beside her.

She shrugged her shoulders. "Not sure," she replied, keeping her gaze fixed toward the road.

"What did he want?" Noah's tone was clipped.

She sighed and turned to face him. "He wants to see Anna. He said he regrets leaving and not being a part of her life."

Grace could visibly see Noah's agitation as his blue eyes blazed. His shirt sleeves were rolled to his elbows, and the muscles in his forearms twitched with tension.

"What makes him think he can just waltz in here after all this time and have any claim at all to Anna?" he exclaimed, throwing a hand up in the direction Chris had just driven.

Grace folded her arms around her waist and looked back toward the road, not responding to his outburst. She worried her bottom lip. She had so much to consider right now, and she certainly didn't need him pointing out the obvious. She was already wrestling with the same thoughts herself.

"Grace," he said, much softer now, "please tell me you aren't considering letting him see Anna. How could you trust him after what he did? What would it do to Anna if he left again?"

She turned back to face him. Both his tone and his expression held genuine concern for the wellbeing of her daughter. She knew he was just being protective, and she should appreciate that. But for some reason, in this moment, it only irritated her. "Don't you think I've thought about that?" she barked. "He is her father, Noah. I have to take that into consideration."

"Why, Grace? Why do you have to consider him at all? Why let him back in your life now?"

She fumed. "Because Noah, she is *my* daughter, and it is *my* decision!" she bellowed, pointing a finger at her own chest.

Noah rubbed his forehead, pinching it beneath his fingers. His jaw was tight, but he spoke softly. "I'm just thinking about what's best for you and Anna. I know she's your daughter, and it's your decision. I just don't want to see either one of you get hurt."

Grace relaxed a little, sighing. "I haven't made any decisions yet. I agreed to spend some time with him before deciding what will happen with Anna."

Noah's eyes blazed again as his entire body tensed. His hands were tight against his hips, his stance clearly communicating his frustration. "Do you really think that's wise? Letting him close to you again?"

Clenching her teeth, she moved closer to him and narrowed her eyes. Her voice was low and direct as she spoke. "I am *not* a child,

Noah! I am a grown woman, and I can handle this! It is my decision to make, and this conversation is over!" she barked, storming off and leaving him standing alone in the driveway.

* * *

Noah watched Grace walk away. He yanked off his hat and raked a hand through his hair as he let out a low growl. Sometimes the stubbornness of that woman drove him mad, and now was one of those times! Why couldn't she see he only wanted to protect her? Wasn't it obvious how much he loved her? He felt like he'd failed to protect her in the past by not being there when she needed him most, and he didn't want to let that happen again.

And what about the girls? He'd come to love them like they were his own. The last thing he would tolerate was allowing Chris to hurt Anna. She'd already lost the only father she'd known up until now, and he certainly would not stand idly by and let Chris walk in and out of her life as he pleased. But at the same time, what choice did he have? If Grace sidelined him on this, which she obviously had for now, his interference would not be welcome despite his best intentions.

He sighed heavily as he slapped his hat back on his head. What had started out as a beautiful autumn day had quickly spiraled into an unforeseen chain of events he was still trying to wrap his head around. Had all of this really happened in just one day? What a mess! Right now, he couldn't make sense of any of it.

He was still standing in the middle of the driveway when Jane approached him. "Well, that was certainly unexpected, wasn't it?" she said, more of a statement than a question.

Noah looked at her, forlorn. He suddenly felt powerless to do anything. It was the same way he'd felt when he found out Grace was pregnant and abandoned, and the way he'd felt yet again when he found out she was marrying Jared and moving away. He felt like he really put his heart out there today when he kissed her, but now he questioned whether or not that was the right thing to do.

"I can tell you have a lot on your mind," Jane said. "Let's take a stroll." She looped her arm through his and started walking. He had no choice but to follow.

"Shouldn't you be with Grace right now?" he questioned. "I'm sure she has more on her mind than I do."

Jane smiled. "You know as well as I do Grace will not talk about any of this until she is good and ready. She'll need some time to process things on her own before she will open up to anyone else."

Of course, Jane was right. Grace would need time to herself. She processed her thoughts and feelings at a depth most people would never reach, and it was just one of the many things he loved about her. As he considered this, it gave him hope. Perhaps her response to him earlier in the day had simply been her need for time to process her feelings for him.

Jane patted his arm with her free hand. "Talk to me, Noah. I can tell something is bothering you."

He hesitated, chewing on the inside of his cheek as he carefully considered his response. Could he talk to Jane about this? *Should* he talk to her? While he considered her a second mother to him, she was first and foremost Grace's mother. He had never shared anything specifically related to Grace with her, and he wasn't sure he should start now.

Jane must have sensed his reluctance because she stopped abruptly and looked him straight in the eye. "Noah, you can tell me anything. I may be Grace's mother, but I consider you my son. Whatever you tell me is just between us, for our ears only," she said. She smiled reassuringly before reengaging in their stroll, her arm remaining looped through his.

Noah sighed. "I don't know where to begin. Today has been one unexpected mix up after another."

"Why don't you just begin with what's bothering you most and go from there. Maybe we can sort it out together," she said confidently.

Noah relaxed a little. Jane Buckner had a way of making a person feel at ease, making it easy to open up to her. Her compassionate, loving manner made him feel safe to share things he wasn't sure he would even share with his own mother.

"Well, for starters," he began, "Mavis kissed me earlier today." He gave Jane a sideways glance, but her expression didn't slip, and she didn't miss a step.

"Oh? And how do you feel about that?" she asked.

Noah guffawed. "It certainly wasn't what I wanted!" he exclaimed. "She's been throwing herself at me for weeks, but I never once gave her the slightest notion I was interested!"

"So why do you think she took it a step further today?" Jane quizzed.

He sighed. "I think she did it because of Grace."

Jane raised an eyebrow but said nothing. She waited for him to continue.

"It's been obvious that Grace and Mavis don't like each other. You could practically cut the tension between them with a knife! And since Grace was standing there when Mavis picked up her horse, I think it was one last jab at Grace before she left."

"And why would Mavis assume it would bother Grace if she kissed you?"

Noah pondered the question. "I'm not really sure."

"Hmm." Jane replied. "And *did* it bother Grace?"

Noah scrubbed his free hand down his face. "I guess so. She took off on Jingle, and I had to go find her. She was pretty upset at me when I did."

"Upset that you went looking for her, or upset for other reasons?"

Noah thought for a moment. "At first, I thought that's why she was upset, because I came looking for her. But come to find out, she was upset over something entirely different." He suddenly felt himself turning red, knowing where the conversation was headed.

"Oh? What was she really upset about?" Jane inquired.

"Well... uh... it kind of goes back to when we visited my parents," he said hesitantly. "Grace sort of... uh... kissed me." He could fully feel the heat in his face as he attempted to swallow the lump in his throat. This wasn't a conversation he ever planned to have with Grace's mother!

"Oh!" Jane exclaimed, surprise evident on her face. "That *is* interesting. What happened?"

"Well... that's when things got a little weird," he said, nervously rubbing the back of his neck. "Grace sort of flipped out about it and said to forget it. So, that's what I did. But then today, I found out she's been upset all along because I never said anything. I thought I was doing what she wanted!" He could feel his muscles stiffening with frustration as his shoulders and neck tightened.

Jane patted his arm again. "Relax, Noah. Take a deep breath." Her voice was calm and even.

Noah obeyed and breathed deep, releasing his breath slowly. He sighed before continuing. "I think I just made things worse and complicated it even more," he said, stopping to face Jane. "She told me she regretted what she'd done because she thought I regretted it, thought it wasn't what I wanted. So... I... uh... I kissed her." He watched Jane anxiously to see her reaction.

"Oh!" she exclaimed, raising her eyebrows. "Is that the *only* reason you kissed her?" she inquired, a smile peaking at the corners of her mouth. "Because you wanted her to stop feeling bad about what she'd done?"

Noah furrowed his brow. "Of course not!" he exclaimed. "I love her!" His eyes grew round as the confession of love came spilling from his lips before he could stop it.

Jane smiled broadly and looped her arm back through his, recommencing their stroll. "It's so good to hear you say that out loud," she said.

Noah glanced sideways at her. "You knew?"

Jane hugged his arm, pulling him closer. "Of course, Noah," she said quietly. "It may not be obvious to everyone, but it's been obvious to me for a very long time."

Noah felt himself blushing again. Up until now, he thought he'd done a pretty job of hiding his feelings. "If you know I love her, why did you ask me why I kissed her?"

"Oh, I knew the answer before you told me," she responded with a smile. "But does *she* know why?"

Jane unhooked her arm from his, squeezing his hand as she did. She smiled once more and then walked away.

Noah was left standing alone yet again. His mouth gaped slightly, and his brow was pinched. He hadn't even considered that Grace might not have discerned his true intentions. He assumed his actions would be enough to tell her, but maybe he assumed too much. Maybe he really had made a mess of things. *You know what they say about people who assume things,* he thought with a roll of his eyes.

And now, with the sudden reappearance of Chris, how and when would he get a chance to talk to her about any of it? He knew her aggravation toward him earlier in the driveway was likely just a culmination of the day's events weighing heavy on her mind. For now, he would have to leave her be and let her have some time to process things. Pushing her to talk would only get him in hot water and wouldn't get him any closer to the end result he wanted more than his next breath. Sighing heavily, he headed toward the back pasture. Not only did he have a lot to think about, he had a lot to pray about.

* * *

Grace could see Noah crossing the pasture field from her bedroom window. She knew it was his quiet place to pray, and she smiled. She regretted snapping at him earlier, but the events of the day left her feeling stressed and short on patience. As she watched him slowly meandering through the field, she felt peace wash over her. She knew him well enough to know he was praying for her at this very moment.

She turned from the window and resumed her own quiet prayer. *Lord, I am definitely in uncharted territory! Today has been a roller-coaster of emotions and events, and I'm not sure what to do. I certainly didn't expect Chris to show up, but I know it was not a surprise to You. Please help me know what I should do. I know I've agreed to spend time with him before I make a decision about Anna, but I'm not sure I'm doing the right thing. Part of me wants to tell him to leave and never come back, but another part of me believes Anna deserves the chance to know her father. Please help me make the right decision for her. You've entrusted her life to me, and I am so blessed to be her mother. Help me not fail her. Or You.*

CHAPTER 11

G race perused the menu in her hands, attempting to focus on the words she was reading. It felt as if every nerve ending in her body was on heightened alert. She occasionally glanced across the table at Chris. He was grinning from ear to ear, clearly thrilled with her acceptance of his dinner invitation. And while this felt oddly like a date, Anna was the only reason she was sitting across the table from this man she thought she'd never lay eyes on again as long as she lived.

"Please, order anything you'd like," Chris said. "While I may have made a mess of my personal life, I've done well on the business side." He grinned even broader.

Grace eyed him guardedly, unsure of his intentions.

He must have sensed her apprehension because he soon began to backtrack. "I'm not trying to boast or anything," he said. "I only wanted to assure you I'm financially capable of caring for Anna."

Grace didn't relax her expression as she continued to stare at him. Money was the least of her concerns with whether or not Chris was fit to be a part of Anna's life. "I don't care about your financial situation, Chris, whatever it might be. I only care if I can trust you with my daughter's heart."

"*Our* daughter," he corrected her with a smile.

Grace felt her jaw clench as she rather forcefully placed her menu on the table. She narrowed her gaze at him. "*You* have not yet earned the right to be anything in Anna's life," she seethed. "We are sitting here now because I agreed to give you a chance. I'd be careful not to get ahead of myself if I were you."

Chris's smile faded, and he leaned forward, speaking softly. "Grace, I'm sorry. I didn't mean to offend you. I know I have to prove myself, and I'm thankful you're even giving me a chance. It's more than I deserve."

Grace eyed him for a moment longer before returning her attention back to her menu. Chris appeared to relax, and the smile returned to his face. Studying him with occasional glances, she was reminded what had drawn her to him when they first met nearly ten years ago - the grey blue of his eyes, his sandy blonde hair, that easygoing smile he so readily flashed. Even now, after all the time that had passed, he was still a handsome man. Age was being kind to him, adding a sort of rugged charm to his already good looks.

He also appeared dressed to impress for this occasion. From his designer jeans paired with a trendy, button front shirt to his luxury wristwatch, he definitely did not look like small-town Texas. Grace couldn't decide if he was attempting to impress her or if this was his typical, everyday attire. There was a great deal she needed to learn about him before deciding if he was fit to be part of Anna's life.

Taking a deep breath, she decided to get the conversation rolling. "So... where are you living now?" she asked, her voice ringing with hesitation.

Chris grinned broadly, seeming eager to answer her question. "I've lived in a few different places over the years," he said. "After

I graduated, I moved from Syracuse to New York. I thought I needed to be in the city to really scope out the job market, and it was a good compromise to keep me close to my family. But things didn't quite work out like I planned," he said, looking red in the face. "I ended up with my first ex-wife and an ex-father-in-law who fired me."

Grace felt her eyebrows raise, surprised to hear such a confession so soon in the conversation. Chris, noticing her reaction, paused briefly, perhaps waiting to see if she would offer some sort of verbal retort. When she didn't speak, he continued.

"I'm ashamed to say, though, I didn't learn my lesson. That wasn't the end of me putting me first and everyone else second. Apparently, I've been pretty good at that," he said, his face turning a light shade of pink as he spoke. "I told you, Grace, I've hurt a lot of people over the years. People who deserved far better than what I gave them."

Grace still opted not to speak. She wasn't sure what to say or if she should say anything at all. She certainly wasn't going to throw him a pity party. He was a grown man who had made his bed, and now he would have to lay in it.

When she said nothing, he went on. "After the divorce was finalized, I moved to Chicago. I had a buddy there from college, and he got me an interview with the company he was working for. They had an opening in their marketing department, and that was right up my ally." He paused again, shaking his head. "That was such a great opportunity. I was really going places. But just like before, I messed it all up," he said, lowering his eyes.

Grace now felt compelled to speak, hoping her question would sound more like concern than just sheer curiosity. "What happened?"

Chris raised his head and met her stare. "I met my second wife and had my son. The only problem was I wasn't faithful. Again. I cheated on Chloe just like I did Rachel."

Grace pinched her brows in confusion. "What does that have to do with your job? Was *this* wife the boss's daughter, too?"

Chris sighed heavily, his body language riddled with guilt and regret, something Grace was all too familiar with. For the first time since the conversation had begun, she found herself feeling sorry for the father of her oldest child. Perhaps he had woven himself a bed of thorns, but she knew he didn't have to lie on that bed forever. She knew he could find healing and forgiveness in the Lord. *Is this why he's here, Lord? Am I supposed to share Your grace and love with him?* She pondered this in her heart as she waited for him to continue his story.

"Megan was the boss's daughter," he said, his voice sounding weary. "I cheated on Chloe *with* Megan. She knew I was married when the affair started, and she thought I would leave my wife for her. When she found out otherwise, she ruined my marriage *and* my career." He let out another audible sigh as a heaviness settled in.

Grace, again feeling compelled to speak, tried to steer the conversation in a more positive direction. "Well, you may have lost a couple of jobs, but you seem to be doing okay now," she said, a slight shrug in her shoulders.

Chris grinned at her. "I guess that brings me to finally answering your question. After my second divorce, I moved back to Syracuse to be near my family. I started up my own company, and it took off like a rocket! Since I obviously mess up every relationship I try to have, I decided just to focus on work. And hey, at least that much has paid off!" he said, laughing half-heartedly.

The rest of the dinner passed uneventfully. Chris answered any question Grace asked with open honesty, and no topic was off limits. And while he also posed some questions of his own to her, she answered with far less enthusiasm and frankness. She was weighing everything he said and did with absolute scrutiny. Her daughter's heart was on the line, and she wasn't letting her guard down just yet.

* * *

After leaving the restaurant, Grace didn't feel like heading home just yet. She decided a long walk alone might help clear her head. Her heart was heavy before meeting Chris, and now she had even more information to sift through. Her life had taken so many unexpected twists and turns in the past few months, and at times, she found herself wondering where God's hand was at in all of it. But anytime she felt herself doubting and her faith slipping, she could feel the comfort of the Holy Spirit with her, reminding her the Lord had never forsaken her or left her side. In fact, when she stopped and really thought about it, she knew beyond the shadow of a doubt she wouldn't have survived the things she had if He hadn't been with her through it all. Despite everything, His blessings were evident all around, including His greatest blessing of all - forgiveness.

Grace inhaled deeply, the cooler autumn air filling her lungs. A gentle breeze rustled the trees and tickled her nose. She tucked her hands in her pockets as she wandered along. The light of day was quickly fading into an evening glow, and she smiled as she let the peace of the Lord settle over her, allowing her cares and worries to slip away.

Her eyes roamed the changing leaves. Hues of red, orange, and yellow swirled to the ground around her. As she watched them floating through the air, she suddenly felt very much like those leaves. At times, all the sudden changes she was experiencing felt like she, too, was swirling through the air with absolutely no inkling where she might land. But despite all the changes and as unexplainable as they may be, she was certain the Lord was making something beautiful from the chaos, just as with the leaves. Grace could feel it in her heart and knew it to be true in her head. A silent tear trickled down her cheek as the love of the Lord wrapped around her like the comfort of a warm blanket. She still didn't have the answers she needed, and she was uncertain what lie ahead. But one thing she knew for sure - the Lord holds it all in His hands, and that was enough.

She paused as she passed a diner. Sitting alone in a booth near the window was her grandmother. Grandma Elaine looked up from her coffee cup and smiled. Grace returned her smile and backtracked toward the door, joining her grandmother inside.

"Grandma, what are you doing here all alone?" she asked.

Elaine smiled again and sipped her coffee. "Your mother needed to do some grocery shopping, so I decided to ride along. I thought I'd sit and enjoy a quiet cup of coffee while she shops."

Grace scanned the diner. "Where are the girls? I thought they were staying with Mom while I met Chris."

Elaine waved off the question, taking another sip before answering. "They're fine. They were in the barn with the men when we left. You know those girls are head over heels for Noah," she said with a grin. "And I'm pretty sure he feels the same about them."

Grace felt a flush of color infuse her cheeks at the mention of Noah's name. She turned her eyes away from her grandmother as a smile played at the corners of her mouth. As much as she tried to push aside thoughts of him, it was impossible. His handsome face, the intense blue of his eyes, and the feel of his lips on hers kept flashing through her mind.

"How did your dinner go with Chris?"

The question drew her back to the present. "It went fine," she answered. "He shared a lot more about himself than I expected."

"I'm assuming that's a good thing," Elaine responded. "Have you decided yet if he can see Anna?"

Grace sighed as she slouched back in the booth. "I don't know, Grandma. I'm not sure what the right thing to do is. I'm not sure I should trust him, *if* I can trust him."

Elaine sat her coffee cup down and looked her granddaughter straight in the eye. "I know this is difficult for you. You've been hurt and disappointed so much, but you can't let the past determine your future. And you must remember that we all deserve a second chance. After all, you or I neither one would be sitting here now if it weren't for the wonderful grace of our Lord Jesus."

Grace sat up and leaned in closer to her grandmother, crossing her arms on the table. "You know, Grandma," she said with a pinched expression, "the strangest thing happened while Chris was telling me about all the mistakes he's made in his life. It was like the Lord was wanting me to tell Chris about Him, tell him he doesn't have to live with all the guilt he's carrying around. Isn't that crazy?"

Elaine simply smiled and returned to sipping her coffee.

Grace sat wide eyed as she waited for her grandmother to respond, to agree that such a thing sounded ridiculous. But Elaine said nothing.

"Grandma? Did you hear me? Isn't that crazy? I mean, seriously, *me* telling Chris about the Lord?"

Elaine lowered her coffee cup, placing it gently to the side. She reached across the table and took her granddaughter's hand. "The grace of our Lord is a free gift to us all if we accept it," she said. "When you find that gift for yourself, there is nothing crazy at all about sharing it with others. And you my dear," she continued, her eyes warm and her smile soft, "you've found that gift. You've found grace."

Grace immediately felt the moisture begin to pool in her eyes as she yet again felt the love of the Lord wash over her. Her grandmother was right. This journey was not solely about finding her way home, finding herself again. It was so much more than that. It was a journey drawing her back to the Lord, back to relationship with Him. She squeezed her grandmother's hand and smiled as she thanked the Lord for the gift He'd given her in this gentle, wise woman.

* * *

Noah tossed one more hay bale before stopping to take a break. He eyed the driveway as he pushed his hat back on his head, sweat stinging his eyes. He lifted his shirt and wiped the perspiration from his face. He was trying in vain not to think about the fancy, silver car parked near the house, and even more so, the driver of that car. Chris had been coming around often enough he should have gotten used to the idea of him being there, but no matter how hard he tried, the whole situation left him feeling uneasy.

He turned away and went back to tossing hay bales, attempting to drown out his thoughts with manual labor, when a voice called out to him. "Whoa now, Noah! You plan to rearrange the whole barn while you're at it?"

He turned to see Caleb walking toward him, grinning broadly. He tossed the bale he was holding before removing his gloves to greet his friend. "Man is it good to see you! I didn't think you were coming until Thanksgiving?"

"Well, I didn't really tell anyone other than Mom. She's been keeping me filled in on what's going on around here. Figured I should come check in on my little sister. Besides, I thought you might need a friend right now."

Noah shook his head, looking to the ground. He folded his arms across his chest and sighed heavily. "This sure has been tough. I'm trying to be positive, trying to be supportive for Grace, but it's hard."

"I can imagine. It's hard on me being her brother. I can't tell you the things I'd like to say, or do for that matter, if I had the chance! But you know Grace, it won't be pretty if you or I interfere where we aren't wanted."

Caleb's words stung a little more than Noah would have liked as he felt himself bristle. "I just don't like it. I mean, what if he up and leaves again?"

"That's between him and Grace. If she's decided to give him a chance with Anna, then that's her choice. Besides, you know she doesn't make decisions like this lightly. She must have some reason she believes she can trust him."

Noah eyed that fancy, silver car again. "Have you met him yet?"

"Nope. But that's partly why I'm here. I'm thinking its time our new friend Chris gets acquainted with Gracie Mae's big brother!" he said, cracking his knuckles and flashing a wicked smile.

Noah grinned and folded his arms across his chest again. But as he looked toward the house, his brows drew together, and his jaw tightened. "What about Anna?" She's the one who stands to lose the most in all of this."

Caleb clapped Noah on the back. "You know as well as I do Grace will protect both her girls like an angry mama bear if it comes to that. Mom says that's why she's been spending so much time with Chris, making sure he isn't planning on running off again."

Noah furrowed his brow even deeper, his blood running hot. "That's another thing. I don't like Grace spending so much time with him. I don't trust him."

Caleb half chuckled. "Now that, my friend, is what's really bothering you, isn't it? Her spending time alone with him."

Noah eyed Caleb and relaxed his posture just slightly. "I can't really say I'm all that fond of the idea! I've barely had a chance to talk to her since he showed up," he retorted, throwing a hand up in the direction of the house. "I'm trying to be there for her in case she needs me, but I've been getting a pretty cold reception lately."

"I'm sure she's just dealing with this the best she knows how. Nothing has changed between you and her."

Noah looked at the ground, heat rising up his neck. "Actually," he said, feeling slightly uncomfortable, "some things *have* changed. The problem is Grace and I haven't ever gotten to talk about any of it because Chris showed up."

Caleb raised his brows, grinning. "It's about time you did something about her!"

Noah cocked his head, eyeing his friend. "What's that supposed to mean?"

"Oh c'mon! You've been in love with her since you two were teenagers! It's about time you do something about it!"

Noah sighed. "That's the problem. Time. Seems like the timing is always off for us. I thought maybe we were finally heading in the right direction, but now I'm not so sure."

Caleb clapped him on the back again. "Talk to her, Noah." And with that, he walked off, heading for the house.

Noah watched his friend leave but didn't follow. He knew Caleb was right, but how was he supposed to talk to Grace about anything right now? She was completely absorbed in dealing with the current situation, and he felt like he was just in the way. Watching her and the girls with Chris created an ache so deep inside him at times it felt like he was being suffocated. And trying to avoid Chris only seemed to be making things worse. He felt a strong will to protect Grace and the girls, and not knowing what was happening was eating him up. Tossing his gloves on the stack of hay bales, he decided maybe Caleb had the right idea after all. Maybe he needed to acquaint himself a little better with the whole situation.

* * *

Grace took a sip from her coffee cup and smiled. Anna was beginning to warm up to Chris. They were sitting on the couch together looking at a scrapbook of her baby pictures, and she was finally engaging in conversation with him. Grace couldn't hear what they were saying, but she could see her oldest daughter's broad smile from where she sat in the kitchen.

Anna still didn't want her mother out of sight just in case she needed her. This whole situation had been somewhat difficult for her to fully grasp. Although she knew Jared wasn't her biological father, he was the only father she'd known up until now. In fact, before now, she knew little to nothing about Chris. Ashamedly, Grace herself didn't know all that much about him so there wasn't much to share with their daughter. And now, with him showing up out of the blue, Anna suddenly had a lot to process and deal with. But just as Grace expected, she was being a champ about it. She was cautious to a fault, but she was also being brave. They'd shared many long talks since Chris's arrival, and Grace was proud to see Anna handling the whole situation with poise and maturity far beyond her years.

Grace, of course, was doing her due diligence as Anna's mother, making sure Chris was doing right by their daughter. She'd had several frank discussions with him, making sure he understood Anna's heart was on the line. She made sure he understood, without giving too many details, that Anna had already been through enough and didn't need a here today, gone tomorrow relationship with him. Chris, of course, kept reassuring her he was in this for the long haul. And the more time she spent with him, the more she believed it.

Grace turned when the back door opened. She jumped from her seat when Caleb came walking in, practically knocking him over with a hug. "What are you doing here? I thought you weren't coming until Thanksgiving?"

"I thought my little sis could use a visit from her *favorite* big brother," he said with a wink. "Besides," he continued, lowering his voice, "I'd kinda like to meet this man claiming to be the father of my niece. I think it's high time he and I were acquainted." He grinned slyly.

Grace stepped back, planting her hands firmly on her hips. She kept her voice low but serious. "Caleb Matthew, you better be on your best behavior! You better not say or do anything!"

He continued to grin and kissed her on top of the head. "I love you, Gracie Mae. I promise to behave. Now, introduce me before I do it myself!"

Grace narrowed her eyes and jabbed a finger into her brother's broad chest. "I mean it!" she said, whispering one last threat before leading him into the family room.

When Anna saw her uncle walk in, she jumped up from where she was sitting. Caleb easily scooped her up, and she wrapped her arms around his neck. "Uncle Caleb! I'm so glad you're here!"

He gave her one good squeeze before setting her down. "It's always good to see my Annabelle," he said, gently flicking her nose with his finger. "Now, who is this?" he asked, turning to Chris.

Chris had already risen from his seat and was smiling somewhat uncomfortably. Anna stepped closer to him and said, "Uncle Caleb, this is Chris. He came to visit me. He is... uh... he's my dad." Her cheeks turned a rosy shade of pink as she grinned shyly.

Grace held her breath as Chris extended his hand to her brother. "Nice to meet you," he said. "I've heard a lot about you."

Caleb extended his own hand, grasping Chris's, the smile never leaving his face. Grace could tell by Chris's subtle wince that Caleb

AMBER WELLIN

was squeezing just a little too firm as he eyed his new acquaintance, holding him there just long enough to get his point across. She had to choke back a giggle that threatened to spill from her lips.

"Wish I could say the same about you," Caleb finally replied, releasing Chris's hand.

Caleb continued to smile as Chris looked awkwardly from him to Grace. Again, she had to stifle her amusement. "Ahem," she said, clearing her throat, "can I get anyone a cup of coffee or something else to drink?"

"I'd love a cup of coffee," Caleb replied as he sat down in the nearest chair, making himself comfortable. "I think I'll stay a while and get to know my new friend here," he said, flashing another grin at Chris.

Grace could see Chris's Adam's apple bob as he swallowed hard. Caleb's size alone would be intimidating without all the pomp and show he was laying on so thick!

Chris slowly lowered himself back down onto the couch. Anna picked up the scrapbook they had been looking at. "Uncle Caleb, do you want to see my baby pictures, too?" she asked sweetly.

Caleb turned his attention to his niece. "Well of course I do," he said, motioning for her to come to him.

Anna smiled and went to her uncle. Grace took the opportunity to make her exit. She knew Chris was safe with Anna in the room. Her brother would never say or do anything to upset his niece.

Grace was fixing Caleb's coffee when Noah walked in. As soon as she saw him, her heart rate ticked up a notch as butterflies swirled in her middle. She offered a hesitant smile but said nothing. She seemed to have a hard time finding the right words with him lately.

"I thought I'd come see how things are going in here," he said, sidling up next to her, leaning against the counter.

"Okay I think," she said, continuing to stir the coffee for far too long. She wasn't quite sure what else to say, but she also didn't want to walk away from him. She knew she'd been avoiding him, and it was taking a toll on her. She still wasn't sure what was happening with their relationship, and she had sidelined dealing with it. With Chris's unexpected arrival, she had to focus on Anna right now and didn't have time to think about anything else. Or so she was telling herself.

"Uh… I think you've stirred that coffee plenty," Noah said, nodding toward the mug and chuckling.

Grace pulled herself back to the present, laying the spoon aside. She leaned against the counter and dropped her head. "I don't think I know what I'm doing half the time anymore," she said, sighing heavily. She suddenly felt like crying.

Noah reached and gently rested a hand at the small of her back. She could feel the hesitation in his touch, and she knew it was her fault he was feeling so unsure. She scooted closer and let her weight rest against him. He tentatively wrapped his arms around her. She leaned in, tucking her head under his chin. "I'm sorry, Noah," was all she could manage. Tears were already clouding her vision, and her throat felt tight.

"Grace," he spoke in a near whisper, "it's okay. It will all be okay."

She encircled her arms around his waist and pulled her body flush against his, clinging to him like a lifeline. Tears spilled down her cheeks, dampening his shirt. She didn't say another word. She stood still and just let him hold her.

CHAPTER 12

Thanksgiving came and went. Chris stayed in Marble Falls for most of November, heading home to see his family just before the holiday. Noah tried to be more open and give him a chance, even putting forth a little more effort to get to know him. And while Chris was polite to Noah, the two men didn't really have much of anything in common. Other than for the sake of Anna and Grace, Chris was not someone Noah would ever choose to be friends with.

He did have to admit, however, the man really seemed to be trying with Anna. He had been nothing other than patient and kind with her, never pushing her beyond her comfort zone. Noah was thankful for that. And while Anna's relationship with her father had grown during his time in Texas, Noah could tell she still had some reservations about the whole situation. Although she introduced him as her father, she still chose to call him by his first name.

Noah was also thankful Grace had quit spending so much time alone with Chris. During school hours, Chris typically stayed in town working remotely. Then, in the evenings, he would come to the ranch to see Anna or would pick her up. Since Anna had grown more comfortable with him, they had been spending more time together just the two of them. Noah could tell, however, it made Grace nervous anytime Chris left with her. She would constantly check her phone until they safely returned. This meant she was still too distracted for him to broach the subject he most wanted to talk about.

"That should be the last strand of lights for the fence row."

The sound of Eli's voice drew Noah back to the present. He stepped back, eyeing their handiwork. The two men had spent most of the day putting up outdoor Christmas decorations for Jane. She liked everything around the ranch decked out as much as possible, and that meant spending one solid day, sunup to sundown, getting it all done.

"I hope your mom is happy with what we've done. I know this is her favorite time of year," Noah said, smiling.

"I think she adds more stuff every year for us to put up!" Eli retorted, chuckling. "But if it makes her happy, then it's worth it!"

Noah and Eli were still admiring their day's work when Jake walked up. "Lookin' good, fellas! I think my bride will be right happy with what you've done," he said, grinning. "And that makes me a happy man! You know what they say - happy wife, happy life!" He winked at them. "Now come on inside. The women have the house all done up and dinner is on the table."

The three men headed for the house. Noah walked slowly, pondering the beauty of the season. While he wasn't nearly as enthusiastic about decorating as Jane Buckner, he could appreciate the sense of hope and peace that always came with Christmas. It had a way of making a man more aware and reverent of what our Lord and Savior sacrificed for us, what He's done for all those who choose to accept Him.

When Noah stepped through the mudroom into the kitchen, he couldn't help but smile. The entire house was decked out from top to bottom in lights and greenery, and a tall, noble tree stood lit and ready to decorate in the family room. He could smell the fresh scent of pine wafting through the air. It was mixing with the fragrant cinnamon Jane was using in her baking, and it smelled like Christmas.

It also felt like Christmas, because for him, Christmas was about family. The Buckner's had become a second family to him, and he smiled as he watched them. Jake was already seated at the head of the large, dining table, and Jane was scurrying around the kitchen finishing her famous mashed potatoes. Eli joined Hannah in the family room where Abby sat playing with the twins on a blanket in the floor, and Elaine was rocking peacefully in her rocking chair. Grace and Anna were standing near the tree looking through boxes of ornaments.

"Find any favorites in there?" he asked Anna, peeking in one of the boxes.

She smiled broadly. "Grandma Jane has *so* many pretty Christmas ornaments! I can't pick a favorite! Are you going to help us decorate the tree?" she asked, still smiling.

Abby jumped up and ran over to him. "Please, Noah? Please?" she squealed, beaming up at him.

As always, his heart melted anytime these two bright-eyed little girls asked anything of him. "I wouldn't miss it!" he said, scooping up Abby. She enthusiastically wrapped her arms around his neck and squeezed. When he looked at Grace, she smiled warmly at him. For that brief moment in time, all in his world seemed right.

"Mama?" Abby spoke, her tone quizzical. "Will I get to see Christmas trees like this one in New York?"

And just like that, his world flipped. Noah felt his chest constrict as his muscles tensed. Why was Abby asking about New York? Chris was from New York. A sense of dread pooled in his stomach as he darted a look in Grace's direction.

* * *

Grace held her breath as her pulse pounded. This was not how she intended for Noah to learn she was going to New York. And based on the wide-eyed stare of disbelief he was giving her, he was not going to take this well. She knew she needed to say something but wasn't sure what. Now was not the time to have this discussion with him, not in front of the girls.

"It's almost time for dinner, Abby. We'll talk about it later," she said, her tone subdued. "You and Anna go wash your hands and get ready to eat."

Abby wiggled down from Noah's arms and obediently scurried off toward the bathroom with her sister. Grace turned to face Noah. She could feel the lump in her throat growing. He remained silent, his jaw tight. She could feel the tension mounting.

"Noah," she said, taking a breath, "I was going to tell you. I promise." She spoke in a hushed whisper as she looked to see if anyone was eavesdropping on their conversation. "This is not how I wanted you to find out."

He moved closer to her, leaning in. He spoke quietly, but his tone held a distinct edge. "When Grace? When was I going to find out? When you left?"

She pinched at her forehead, a forlorn sigh escaping her lips. "Walk outside with me so we can talk."

Noah silently followed her out the front door. He stopped and leaned against one of the stone pillars, shoving his hands in his pockets. He did not look happy.

"Noah, please. Let me explain. I don't like it when you're mad at me."

His expression softened as he let out an exasperated sigh. "I'm not mad at you, Grace. I just wasn't expecting this."

"I'm sorry I didn't tell you before now," she responded, moving closer to him.

"Why are you going to New York? I'm assuming it's for Chris."

She sighed heavily. "He told me before he left that he wants Anna to meet his parents. He wants her to come ahead of Christmas. But you know she's not comfortable enough with him yet for me to send her all that way on her own."

"So why don't they just come here?"

"Chris's dad had a stroke a few years ago and can't travel. If Anna is going to meet her grandparents, she has to go to them."

"What does Anna think about all this?" Noah asked, looking skeptical.

"She was hesitant at first, not so sure about it. But we had a long talk the other night, and she decided she wants to go as long as I go with her."

"How do *you* feel about going?" he asked, his brows pinching together.

Grace sighed again. "I don't honestly know. I can't say I'm excited about it, but I'm not dreading it either. I'm doing it for Anna, and that's all that matters."

Noah turned his head, staring out across the yard. His jaw worked for a moment before he spoke again. "How long will you be gone?"

"A week. We fly up Monday and come home Sunday."

Noah turned his gaze down to his boots, his posture remaining tense. Grace could see him breathing deep as his jaw remained tight, lips pursed.

"I don't like it, Grace. I'm not going to stand here and pretend like I do."

"You don't have to like it," she retorted, "but I'm going. It's already decided."

His fierce gaze shot to hers, his expression unyielding. Even in the dim light of evening she could see his blue eyes blaze at her. "Do I ever get a say in anything? Are we ever going to talk about what we both know you've been avoiding?"

Grace swallowed hard, resisting the urge to snap back at him. Being too quick with her tongue had gotten her into enough trouble plenty of times, and she didn't want to make this any worse than it already was. Taking a deep breath, she responded, "I have to focus on Anna. I can't deal with anything else right now. I just need time."

Noah stared at her, his expression hard. He chewed the inside of his lower lip, slowly nodding his head. "Time. Sure, Grace. Whatever you say."

He started to walk away, but she reached for his arm, stopping him. "Noah, please, don't walk away like this. Can we just talk about things when I get back? *Please?*" She knew there was desperation in her voice, but she didn't care. This was not how she wanted their conversation to end.

He turned to fully face her. His expression was tense, unreadable, but his eyes had softened. He reached and gently cupped her cheek with one hand. She covered his hand with her own, her eyes pleading with him. He said nothing. Instead, he placed a gentle, feather light kiss on her lips. When he drew back, his eyes searched hers. Then he dropped his hand and walked away.

Grace watched him until he was out of sight. That kiss felt too much like goodbye, and her chest ached with the sorrow of it. She plopped down on the cool concrete, leaning her shoulder against a pillar. She closed her eyes and inhaled deeply. Part of her wanted to run after him, but part of her felt frozen, unable to move. Fear was keeping her right where she sat.

"Mom?" A quiet, little voice interrupted her thoughts. "Are you okay?"

She turned to see Anna approaching, uncertainty pulling at her little brow. Grace shifted her weight and patted the spot beside her. Anna sat down, and Grace put her arm around her, kissing the top of her head.

"I'm fine, baby. Why do you ask?"

Anna hesitated. "I saw you and Noah out here. But I wasn't trying to spy, Mom! I promise!"

Grace sucked in a breath, unsure exactly *what* her oldest daughter had witnessed. "What did you see?"

Anna shrugged her shoulders. "Well..." she hesitated again. "It looked like you two were arguing, but I couldn't hear what you were saying. I wasn't trying to listen! I promise!" She looked at her mother, her expression remorseful.

"Go on," Grace urged.

Anna looked at the ground as her cheeks turned a light shade of pink. "I saw him kiss you." She looked up at her mother, her eyes pleading for forgiveness. "I'm sorry," she said quietly.

Grace sighed. "It's okay, honey. I'm not mad." She pulled her daughter close, resting her cheek against the top of her head.

Anna sat up, pulling away slightly. "Mom?" She seemed hesitant again.

Grace gave her daughter an encouraging smile as she raised her brows. "What is it?"

"Do you love Noah?" Her daughter eyed her curiously.

Grace felt her heart stutter as she weighed her response carefully. "Of course. He's my friend."

Anna rolled her eyes. "No, Mom, that's not what I mean. Do you *love* him? Because if you do, that's okay. I really like him, and so does Abby. He would be a good dad, and I think he really likes you. Like *a lot!*"

Grace felt her eyes well with tears. Her wise-beyond-her-years daughter was sitting on the front porch giving *her* relationship advice. "Oh, my sweet, sweet girl," she said, cupping her cheeks, "Are you worrying about me? Because you don't have to. I'll be fine. Besides, I have you and your sister. What else do I need?"

Anna huffed out a sigh. "I want you to be happy, Mom. Happy like Grandpa Jake and Grandma Jane. Happy like Uncle Eli and Aunt Hannah." She paused, looking at the ground. And when she looked up, her normally bright eyes were muddled with tears.

"Oh, baby, what is it? Why are you crying?" Grace lovingly stroked her hair, pulling her close again.

Anna leaned into her mother, her little body softly shuddering as her tears fell. "I know Dad wasn't nice to you before he died. I know he said mean things." Her body now shook with violent sobs. "I know... I know he... he hit you." She buried her face in her mother's shoulder and cried.

An uncontrollable flood of tears poured from Grace and fell in wet droplets onto her daughter who clung tightly to her. She had tried so hard to hide the awful truth from both of her girls, but apparently, she had not been as successful as she thought.

"Oh, baby, I'm so sorry! I didn't want you to know. I'm so sorry! It's okay now! It's all over." She continued to stroke Anna's hair.

Anna pulled back, sitting up straight. She sniffled and wiped her eyes. "I know, Mom. Sometimes I'm sad he's gone, but other times I'm just glad he can't hurt you anymore. Does that make me a bad person?"

"Oh Anna, absolutely not! You are a *good, kind, loving* little girl! And I am *so* thankful you are mine!" She said, kissing her on the forehead. "There is *absolutely nothing* bad about you!"

Anna sniffled again and looked her mother in the eye. "I don't think Noah would ever hurt you. I think he would protect you."

Grace sucked in a breath as her eyes again filled with tears. She hugged her daughter close but said nothing. She didn't know what *to* say. This was a very grown-up conversation coming from an eight-year-old little girl, a little girl who knew and understood far more than her mother ever thought. *What did I ever do to deserve the blessing of this amazing child?*

Grace and Anna sat together on the front porch a little while longer, holding each other close until the tears stopped flowing. Sitting up, Grace swiped the leftover tears from her own cheeks and then from her daughter's. Anna stood up just as Jane opened the front door.

"There you two are. Dinner is ready."

Grace stood, attempting to avoid her mother's scrutinizing gaze. She knew she would ask questions if she saw her puffy, red-rimmed eyes. But it was too late. Anna's sniffles already had her on high alert.

"What on earth is going on? Are you okay?" Jane asked, hugging her granddaughter. She looked at Grace, her brows pinching together. "And you, too? What has my girls so upset?"

Grace attempted to answer but found herself choking back more tears when she started to speak.

Jane, noticing her daughter's struggle to maintain her composure, ushered Anna on inside. "Go inside, honey, and let Aunt Hannah know your mom and I will be a minute," she said, patting her on the back.

Anna looked at her mother but was obedient to her grand-mother's request.

Grace slumped back down onto the concrete, and her mother sat down beside her. "What's been happening out here?" Jane questioned.

Grace wiped her eyes and took a deep breath. "Anna and I just had a very serious talk. That's all."

"Well, it must have been serious as upset as you are. Is everything okay?"

"I don't know, Mom. I think so."

Jane let out a humph. "You *think*? Things are either okay or they are not, Grace. Tell me what's going on."

Grace felt her eyes sting with fresh tears as a lump formed in her throat. She swallowed hard. "Anna knew about the abuse. She knew about Jared. I tried so hard to hide it from her, but she still knew." Grace began to cry harder. "I thought I protected her, but I didn't!"

Jane hugged her close. "Oh, honey, it's okay. You *did* protect her. You protected both of your girls. Jared never once hurt them so I would say you did your job as their mother." She loosened her hug and turned to look her daughter in the eye. "You are a *good* mother, Grace. Do not beat yourself up over this."

Grace sniffled. "I didn't want them to know how bad it was. I wanted to protect them from the truth. But I failed." She lowered her head and covered her face with her hands.

"Grace," her mother said sternly, "you stop that nonsense right now! You cannot always protect your children from the harsh realities of life. All you can do is teach them how to handle tough situations when they face them, teach them how to be good people no matter what happens. And I think you've done that. Those two little girls in there are resilient and full of hope," she said, motioning toward the house. "They are *courageous, kind, forgiving* human beings because you've taught them that! Those little girls are who they are because of you, Grace! Do not discount yourself as a mother."

Grace took a deep breath and wiped at her tears. She knew her mother was right. She was letting her emotions get the best of her, partly because of what Anna had just told her but also because of what had happened with Noah.

"Thank you, Mom. I don't know what I would do without you," she said. "You taught me to be braver than this. I should be handling this better."

"No," her mother replied, "you are handling this the best you know how. And I think you're doing a pretty darn, good job of it! I'm proud of you, Grace. You've had to deal with a lot of tough situations, but you haven't given up. You've picked yourself up and moved on with life. I don't think anyone can expect any more than that."

Jane hugged her tight and then stood. "Now, let's get inside and enjoy our dinner," she said. She started toward the door but turned back, squinting into the darkness. "Where's Noah? Didn't he follow you out here earlier?"

Grace looked in the direction Noah had gone. "I don't know. He walked off toward the barn."

Jane put her hands on her hips. "Isn't he joining us for dinner? He worked so hard with your brother today putting up all my decorations. I made his favorite dessert to say thank you."

Grace shrugged her shoulders but said nothing. She didn't want to go into any details about her conversation with Noah. She'd cried enough for one night.

Jane eyed her daughter. "What are you not telling me?" she probed.

"I'd rather not talk about it right now. But I doubt he joins us for dinner."

Jane looked back toward the barn. "You go on inside. I'll go find him."

"Mom, no!" Grace said, her voice a little more commanding than she intended. "He's upset with me. I doubt he wants to be around me right now."

Jane looked at her daughter but said nothing. Instead, she started toward the barn, calling Noah's name as she went. Grace clenched her fists and let out a low growl. There was no stopping Jane Buckner once she set her mind to something!

* * *

Noah heard Jane before he saw her. Part of him wanted to hide and pretend he didn't hear her calling his name, but he knew he'd be in a world of trouble if she found him hiding! He stepped into the long hallway where she could see him.

"There you are!" she exclaimed. "Come on inside. You're missing dinner," she said, motioning for him to follow her.

"I think I'm going to skip dinner tonight," he responded. "I've got some work I can get done out here." As the words left his mouth, he already knew she wasn't taking no for an answer.

"Absolutely not!" she said, wagging her finger at him. "You worked hard all day putting up my decorations, and now you're coming inside to have dinner. I made your favorite dessert."

He tried to think of some excuse why he couldn't, but his mind was blank. It would be a lie if he said he wasn't hungry because she likely could hear his stomach growling from where she was standing! He knew he would have no choice but to go with her.

Jane moved closer. "Noah, I don't know what happened between you and Grace, but it shouldn't stop you from eating. Besides, you promised two little girls you would help decorate the tree after dinner. You aren't going to disappoint them, are you?"

He sighed. Jane sure knew what to say and how to say it to get him to concede defeat. Just like Grace, she wouldn't let up until she got what she wanted. "I'll come inside," he said. "Just give me a minute."

Jane smiled. "Okay, but don't take too long. Your dinner will be cold." And with that, she turned and started back down the hall.

Noah watched her exit the barn. He sighed and rubbed his forehead. These strong-willed Buckner women were putting his patience into practice today! But he knew Jane was right. He did not want to disappoint Anna and Abby. He told them he would help decorate the tree, and he was a man of his word.

He walked back into the stall of the young filly he had been brushing down. "Well girl," he said, "guess you and I will have to finish this later." The young horse seemed to nod her head in agreement.

Laying the curry comb aside, he latched the stall door and headed down the hallway, praying as he went. *Lord, this whole situation is in Your hands. I trust Your plan and Your will for my life and Grace's. Please watch over her and the girls on their trip. I love them more than they know, and I want what's best for all three of them. They deserve to be happy.*

CHAPTER 13

G race gazed out the window at the approaching cityscape. The buildings were growing closer. The fasten seatbelt sign was illuminated, and the pilot announced they would soon be making their descent into Syracuse. From this altitude, the world below reminded her of a jigsaw puzzle, the interstates and highways creating definitive lines dividing the pieces. The brilliant white of freshly fallen snow stood out against the charcoal gray of the roadways, further defining the lines. It looked like a perfectly complete winter puzzle.

She looked at her girls. They were eagerly watching the landscape below. Since snow in Marble Falls was a very rare occurrence, they were excited to see snow this close to Christmas.

"Wow, Mommy," Abby exclaimed, "look how pretty it is!" Her face was alight with joy.

Grace smiled. Her girls had seen snow plenty of times while they lived in Idaho, but this was a first - seeing it from miles above. This was also their first time on an airplane. Since they never went on family vacations and never traveled with Jared for work, the girls had not yet had the opportunity to fly before today. And although both were a little nervous beforehand, Grace was glad to see they were enjoying it.

"What do you think of flying in an airplane now?" she asked.

"I love it!" screeched Abby.

Grace put a finger to her lips, shushing her youngest. "Not so loud," she said in a whisper. Abby grinned at her mother as her cheeks turned pink.

"And what about you?" Grace asked, playfully poking Anna in the ribs.

Anna turned from gazing out the window and smiled. "I like it. I'm glad we didn't have to drive. That would have taken *forever*!"

Grace chuckled. "Yes, flying is much faster than driving. And you can't beat the view," she said, nodding her head toward the window.

Anna's face scrunched in uncertainty. "Mom?"

Grace turned to her oldest daughter, raising her brows in question.

Anna hesitated a moment before continuing. "I'm a little nervous about meeting my grandma and grandpa."

Grace reached and gently tucked a strand of Anna's long, blonde hair behind her ear, offering her a comforting smile. "It's okay to be nervous. They're probably nervous about meeting you, too."

Anna kept her face scrunched. "What if they don't like me? I mean, they've never met me, so I don't know. I don't even know what to call them."

"They will *love* you, Annabella Jane, just like everyone else who meets you," Grace spoke reassuringly. "Why don't you just call them grandma and grandpa? I think that would be okay."

She looked at her mother anxiously. "Yeah, I guess I can. I just don't want to hurt Chris's feelings because I don't call him dad."

"You are not hurting his feelings. He is fine with whatever you want to call him. He told you that, remember?"

"Yeah, I know. It just seems weird to call him dad. I mean, I know he is my dad and all, but I don't know if I'll ever call him that. Is that okay?"

"It's your choice, sweetie. He will be fine with whatever you choose."

Anna paused, fiddling with her fingers. "Mom?"

"Yes?"

"What if you marry Noah, and I want to call him dad? Will Chris be okay with that?"

Grace nearly choked on air! That was the last thing she expected her daughter to ask! She knew she was gaping, wide-eyed and frozen. Her mind quickly searched for an answer. *Come on brain! Respond!*

"I'm sorry. I shouldn't have asked that," Anna said, slumping back in her seat.

The sight of her daughter looking dejected snapped her out of her state of shock. "Oh honey, no! Don't apologize. I always want you to know you can ask me anything. I was just... surprised. That's all."

Anna looked at her mother, her expression tentative as she waited for an answer. Grace took a deep breath. "*If* I ever get married again, you can call that man dad if you want to. It will be fine." She hoped this would be enough to satisfy her daughter.

Anna furrowed her brow but said no more. Thankfully Abby was distracted by the view from the window and didn't seem to notice the conversation. Grace breathed a sigh of relief. She had no desire to try and explain something so serious to her now four-year-old daughter!

Once they landed and retrieved their luggage, Grace led the girls just outside of baggage claim where they were to meet Chris. Sure enough, he was on time and waiting for them. He waved and smiled broadly as they walked toward him.

"How was your flight? Did you girls like it?" he asked, bending down to talk to Anna and Abby.

"It was so fun!" Abby squealed.

Chris turned to Anna. "What about you, ladybug? What did you think?"

Anna returned his smile. "I liked it."

Chris pulled her into a hug. "I'm so glad you're here," he said, releasing her and standing. He looked directly at Grace. "I'm so glad you're all here."

Grace felt a twinge of heat rise to her cheeks as nervousness settled in her middle. *Why is he looking at me like that?* She shook the feeling away and responded. "I'm glad we could do this for Anna," she said, putting her arm around her oldest daughter's shoulders. She looked past Chris toward the exit. "Where are you parked?"

Chris leapt into action, grabbing their luggage. "Not far," he answered. "Follow me." He was still smiling broadly as he led them outside.

Grace took her daughters by the hand as she followed. Chris led them to a silver Land Rover and loaded their luggage. He opened a door to the backseat and grinned. He had apparently purchased a brand-new booster seat for Anna and a brand-new car seat for Abby. "I wasn't sure if Abby was out of a car seat or not, so I got one just to be safe," he said.

Grace smiled. "No, she hasn't grown quite enough yet for a booster. Thank you for doing that."

Chris grinned even broader. "Ah, it was nothing," he said. "I'm just happy you all are here."

The girls climbed in, and Grace buckled Abby in her new seat. Anna took care of getting herself buckled in her booster. When Grace moved to the passenger side to get in, Chris raced ahead of her, opening the door. She smiled at the gesture but again felt slightly uncomfortable. She took a deep breath and exhaled the nervousness in her stomach. Her mind was likely just over-analyzing the situation. *As always...* she thought to herself.

AMBER WELLIN

The drive to Chris' parents' house was beautiful and serene. They wound their way through curves and over hills as they exited the city and headed just beyond the eastern suburbs. The freshly fallen snow and plentiful Christmas decorations nearly everywhere they looked created a winter wonderland. As they drove, Grace noticed the homes were growing grander in both size and design. Even under the snow, it was obvious the expansive lawns were perfectly manicured and pristine.

Chris turned into the driveway of a sprawling estate. They halted briefly at a large stone and iron entryway. Christmas greenery and bright red bows trimmed the gate. Grace immediately noticed the ornate letter *A* centered directly in the middle. With the push of a button, the gate parted, dividing the letter in half to allow them passage. As they drove forward, snow covered shrubbery and trees with barren, winter branches flanked both sides of the long lane. White lights filled the trees, softly glowing even in the light of day.

Off to her left, Grace could see an elaborate fountain crafted with the same stone used at the entryway. It stood alone, both imposing and grand in its design. It was covered in soft, white snow and for now, no water flowed. She imagined it was a sight to behold on a warm spring or summer day, running water sparkling in the sun.

As they drove closer to the home, Grace could see it was impressive in both appearance and size, looming proudly over the white landscape. An abundance of Christmas greenery, magnificent wreaths with sparkling red bows, and regal white lights trimmed nearly every inch of the exterior. This was by far her definition of a mansion if she ever saw one!

Its stately appearance and sheer size caused her stomach to lurch, bringing about unexpected thoughts and memories. Every intricate detail appeared precise and perfect, and she found herself thinking of

Jared. She took a few deep breaths to slow her heart rate as uncertainty settled over her. She was on the verge of hyperventilating, and she found herself praying these people were nothing like her deceased husband. *Please God, watch over us. Please keep us safe and let this go well for Anna's sake.*

Chris drove past what Grace assumed to be the formal entrance of the home where majestic stone steps led to a wide, double-door entryway with a large window highlighting a rather grandiose chandelier hanging from the high ceiling. He pulled around to the side of the house and stopped under a large, covered entryway. He quickly exited the vehicle, hurrying to open her door. As she stepped out, Anna had already unbuckled and was climbing down. She hopped to the ground as Chris unbuckled Abby from her car seat and lifted her out.

As Grace turned toward the door of the home, it opened. A woman appearing around the same age as her mother stepped out. She paused, smiling sweetly at her guests.

Chris stepped forward. "Grace, this is my mother, Peggy Atchison. Mom, this is Grace, Anna, and Abby," he said, looking hopeful as he made the introductions.

Peggy stepped away from the door and moved closer. She was a slender woman with kind eyes and a welcoming smile. She was close to the same height as Grace, and as she approached, she fidgeted nervously with her hands. "I'm so grateful you've come. You have no idea how much this means that you've brought our granddaughter all this way. I can't thank you enough." Her eyes welled with tears as she turned to Anna. "It's so nice to meet you, Anna. I've been anticipating your arrival ever since I found out you were coming."

Anna blushed bashfully but bravely stepped forward and hugged her grandmother. Grace gave her daughter an approving nod as she quickly blinked away the moisture attempting to cloud her vision. This child of hers never ceased to amaze her. And as she looked at Peggy, she could see she also was overcome by the kind, generous greeting from her granddaughter.

"You have a pretty house," a little voice piped up. Grace turned to Abby. Chris was still holding her in his arms as her eyes twinkled and roamed, taking in all the new sights. "I like your Christmas things," she said sweetly.

Peggy smiled warmly at Abby. "Well, you just wait until you see the inside," she said. "Christmas is my favorite time of year, and I love to decorate." She reached for Abby's hand as Chris lowered her to the ground. Abby willingly took it as Anna had hold of her other hand. "Come on," Peggy coached, "let's go inside."

And with that, they all headed through the door.

Once inside, they were greeted by three new faces. "Grace, Anna, Abby," Peggy began, "this is Angela, Christina, and Tom," she said, making the introductions. "Angela takes care of all the daily needs around the house. Christina is our chef and takes care of all the cooking. And Tom is a man of many talents," she said smiling. "He takes care of countless things around here, inside and out."

Tom nodded his head in greeting, and the two women offered warm smiles and welcomes. Grace just smiled. Being in a home employing full-time staff was a first for her, and she felt a little awkward and out of her element.

As Angela offered to take their coats, Peggy asked Tom to retrieve their luggage from the vehicle and take it to their rooms. "Put the girls' things in the bedroom we have set up for them and put Grace's things in the room just across the hall," she instructed. "That way she won't be far away if they need her." She turned to Grace. "I hope that's okay," she said, a hint of question in her tone.

Grace, still somewhat astonished, nodded and smiled. "Of course. I appreciate your hospitality. I hope we aren't being too much trouble."

"Nonsense," Peggy replied with a wave of her hand, "You are family to us. I wouldn't have it any other way." She smiled kindly. "Now," she said, turning to Anna and Abby, "let's go meet your grandfather."

Abby wrinkled her nose. "Is he my grandpa, too?" she asked quizzically.

Peggy knelt in front of her and gently took hold of her hands. "Of course he is, darling. Just like I am your grandmother."

Abby smiled. "Does that mean I can call you grandma and grandpa just like Anna?"

Peggy grinned broadly. "Absolutely!" she answered.

Grace again felt as if her heart might burst. This introduction was going far better than she could have imagined. Peggy seemed nothing other than kindhearted and loving, and she was being so welcoming. Grace swiped away a lone tear and felt a hand grasp her shoulder. It was Chris. He was standing just behind her, and his gaze pinned her to the spot. She quickly looked away as she felt a flush begin to creep up her neck. She stepped away from his touch and knelt in front of her girls.

"Now remember," she said, "Chris told you both how his daddy has been sick and won't be able to answer you when you talk to him."

"Yes," Peggy chimed in, "your grandpa can't walk or talk on his own anymore. But he understands when you talk to him, so don't be afraid. He is just as excited to meet you as I was," she said reassuringly. "Are you ready to go find him?"

Both girls nodded, and Peggy led the way.

As they moved through the house, Grace was awestruck by the grandeur around her. She had lived in some exceedingly nice homes while married to Jared, but this one far surpassed any of them. She turned to Chris and whispered, "You didn't tell me your family lived in a mansion! And has *staff*!" she exclaimed just loud enough for him to hear.

He chuckled. "I didn't think that would matter to you," he whispered back, smiling down at her.

She rolled her eyes. "It doesn't matter, not like *that*," she retorted. "It just would have been nice to have had a heads up!"

He chuckled again, placing his hand at the small of her back, his touch feeling almost intimate. He whispered near her ear, his breath warm against her skin. "I really am glad you're here."

Her breath caught as she felt her cheeks heat yet again. Before she could think what to say or how to respond, they entered the room where Chris's father sat in a wheelchair. He turned his head at the sound of their entrance and attempted a smile. Grace observed the left side of his face wasn't fully cooperating with his efforts to greet them.

Peggy led the girls over to him. "Girls, this is your grandfather, Bruce. And honey, these are your granddaughters, Anna and Abby," she said, beaming with pride. "And this is Grace," she continued, motioning behind her, "mother of these two beautiful, little angels."

Grace stepped forward. "It's so nice to meet you," she said, taking his outstretched right hand. "Thank you for inviting us to stay with you."

Bruce nodded and smiled feebly at Grace before turning his attention back to the girls. Anna held Abby's hand and moved closer. "Hi Grandpa," she said. "It's nice to meet you."

He continued to attempt a smile with renewed effort as his eyes misted with tears, clearly overcome with emotion at meeting his grand-daughter for the first time.

Abby stepped even closer. "I'm Abby," she said, introducing herself. "Grandma says I can call you grandpa just like Anna." She reached to take his hand. "I know you can't talk, but that's okay. I know you can still hear me. Grandma told me so." Her little face beamed up at him.

Grace felt her heart swelling yet again, beyond proud of the courage her girls were exhibiting. *Maybe my mom is right. I haven't done such a bad job after all being their mother*, she thought to herself.

It wasn't long at all before everyone had settled comfortably into conversation. Peggy asked numerous questions of Grace about her parents, siblings, and her childhood. She didn't broach the subject of her marriage to Jared, but she did offer her condolences on his passing.

She also praised Grace for her bravery and resiliency in picking herself up and moving on with life. "I'm sure it hasn't been an easy task, moving forward without your husband. But I must say, just this little time we've spent together already tells me how courageous you've been, for you and for your girls."

Grace shifted uncomfortably and looked at the floor. While she appreciated Peggy's kind words and the intent behind them, she desired to move on from this topic of conversation.

Peggy appeared to take notice and obliged. "Now Grace, dear, what would you like to know about Chris? I can tell you stories for days!" she said, chuckling.

"Mom, seriously?" Chris interjected, "I don't really think Grace wants to hear all the embarrassing stories you could tell."

"We will let Grace make that decision for herself!" Peggy quipped, giving her son a stern look, followed by a playful wink in Grace's direction. "Why don't you take the girls on a tour of the grounds while Grace and I chat? It appears we've already exhausted your father," she said, gesturing to her dozing husband.

Chris sighed in overly dramatic fashion. "Absolutely mother, whatever you wish," he said, rising from where he sat. He bowed pretentiously, winking at Grace as he did.

Once he had exited the room with the girls, Peggy moved to a seat closer to Grace. "There is something I've been wanting to say ever since you arrived, but I didn't want to say it in front of Chris or the girls," she began, shifting her gaze to the floor. When she finally raised her chin, her eyes were filled with tears. "Grace, I can't begin to tell you how very sorry I am for the way my son has treated you. We had no idea about you or Anna until right before he left for Texas to find you."

Grace offered a slight smile. "It's okay. I don't blame you. You aren't responsible for what happened."

Peggy shook her head in disagreement. "No, Grace, I am responsible. I was too easy on him growing up, spoiled him far too much. Bruce always tried to tell me I needed to toughen up on him, make him take more responsibility. But I didn't listen. I gave him whatever he wanted and came to his rescue whenever he was in trouble. So, you see, I *am* to blame for how he treated you." Tears flowed down her cheeks as she dabbed at her nose with a tissue.

Grace shifted to place her hand on Peggy's. "Please don't blame yourself. I know what it's like to do that, and it's not a good place to be. Regret keeps you from moving forward. I've had plenty of experience with that. So please, let's just leave all of this in the past and start from where we are now," she said, smiling warmly. "I have a good life now with two beautiful girls, and that's all that matters."

Peggy sniffled and dried her tears. "Grace, you truly are amazing. So forgiving. I can already tell we are all lucky to have you in our lives," she said. "I just wanted you to know how truly sorry I am, and that's the last I'll say of it."

"We've all made mistakes," Grace responded, "but I'm thankful that by the Lord's grace, we don't have to let our failures define who we are."

Peggy patted her hand. "You are so right. If only I could get Chris to believe that. I know he continuously punishes himself for so many things. I've tried getting him to come to church with me, but he hasn't been since he was a teenager I don't think. He always says God has no need for someone like him, and it just breaks my heart."

Grace felt an awareness flutter from somewhere deep within as her grandmother's words suddenly came to the forefront. *The grace of our Lord is a gift to us all if we accept it. And when you find that gift for yourself, there is nothing crazy at all about sharing it with others.* Grace pondered this in her heart as she prayed silently. *Lord, if this is what You want and why I'm here, then You're going to have to help me. I can't do this on my own.*

* * *

Grace found herself enjoying the rest of the evening with Chris's family. Peggy gave her a tour of the home and grounds while Chris entertained the girls. Christina prepared a wonderful dinner for everyone, and Chris's sister and brother-in-law came for coffee and dessert with their two boys. Grace found Bruce often fell asleep during most activities, including dinner. Peggy explained it was typical for him to sleep more than he was awake since having the stroke.

"He really tries," she said. "He wants to be a part of everything, but sometimes I have to insist he stay behind and rest. If it wasn't for Chris helping me, I don't know what I would do. Bruce doesn't want anyone other than family caring for him, even though we do have a nurse who visits a few times a week just to keep check of his overall health."

"Is that why Chris moved back in with you, to help care for his dad?" Grace inquired.

"Yes, he sold his home and moved in here with us. He saw how much I was struggling to handle things on my own and how stubborn his father was being about hiring someone to care for him. I think Bruce's pride has been so wounded by all he's endured, and he can't bear the embarrassment of a stranger taking care of his daily needs." She sighed. "But for me, it was just becoming too difficult. I was trying to do everything on my own – bathing Bruce, dressing him, helping him in and out of bed, helping him use the bathroom, managing the house and staff. I was physically and mentally exhausted. I often cried myself to sleep at night. You see, before the stroke, Bruce was a very different man. He was the head of our household in every sense of the word. He took care of everything. After the stroke, our roles completely reversed. Suddenly, I was responsible for not only him but everything else. It was a lot to handle. But thankfully, Chris convinced his dad we needed to employ a house manager. We already had Christina and Tom on staff full time, along with other part-time staff, but we needed someone to take care of the daily operation of our household. That's when we hired Angela. And let me tell you what a blessing she has been! Having her here has allowed me to solely focus on caring for Bruce while also taking care of myself. I probably tell her how grateful I am at least a hundred times a day!" Peggy said with a chuckle.

Grace smiled. "We all have to recognize that sometimes we need help and can't do everything on our own, no matter how stubborn we are."

"You are so right!" Peggy nodded her head in agreement. "I knew I needed help, but I didn't know how to ask for it. My husband was always the one I would go to, the decision maker. And when that changed, I felt lost."

"I'm sure you're thankful Chris recognized you needed help. It sounds like he's been a good son."

"Yes," Peggy replied. "He certainly has been these past few years. I think it's his way of trying to make up for some of the past. He and Bruce butted heads so much when Chris was growing up. They didn't have a very good relationship. Although I was too soft on him, Bruce could be quite harsh and impatient. He worked a lot and worked long hours, and it always frustrated him that Chris wasn't more responsible. He would come down very hard on him anytime he got in trouble, whether it was at school or here at home. But," she said, waving away her words, "that's all in the past. Even though Bruce can no longer tell Chris how he feels, I can see it on his face how proud he is of him. Chris has worked hard to build his business. That was all Bruce ever wanted, for him to be successful."

Grace turned and looked at Bruce who was snoozing peacefully in his wheelchair. She tried to picture what he must have been like before the stroke robbed him of his strength and independence. It was hard to imagine the frail man before her as anything other than that. While he seemed mostly there from a mental standpoint, his battered body must be a shell compared to its former state. Her heart ached for both Peggy and Bruce, and she also felt more thankful than ever for the good health of her own parents.

* * *

As their days with the Atchison's ticked by, Grace was thankful she'd chosen to bring the girls for this visit. Getting to know Peggy was an absolute pleasure, and she was beyond thankful her girls had yet another wonderful woman to call grandma. Peggy also remarked several times that this was the most lighthearted she had seen her son in years. Chris had surpassed Grace's expectations as far as being attentive and understanding. He and Anna were developing a healthy father-daughter relationship, and he never once denied Abby tagging along if she asked.

While Grace was thoroughly enjoying getting to know Chris's family, she also took time to herself, reading quietly in what had become her favorite room in the house. When she had explained her intentions of allowing Anna some space to get to know her father and grandparents, Peggy shared her personal little reading nook with Grace - a cozy, little study with its' own fireplace and Christmas tree. A large, overstuffed chaise lounge sat near the fireplace, the perfect spot for relaxing and getting lost in a good book.

One evening, snuggled up by the fire with book in hand, Chris unexpectedly joined her. "There you are," he said, walking over to where she sat. "I've been looking for you."

Grace furrowed her brow. "Oh? Is everything okay?"

"Fine, fine," he answered. "I just wanted to talk to you about something."

She closed her book and laid it aside, waiting for him to continue.

"May I sit with you?" he asked.

She hesitated. "Sure... I guess." She eyed the lounge she was resting on, trying to decide if she wanted him seated that close to her. She obliged, however, scooting over and giving him some space.

Chris sat down next to her and sighed. "Grace, I can't thank you enough for coming here and doing this for me."

She stopped him. "Umm... no, I did this for our daughter. She deserves to know her grandparents."

"Yes, yes, I know," he said, waving off her comment. "But I'm a part of that. And you allowing her to be here, having you all here, it just means so much to me."

Grace didn't respond. She could tell there was more he intended to say so she remained silent.

"I know I've told you this before, but I've made such a mess of my personal life. I know I don't deserve a second chance, but you've given me one anyway. Somehow, some way, I hope you can find it in your heart to forgive me for everything."

His voice and his eyes were pleading with her. She could see the brokenness in his expression, hear the desperation in his tone. *Now is the time,* a still, small voice was saying. She knew it was the Holy Spirit prompting her. Taking a deep breath, she started the conversation she knew beyond the shadow of a doubt the Lord wanted her to have.

"Chris, there are some things I need to share with you. Please don't say anything, just listen."

She looked at him, and he nodded his agreement. She took another deep breath. "You aren't the only one who's made mistakes. You know I was married, and he was killed in an accident."

Chris nodded again.

"His name was Jared, and I married him when Anna was just a baby. I'm not going to lie to you about the circumstances. I felt broken and alone, a teenage mother who felt like no one would ever want her again. So, when Jared came to town and showed interest, I jumped at a chance with him. I wasn't in a good place emotionally or mentally, and I convinced myself he might be the only man who would ever want me."

"Grace..." Chris started to interrupt.

She shook her head and raised a hand. "No, you are listening. Remember?"

He sighed and nodded.

She continued. "Marrying Jared was not the first mistake I made, but it was the one mistake that took my life in a direction I never thought possible, to a place I never thought I'd be." She looked down, fighting back the tears that wanted to come. "I found out all too late I had married a monster. He was controlling, abusive, and a master manipulator. He took me away from my family, and he took any self-worth I had left. The only thing good that came from my time with him is my beautiful, kind-hearted Abby."

Tears were now flowing down her cheeks of their own free will. Chris looked like someone had just knocked the air out of him. His expression was pained and his breathing shallow. His lips parted as if to speak, but Grace raised a hand again to stop him. "I am not telling you this to make you feel any worse than you already do. The choices I made with you were mine to make, and the choice I made to marry Jared was mine. But because I chose not to deal with the guilt and shame I was feeling, it led to a very long road of painful mistakes. I put myself in that situation," she said, patting her chest with one hand, "because I chose not to ask for forgiveness and chose not to look beyond my failures."

She paused, taking a breath. "When I moved back home to Texas and was with my family again, I finally found what I'd been missing all along. And no, my family wasn't the answer. Yes, of course, I'm thankful they are a part of my life again, but they are not where I found my healing and forgiveness."

Her heart thrummed as her tears flowed faster, more freely. "I am forgiven and have accepted that forgiveness because I gave it all to Jesus, my Lord and Savior. I *chose* His grace and *chose* to give Him all my pain and mistakes. I made an absolute wreck of my life, but that didn't matter to Him, doesn't matter to Him! He picked up all my broken pieces and put me back together. He loves me!" Her voice was heavy with emotion. "And Chris, He loves you, too! He wants to take all your pain and all your mistakes just like He did mine." She leaned closer to him, her voice emphatic. "He *wants* to forgive you and for you to accept that forgiveness. All you have to do is ask."

Chris was now sobbing, tears streaking his face. "How Grace, how can I do that? I've done too much!"

She reached to take his hand in hers. "No, Chris. No. That's not true. He loves you and is waiting for you to choose Him. Just let it all go and let Him have your life."

He searched her eyes before responding. "How? How do I do it? What do I say? What if He doesn't hear me?"

"He hears you. I promise. Just talk to Him. Ask Him to forgive you. Ask Him to be Lord of your life. Tell Him you're choosing Him!"

Grace squeezed Chris's hand in encouragement as he slowly started to nod his head. For the next several moments, she sat quiet, reverent, as he poured out his heart to the Lord. The sincerity of his prayer touched her heart, and she found herself thankful God had trusted her with this opportunity. She felt her own faith strengthened, and her joy was practically bubbling over. She offered a silent prayer of praise. *Thank you, Lord! Thank you! You are such a good, good Father! Thank you! Thank you! Thank you!*

CHAPTER 14

It was Saturday evening, and Grace was packing the girls' suitcases so they would be ready to leave bright and early the next morning. The week had flown by, and it didn't seem possible it was already time to head home. She was, however, ready to be back in Texas with her family. While this trip to meet Chris's family had gone far better than she could have anticipated, this was not a lifestyle she was accustomed to, from having full time staff in the home to Chris chartering a private jet to fly them all to New York City for the day. This was all wonderful for a vacation, but it wasn't a life Grace envisioned herself living. She missed the daily grind of the ranch, checking cows and working horses, and she missed being in the kitchen with her mother, the smell of some freshly baked treat filling the air.

She had just finished folding the last of Anna's clothes when Chris entered the room. He fidgeted nervously as he smiled awkwardly at her. She returned his smile and waited for him to speak. When he said nothing, she stopped what she was doing and furrowed her brow at him. "Do you need something?"

He smiled awkwardly again. "Will you take a walk with me?" he asked, moving closer as the nervous fidgeting continued.

She felt her heart lurch. His nervousness coupled with the sudden awkwardness put her on high alert. What could he possibly want? Her mind immediately went to Anna. Surely, he wasn't going to ask for shared custody, was he? She gulped. "I guess," she managed to choke out.

Grace followed Chris downstairs and willingly took her coat when he offered it. "I thought we could take a walk outside," he said. "I know it's cold, but it's a beautiful evening. The moon is really bright tonight."

She nodded her head as she zipped her coat and retrieved her gloves from her pockets. She was still on high alert as she eyed him with suspicion. All she could think about was how to answer him if he asked for anything to do with Anna. While he was so far proving himself to be a decent father, she didn't feel ready to fully share their daughter with him. In fact, the thought made her feel downright sick to her stomach. *Calm down, Grace,* she silently coaxed herself. *You don't even know what he wants. Just relax.*

Chris led her along a snow-cleared path to the large pond that bordered the backside of the property. The moon shimmered across the semi-frozen water, and a quaint, little covered dock glowed with soft, white lights. Christmas greenery and bright, red bows rimmed its' edges. The scene looked like it had been taken straight from a movie, like it was intentionally fashioned for such a night. This only increased the feelings of unease swirling inside her.

Following him onto the dock, she finally asked, "What's this all about? Why are we out here?"

Chris offered a warm smile and motioned for her to take a seat. She obliged, waiting for him to answer. When he joined her on the bench but didn't respond to her questions, she spoke what was worrying her most. "Chris, if this is about Anna, about you wanting to share custody or anything like that, I don't think..."

He cut her off before she could finish. "This isn't just about Anna, Grace. This is about her, Abby, *and* you." He paused, looking nervous again as he rose to his feet, standing just in front of her. "This is about us, Grace. This is about the life I can provide for all of us." He knelt in front of her and took her hand in his. "Grace, you are a *beautiful, kind, amazing* woman and mother. I was a fool to walk away from you like I did. I want nothing more than to spend the rest of my life making up for so much lost time. Will you marry me?"

Grace inhaled sharply, the frigid air burning her lungs. Her heart pounded a wild cadence as the blood roared in her ears. She knew her eyes were wide, her mouth agape. Of all the things she'd envisioned, this never once crossed her radar. Her mind raced, trying to find the words to answer him.

Finally speaking, she found herself stammering. "Chris... I... uh... I don't think..."

He stopped her again. "Please, don't answer right away. I know this is unexpected. It's unexpected for me, too! I didn't plan this. I didn't know this was going to happen. But this week has been so amazing, having you all here. I know I don't have the best track record, and I've made a lot of mistakes. But I really believe we could build a wonderful life together, for us and for the girls." His eyes searched hers, pleading with her.

He pulled a small, black box from his pocket and popped it open. The glow from the soft, white lights danced across the most stunning diamond ring she had ever laid eyes on. He removed it and placed it gently on her finger, smiling affectionately as he did. She didn't know what to say. This should be a simple decision. And yet, she found herself questioning what to do.

As she looked from the ring to him, he leaned in close, his lips brushing her cheek. He lingered only a moment, and Grace felt the warmth of his kiss in contrast to the swirling winter wind. When he drew back, a tender smile tugged at one corner of his mouth. "Just think about it. Please."

And with that, he rose and walked away, leaving her alone with her racing heart and a diamond ring on her finger.

* * *

And all my life you have been faithful. And all my life you have been so, so good. The melody of the ringtone reverberated through the kitchen. Jane reached for her phone, looking at the screen. "Oh, it's Grace!" she said happily, answering the call.

Her brow quickly furrowed. "Grace, slow down. Take a breath!" she commanded. "What happened?"

Noah straightened in his chair at the kitchen table, quietly laying his fork on the plate in front of him. He could tell from the tone of Jane's voice that something wasn't right. His stomach dropped. If Grace or the girls were in trouble, he wouldn't hesitate to hop on a plane and fly to New York this very minute!

"Oh!" Jane exclaimed, "That certainly *is* unexpected, isn't it? What did you say?"

Noah waited, albeit impatiently, as Jane continued listening to whatever Grace was saying, responding now and then with an occasional utterance. She hadn't yet said anything that would give him any indication as to what was happening. Maybe this was nothing more than their flight being cancelled or changed. He knew they were supposed to fly home first thing in the morning.

He was still listening intently when Jake walked in. "You save me any of that pie?" he joshed, his booming voice startling Noah.

Noah waved a hand, shushing Jake as he joined him at the table.

Jake eyed him curiously, leaning in. "What on earth is going on? Why are we whispering?"

Noah motioned toward the counter where Jane was standing. "Jane is talking to Grace, and something's up," he whispered.

Jake looked in the direction of his wife and furrowed his brow. "Is everything okay?" he whispered in response.

"I don't know yet. I can't tell."

Noah and Jake remained silent until Jane's call with Grace ended. Then, Jake being Jake, loudly called to her. "What's going on with Grace? Is everything okay?"

Jane turned and joined them at the table. Her face was scrunched with worry. She slowly lowered herself into a chair. She looked at Noah and sighed wearily, her eyes filled with concern. "Something very unexpected has happened."

Jake shifted in his chair. "What is it? Is Grace okay? Are the girls okay?"

Jane nodded. "Yes, yes, they are all fine. It's nothing like that."

"Well, then spit it out already! What happened?" Jake demanded, a sharpness to his tone. Noah knew the only time Jake was ever short with his wife was when he was worried.

Jane gave her husband a serious look before returning her gaze to Noah, the same look of concern still evident. "Chris has proposed to Grace."

Her words hit him like a ton of bricks slamming into his chest. It was hard to breathe, like all the oxygen had been sucked out of the room. The room was spinning even though he was sitting perfectly still. A buzzing settled into his ears, drowned out only by the pounding of his own heart.

Jake slapped a hand down on the table, letting out a growl of disapproval. "She wouldn't actually consider marrying him, would she?" he asked, his volume rising as he spoke.

Jane shook her head, shrugging her shoulders. "She hasn't given him an answer yet."

Noah pushed back from the table, standing as he did. The weight of Jane's words hung heavy in the air. His mind was clouded as he struggled to breathe. The room continued to spin as his chest constricted.

Jane stood. "Noah, please, don't overreact," she spoke calmly. "We don't know what she's going to do yet. Let's all just take a breath."

He looked at Jane, her eyes pleading with him.

Jake broke the silence. "Has she lost her mind!" he bellowed. "She is *not* marrying that man!"

Jane shifted her attention to her husband. "You know as well as I do, we cannot make that decision for her. She is a grown woman, John Jacob. Now, *please*, just calm down!"

Jake ran both hands through his hair, letting out another growl before resting his head in his hands. Jane sat down beside her husband, gently placing a hand on his knee. "It will all be okay. You just wait and see," she offered encouragingly.

Noah, however, didn't feel at all like things would be okay. For him, it didn't feel like things would ever be okay again. It felt like the walls were closing in around him, suffocating him. Walking to the mud room, he retrieved his cowboy hat from a peg by the door and placed it firmly on his head.

Jane shifted her attention back to him. "Noah, please, wait! Come sit back down. She hasn't given Chris an answer yet. We don't know what she's going to say!"

He loosened his jaw just enough to speak. "She's said enough. I've heard all I need to hear." And with that, he walked out.

As he strode quickly toward his truck, wanting nothing more than to get away, his phone rang. It was a number he didn't recognize. He almost didn't answer, but something inside was prompting him to take the call.

"Hello," he answered gruffly.

"*Bruder,* is that you?"

He froze mid-step at the sound of Levi's voice. "*Jah,*" he answered in *Deitsch.* "Is everything okay?" He knew his brother calling him out of the blue from an unknown number could mean only one thing. Something was wrong.

"*Daed* is hurt. He's hurt bad."

"Where is he?"

"The hospital. *Mamm* is there also."

"Is she hurt, too?"

"*Nee.* She is fine."

"I'm on my way."

And with that, he ended the call. The details of what happened could wait until he arrived. His family needed him, and that was all that mattered right now. He pushed his thoughts of Grace out of his mind. As far as he was concerned, she'd told him all he needed to know without saying anything at all.

* * *

Grace watched both girls resting peacefully beside her. The early hour of the morning combined with the roar of the plane had lulled them both to sleep. She sighed and looked down at her empty finger, knowing she had disappointed Chris with her answer. Thankfully, he was gracious and understanding. She didn't want this to make things awkward between them and had taken great care to fully explain her reasons for rejecting his proposal. While she knew he could financially provide anything her or her girls would ever need, she knew he could not provide for the needs of her heart. She had married once for the wrong reasons and knew what it was like to live in a marriage where love did not exist. If she ever chose to marry again, it was going to be for love.

The flight home passed uneventfully, and Jane met Grace and the girls at the airport. "Your taxi awaits," she said, after hugging their necks. "I can't wait to hear all about your trip, especially from *you*, Grace," she said, eyeing her daughter inquisitively.

Grace flashed her left hand for her mother to see. "Not much to tell, Mom," she responded.

Relief washed over Jane's face. "Well, good," she said. "Then I can't wait to hear everything my beautiful granddaughters have to tell me!" she exclaimed, hugging their necks again.

On the drive home to the ranch, it didn't take much coaxing and Abby was soon relaying every detail of their trip. She enthusiastically shared about their trip to New York City to see Christmas decorations and go ice skating, and she shared numerous details about everyone she had met. "My new grandma and grandpa have a huge house!" she said excitedly. "They have people who work at their house every day. My new grandma never has to cook!" she exclaimed, still in disbelief.

Jane chuckled. "I don't know what I would do if I didn't have to cook. It's one of my favorite things to do," she said, smiling at her granddaughter.

"Oh, and I'm glad Grandma Jane! You are the best cook!" Abby said, smiling sweetly at her grandmother. "Except for maybe Mommy. She cooks good, too!"

Grace smiled at her youngest. "That's because your grandma taught me everything I know," she said.

Jane smiled at her daughter before turning her attention to Anna. "What about you, sweetie? What did you think of your trip?"

Grace looked at her oldest daughter. She had been mostly quiet since leaving New York.

"It was good," Anna replied. "I'm really glad we got to go." She looked out the window beside her. "I'll miss everyone there, but I'm really glad to be home," she said. "I missed you and Grandpa Jake. And Noah," she added.

Grace felt her heart flutter. Truth be told, she had missed Noah, too. But she also felt a healthy dose of nerves about seeing him. She wasn't sure if he was speaking to her or not. She hated the tension that was always lurking just below the surface between them. She knew she was going to have to face the cause of it sooner or later, and she decided it might as well be sooner.

"Oh, sweetie," Jane responded, pulling Grace from her thoughts, "you might be missing Noah a little while longer," she said, her expression sad.

"Why?" Grace blurted, not giving her mother a chance to explain any further.

Jane gave her daughter a scolding look. "As I was trying to say, he's not at the ranch right now. He left last night after getting an emergency call from his brother. His father was hurt in an accident."

Grace felt her heart clench in her chest. "Oh no! What happened? Is Sol going to be okay?"

"Well, Noah called me this morning from the hospital. His father was in a buggy accident yesterday evening. A car hit him from behind. Apparently, it was a teenage girl who was texting and driving," Jane said, shaking her head. "Poor Sol. Noah said he's in rough shape right now. His left lung is punctured, he has multiple broken ribs, his pelvis is fractured, and he has a concussion along with some minor neck injuries. He was thrown from the buggy on impact."

Grace's mind whirred with the information. "What can we do? We have to do something to help them. This is just awful!"

"I already told Noah to let us know if there is anything we can do for him or his family. He assured me the community is already rallying around them, and he will stay and help for as long as he is needed."

The last statement stole Grace's attention. *For as long as he is needed.* She mulled it over in her mind. "So... he didn't say when he was coming back... here?" She drew out her question.

"Of course not, Grace," her mother retorted, sounding indignant. "You know as well as I do, he won't leave if his family needs him. And your father and brother will keep things running like normal at the ranch, especially since you're home now. Noah is right where he needs to be."

If there was a hole to sink into, Grace would have done just that. Her mother's tone told her exactly how selfish her question sounded. And she was right. Noah was where he should be. But it didn't change the fact she felt a gnawing ache not knowing when she would see him again. And that ache only grew when she realized her first Christmas back home in Texas would likely be spent without him. She sucked in a breath and straightened in her seat, not giving in to her own pity party.

Stop it, Grace! Stop feeling sorry for yourself and start praying! She shifted her focus to Sol, Katie Ann, and the whole Miller family. If she couldn't be there with them, at least her prayers would be.

* * *

Grace spent the rest of the day repeatedly checking her phone. She'd kept it with her all day, so it wasn't likely she'd missed any calls or texts. She thought Noah would have called her by now, or at least sent a text message, letting her know how his father was doing. But since the clock now read 9:23 p.m., she assumed that wasn't going to happen. Maybe he forgot she was coming home today and didn't want to bother her. But how could he possibly think he would be bothering her considering what was going on with his father? Didn't he know she would want to hear from him? Surely, he must.

She huffed a breath. She couldn't seem to focus as her insides buzzed with nervous energy. She thought rocking might help, but she'd practically rocked the legs off Grandma Elaine's rocking chair! When her father raised his head from his bible reading to peer at her through furrowed brows, she abruptly stopped rocking. She offered a sheepish grin and exited the room.

Once outside on the patio, she took a seat on the step and stared at her phone, sighing heavily. The warmth from her breath mixed with the unusually cold, night air created a fog in front of her. She rubbed the phone screen with her sleeve to clear the moisture from it. Still no calls or texts. Sighing again, she brought up the home screen and selected the call icon. Scrolling through her list of favorites, she found Noah's name. Taking a breath and hesitating only briefly, she touched his name and placed the phone to her ear.

"This is Noah Miller. Please leave a message, and I'll get back to you as soon as I can. Thank you."

Voicemail. His phone went straight to voicemail. She rolled her eyes and ended the call, growling in frustration. *Why is his phone off? Doesn't he know people will be calling to check on his dad? This is so frustrating!* She anxiously tapped her foot as she stared into the darkness. *Just go to bed, Grace. Nothing you can do tonight. Maybe he will call tomorrow.*

* * *

Grace rolled out of bed the next morning, wincing as she did. Her back felt stiff, and a dull, throbbing ache had settled just behind her eyes. She hadn't slept well at all, tossing and turning as she fought for sleep to come. Unfortunately, she couldn't convince her mind to shut down long enough to enjoy any type of restful sleep. She had spent most of the night praying, not only for Noah and his family but also for the Lord to quiet her worries and anxiety over the whole situation.

She rubbed at her temples as she blinked several times, trying to focus on the clock. 7:19 a.m. Her father would already be in the barn starting morning chores, and her mother was likely starting breakfast. As she tiptoed past her girls' room, she peered through the cracked door. Both were still sleeping soundly, likely tired from their early morning flight the day before. She pulled the door closed and headed downstairs.

As she rounded the corner into the kitchen, the aroma of freshly brewed coffee enticed her senses. Maybe a little caffeine would send her headache into submission and lessen the pain in her back. "Morning, Mom," she said, reaching for a coffee mug.

Jane turned from where she was placing homemade, hand-cut biscuits on a buttered baking sheet. "Morning, sweetie," she replied, giving her daughter a once over. "Are you feeling okay?" she asked, her brow creased in concern. "You don't look so well."

Grace rolled her eyes. "Gee, thanks, Mom," she retorted. "I'm fine. I just didn't sleep well." She filled her mug with coffee, adding a splash of cream, and took a sip. "I couldn't stop thinking about Sol. I tried to call Noah last night, but his phone was off."

"Oh, that's because his battery is dead," Jane responded, now brushing the tops of her raw biscuits with melted butter.

Grace peered at her mother over the rim of her coffee mug. "And how exactly do you know that?" she quizzed.

"He called this morning a little before 7:00. He told me his phone had died, and he forgot his charger when he left in such a hurry the other night."

Grace plunked her mug down a little harder than intended. Hot coffee sloshed over the rim and onto her fingers and the counter. She jerked her hand back instinctively.

Her mother handed her a towel. "Are you sure you're okay?" Jane eyed her daughter with uncertainty.

Grace wiped the coffee first from her hand and then from the counter before responding. "No, actually I'm not okay," she said, plopping the towel down. "Why did Noah call you and not me? I've been worried sick about his dad all night!" she said, her volume rising.

"I have no idea, but you need to take a breath and calm down. This is not something to get upset over," Jane said, chiding her daughter. "I can't imagine what Noah must be thinking or feeling right now with his father being hurt. I just appreciate him taking the time to call and let us know how Sol is doing."

There it was again, that same convicting feeling from yesterday, only magnified by her mother's chastising tone. Grace looked at the floor, wishing it would open up and swallow her.

Nope, no such luck.

"I'm sorry," she said sheepishly. "I don't know what's wrong with me."

"It's probably just the lack of sleep and concern over Sol," her mother said reassuringly. "Besides, you just came home from your trip yesterday, and it sounds like you've had a lot to deal with yourself. It's not every day a girl gets proposed to," Jane said, raising one eyebrow.

"I don't know that I consider it a *real* proposal," Grace said, picking up her coffee cup again and taking a sip. "I think Chris just wants to make up for the mistakes of his past, and he saw marrying me as one way to do that. He beats himself up a lot and has struggled to let go and move on."

"Hmm." Jane responded, "I think I know someone else who did that same thing at one time," she said, winking at her daughter.

"Yes, I know. But that's in the past. I've found the healing and forgiveness I need to move forward." She paused, reflecting on what she'd shared with Chris. "And I told Chris about it, too. I told him he can find that same forgiveness for his mistakes.

Jane stopped what she was doing. "Oh, Grace!" she exclaimed. "That's just wonderful!"

Grace smiled. "You know, it really is. I'm thankful the Lord gave me the opportunity. I really believe Chris will follow through with it, too. He's got Peggy to encourage him, and I told him I'm always here if he ever needs to talk. But I also made it perfectly clear that our relationship will never go beyond friendship."

She paused for a moment. "I think what made me even consider marrying him didn't really have anything to do with him at all. I guess, in a way, a piece of my heart will always be linked to his because we share Anna. That was what was driving my thinking. I want Anna to be happy and have her father in her life, but I don't have to be married to him for that to happen. I don't ever want Anna to make the same mistakes I made. Some day when she's grown and ready to marry, I want her to do it for the right reasons. For love."

Jane smiled as her eyes misted. "I'm so proud of you, Grace. You've grown so much these past six months, and it does my heart good to see you living life again."

"Thanks, Mom," she replied, turning somber. "You still haven't told me how Sol is doing."

Jane swiped at her tears with the hem of her apron before slipping her tray of biscuits into the oven. "Noah said he's about the same. He's still in ICU so they can keep a close eye on him, and they're keeping him mostly sedated so his body can rest. So far, all the tests they've run point to him making a full recovery, but it's going to be a long road. The doctors are saying at least four to six months to heal, and then who knows how long after that before he'll be able to fully return to work."

Grace felt her heart drop to her stomach. "Who's going to keep his business running while he recovers? I know Noah's brother-in-law works for him, but I don't think one person could keep up with every-thing. And his brother Levi is still learning."

"That's one reason Noah said he will stay as long as he's needed. He learned from his father so he will keep things running smoothly until Sol is ready to take back over. It will all work out," Jane said, returning to her cooking.

Four to six months and who knows how long after that. Grace couldn't imagine Noah being away from the ranch for that long, not seeing him for weeks on end. Of course, she could go visit but that wouldn't be all that often. And, at the moment, she was wondering if she would even be welcome since she hadn't spoken to him since she left for New York. *He will call,* she told herself. *Just give him some time. He's got a lot to deal with right now. That's all.*

CHAPTER 15

Noah removed his hat and wiped the sweat from his brow. Although it was only a few days until Christmas and the weather had turned cooler, working anywhere near the forage in his father's shop could heat a man up faster than just about anything. Placing his hat back on his head, he finished the horseshoe he was working on and quickly carried it to where Samuel was standing with the two-thousand-pound draft horse they were shoeing, their last client of the day.

He placed the hot shoe against the horse's hoof and smoke billowed. He repeated this process a few times before cooling the shoe in a bucket of water. Samuel nailed and clinched each shoe as Noah finished the prepping, finally fitting the last shoe and lowering the horse's massive hoof to the ground. Samuel straightened to his full height, stretching his back as he did.

"Here, let me rasp, and you take a break," Noah offered.

Samuel stood tall and stretched again. "*Jah, danki.* I think my back is done for the day," he said, wincing as he rubbed his lower back.

Noah made quick work of the rasping, smoothing out any rough or sharp edges left by the nails. "I guess my back is just younger than yours," he quipped to his brother-in-law as he lowered the horse's hoof to the ground for the final time.

Samuel let out a guffaw. "*Nee, bruder,* we are the same age. My back just works harder than your back. That's all," he said, grinning.

Noah laughed. "Maybe so, maybe so. But either way, I'm glad this was the last horse for the day. I'm ready for supper."

Samuel clapped him on the back, chuckling as he did.

Noah made quick work of closing the shop for the night and headed for the house. After washing off the sweat and grime from the day, he walked to his parents' bedroom and knocked on the door.

His father answered his knock. "*Kumme* in."

Noah entered and went to sit in the chair beside the bed. *"Wie bischt du heit?"* he asked, greeting his father.

Sol attempted to shift his weight and sit up straighter before answering his son. The look of pain that paled his face told Noah all he needed to know.

"*Daed,* you are not supposed to do that. You can only move with help."

Noah put his arm gently under his father's back and lifted just enough for him to change positions ever so slightly. While he was thankful to have his father home, it was hard to watch him struggle in so much discomfort.

"*Jah,* I know. Your *mamm* has been reminding me all day. It has only been a few weeks, and I am tired of this bed," he said, grimacing as he did. "We must pray to *Gott* for this to pass quickly."

Noah smiled. "You have many people praying for you. But you have to listen and do what the doctors say, otherwise it will take you even longer to get better."

"*Jah, jah,* that's what my *fraa* reminds me," Sol answered, rolling his eyes.

Noah stifled a chuckle. Solomon Miller was not one to roll his eyes. In fact, Noah remembered his sisters being scolded as children for that exact behavior. At this point, however, he supposed the only body part his father could move without pain just might be his eyeballs!

"Can I get you anything? Do you need more pain medicine?"

"Nee, your *mamm* has taken care of it."

"Well, in that case, I guess I'm going to go eat. Samuel and I shod a few draft horses today, and I worked up an appetite. I forgot how much work their hooves are," he said, shaking his head.

Sol smiled. *"Danki, sohn.* I am grateful you are here."

"I'm here for as long as you need me. I won't leave until you're one hundred percent ready."

Sol creased his brow. "That could be many weeks. I cannot keep you away from Grace for so long. That would not be good."

Noah looked away, not wanting to discuss her. He'd been working overtime to try and keep his thoughts elsewhere, although she always seemed to find her way in. His jaw grew tight, and he could feel his muscles tensing. "It's fine. I'm here, and she's there."

Sol's expression shifted to a look of concern. "What has happened with you and Grace?"

"I'd rather not talk about it," Noah responded curtly.

"Sohn," Sol's tone was sympathetic. "If you do not talk, things will not get better."

Noah sighed, relaxing slightly. "I tried, *Daed.* I've tried to talk to her, but she just pushes me away. Says she needs more time. And now, I think time has run out."

"Have you prayed and asked *Gott* to show you what you must do?"

Noah nodded. *"Jah,* I've prayed a lot about it, but now I'm not so sure."

"Do not give up now, *mei sohn*. If you are unsure, you must keep praying."

Noah appreciated his father's efforts to encourage him. Despite being in pain and uncomfortable, he was still thinking of his family's needs, just like he'd always done. Noah also knew he was right. As much as he wanted to push Grace out of his mind, that wasn't the right response. The fact that she was even considering marrying Chris hurt him far deeper than he wanted to admit to anyone. And he didn't want to hang around to find out what her answer was. For all he knew, she was engaged. The thought made him physically ill.

He was reminded of the saying *time heals all wounds*. He wasn't sure that was true, but right now he definitely felt wounded. Maybe he would give Grace, and himself, what she'd been asking for all along. Time. With their relationship, it seemed only time would tell. Time and prayer.

* * *

Christmas and New Year's came and went. Chris made a surprise visit to see Anna, flying down on Christmas day. The entire Buckner family was there, minus Caleb who had to work, and it was the first time for many of them to meet Chris. Everyone was gracious and hospitable. Even Jake was warming up to him, albeit ever so slowly. And thankfully, things were not nearly as awkward between Grace and Chris as she'd feared they might be. He only stayed for the day, flying home the next morning. But it was a nice surprise for Anna just the same.

While this was by far the best Christmas Grace could remember having in years, she found herself feeling less enthusiastic than she ought to be. She missed Caleb, not having his lighthearted humor and teasing to distract her from the funk she seemed to have slipped into. He was her go-to sibling when she needed a friend the most, and talking over the phone just wasn't the same.

She also missed Noah. She didn't realize how much she was looking forward to spending the holidays with him until he wasn't there. He called now and then to give Jane updates on Sol and to talk to Jake or Eli about the horses, but he never once asked to talk to her. She had tried to call him a few times to no avail, although she didn't share that with anyone else. It seemed he was keeping his phone off other than when he needed to make a call or check his messages. She, however, had chosen not to leave any messages.

Jane received a letter from Katie Ann the first part of January, thanking her for the card she sent at Christmas and for their prayers. She said Sol was healing and making progress, but it was a slow process. She said his restlessness was making it more difficult, and he needed many reminders to be patient and give his body time. She also shared what a blessing it was having Noah home. She said he was settling back into life without modern conveniences much easier than she had anticipated and was even attending Sunday gatherings with them.

Grace felt her heart lurch and her chest tighten as her mother shared the letter aloud. Her mind raced. *What if Noah isn't planning on coming back? What if he's changed his mind and has decided to stay? What if he's decided he does want to be Amish and join the church? Will I ever see him again?* She wanted to run from the room crying but opted to use more self-control than that. *You are not some overly dramatic teenage girl,* she scolded herself.

She quietly stood and walked to the backdoor to retrieve her coat. "I think I need some air," she said, not looking back. She didn't want her mother to see the tears she was struggling to hold back.

Grace opened the door and stepped outside before her mother could respond. The harshness of the unusually cold weather smacked her in the face, burning her lungs as she inhaled sharply. It was colder than she had anticipated, but it didn't matter. In some ways it felt like relief, the cold air washing over her, offering a temporary reprieve from the searing pain branding her heart. The winter wind stung against the exposed skin of her face, drying the tears that were attempting to spill.

She walked briskly to the far pasture and leaned against the fence, watching the horses as they trotted across the field. The breeze whipped around as they pranced, kicking up playfully. The cold weather had them feeling frisky and full of energy.

As she watched them, her eyes settled on Jingle. She was by far the most beautiful animal among them all. The silver streaking her mane and tail glistened in the bright sunshine, contrasting against the blue-gray shade of her coat. As Grace continued to watch, a sad smile formed on her lips. Noah knew his way around a horse, and he knew how to choose the best. A lone tear trickled down her cheek, the cold wind drying it up before it could fall to the ground.

Her attention was diverted when she heard a truck coming up the driveway. As she turned, Caleb was coming to a stop a few feet away. She immediately took off toward him, practically jumping in his arms as he stepped from the driver's seat.

"Hey, whoa now, Gracie Mae! I'm glad to see you, too," he said, chuckling. "Too bad I can't find a woman other than my sister who's this happy to see me!" He quipped as he squeezed her tight before letting go and stepping back.

Grace wiped at the tears now streaming down her face. Her cheeks stung as the wetness mingled with the winter breeze. "I'm so glad you're home," she said, tears still coming. "I've missed you."

Caleb gently grasped her shoulders, bending down so he was face-to-face with her, his brow pinched in concern. "I'm glad to see you, too," he said, "but I don't think all this is just because you missed me." He continued to search her face. "What's going on, Grace?"

She sniffled and sucked in a breath, forcing the tears to stop. She took one more wavering breath before answering. "I'm fine," she said. "Just glad you're here." She attempted a smile.

Caleb continued to eye her questionably. "I'm not sure I believe that, but I'll let it go for now." He pulled her into another hug. "But you and I are gonna talk later, you hear me?"

Grace squeezed him tight one last time before letting go. "Did you tell anyone you were coming?" she asked, wiping her eyes with a gloved hand.

"Yep," he answered. "Mom knows all about it. But I swore her to secrecy," he said with a wink. "Couldn't have her spoiling my surprise!"

Grace smiled a genuine smile this time. Having her brother here was already lightening her mood. "Anna and Abby are going to be so excited to see you. We all were sad you couldn't make it for Christmas."

"Me, too. But work is work," he said with a shrug. "You know I usually take the holidays so the guys with families can be home."

She smiled again. True to his character, Caleb put the needs of others before his own. That's what had made him a good soldier and also what made him an outstanding brother. She found it hard to fathom why some lucky woman hadn't already snatched him up and made him a husband. Although, in her opinion, it would be hard to find a woman deserving enough.

* * *

Grace relished the second Christmas she was having with her family. Her mother basically had them doing everything on repeat since Caleb missed out during their first family Christmas. But no one seemed to mind. Grace herself was enjoying this round much more than the previous one. It seemed whenever Caleb was around, the smiles and laughter never ceased. It gave her mind and heart a reprieve from what was bothering her most. It was now the middle of January and still no call from Noah, at least not for her. It hurt far more than she wanted anyone to know that the man she once considered her best friend hadn't bothered to speak to her in over a month.

Caleb plopped down on the couch beside her, jostling her as he did. "What's my dear sister thinkin' about over there?" he asked, lightly elbowing her in the ribs.

She smiled slightly as she pretended to shove him away. "I'm trying not to think about anything at all if you must know. Just trying to enjoy these last few days of extended Christmas before you have to leave."

"Hmm... trying *not* to think about anything at all, huh?" he said, rubbing his chin. "That pretty much tells me you're thinkin' about *something*! I think it's high time we had that chat I promised was gonna happen!" He moved to stand, yanking her up with him as he did.

Grace rolled her eyes but obliged her brother and followed him to the door. "Where are we going?"

"Let's go for a walk and see where it leads," he said, grinning as he held out her coat.

Once outside, they strolled in peaceful silence. A brilliant moon shone overhead, and the sky was littered with millions upon millions of twinkling stars. The air was brisk, but not nearly as cold as it had been a few days prior.

"It sure is somethin'," Caleb finally spoke, breaking the silence. "I don't think I'll ever stop being amazed by a sky that looks like that." He nodded his head upward, his hands remaining tucked inside his warm pockets. "Sure has a way of makin' a man feel small. But in a good way. It's a good reminder that someone far greater holds it all in His hands." He grinned as his eyes remained focused on the sky above.

Grace smiled, letting the peace of the moment resonate in her soul. "He really does hold it all," she said, her voice barely above a whisper. Moisture was beginning to cloud her vision.

Caleb turned his attention to his sister. "Are you ready to tell me what's going on? I can tell something is really eating away at you." His voice lost some of its Texas drawl when he turned serious.

She lowered her face and closed her eyes, breathing deeply. "I don't know where to start," she said. "So much has happened."

"Well, then just start from the beginning," he replied. "I've got all night." He gently nudged her shoulder with his elbow.

For the next half hour or so, Grace filled her brother in on as much as she could concerning everything with Noah and with Chris. While it felt like something released on the inside of her, finally speaking everything out loud, it also brought everything she was trying not to think about to the forefront.

"So, that's it," she said, turning toward Caleb. "That's the story."

He didn't respond right away. Instead, he just grinned at her. She could feel her annoyance building. "I just poured my heart out to you," she said, sweeping her arms open, "and you have nothing to say?" Her volume rose as her irritation grew.

Caleb chuckled. "Calm down, just wait a minute! I have plenty to say if you'll just be patient. And for the record, I was filled in on some of this already."

She pinched her brow. "What? By who? Mom?"

He chuckled again. "No, not Mom. Who do you think? Noah isn't just your friend in case you didn't know."

Her eyes grew wide as her brows raised. "Has he called you?"

"Yep. Several times."

Her irritation level rose to new heights as a red-hot rush of frustration coursed through her. "That man is so maddening!" she bellowed. "It seems he's perfectly happy communicating with everyone but me!"

Now Caleb laughed out loud, tossing his head back as he did, only increasing her aggravation. Grace glared at him. "Oh, great! You think this whole thing is funny? Just great!" She started to storm off.

Caleb grabbed her arm, still halfway laughing. "Grace, just stop! You haven't even given me a chance to explain anything. No wonder Noah has been having a hard time trying to talk to you!"

She froze. "Did he tell you that?"

"He did. And a whole lot more."

She folded her arms across her chest and eyed her brother with scrutiny. "If you have all the answers, then why don't you just fill *me* in on what's going on?"

Caleb shook his head. "Gracie Mae, you are one hardheaded woman, you know that? If you haven't figured out by now what's going on, I don't think there's anything I can say that would help."

She furrowed her brow at her brother. "What are you talking about?" Her pulse began to pound in ears.

Caleb grasped both of her shoulders and looked her square in the eye. "How would you feel if you found out the person you are head over heels in love with was proposed to by someone else? And how would feel if that person was considering saying yes to said proposal?"

Her mouth gaped as realization dawned.

Her brother slowly nodded his head. "Yes, that's right. Noah knows about all of it."

She closed her gaping mouth, taking in everything Caleb was saying. "I didn't tell him about any of it. I haven't even spoken to him since before I went to New York."

"He was at the house when you called Mom and told her. Trust me, he knows."

She shook her head at her brother, pinching her brows together. "I don't understand. Why does it matter?" Her pulse quickened. "What do you mean he's in love with me?"

Caleb shook his head and chuckled before turning serious. "Grace, that man has been in love with you since the first time he laid eyes on you. And he's been trying to tell you just that since the moment you came home."

"I... uh... I... I didn't know," she said, her mouth gaping again. "I mean, I guess I kind of knew. Or at least the thought crossed my mind. But I wasn't sure. I haven't been sure about anything. I just know things have been different between us."

"You're an intelligent woman, Grace. I can't honestly believe you didn't know. I think you *did* know. But you're scared." His gaze pierced hers. "And I think what scares you the most is you know you love him, too."

She lowered her eyes as the tears started to come. Now that someone had finally voiced out loud what she'd been feeling for months and trying to avoid, there was no more denying it. Her heart was wide open, exposed. She couldn't pretend she didn't know anymore, and she couldn't keep asking for more time. But that's when it hit her. Maybe what she feared all along was coming true. Maybe she'd tried to hide from it for too long. Maybe too much time had gone by, and maybe too many things had happened. Maybe she was being forced to face her greatest fear after all. Maybe Noah was gone from her life for good.

Her brother drew her into his arms as she softly sobbed. He didn't say anything. He just let her cry. It was her who finally pulled away, looking to him for some sort of reassurance. "Is it too late, Caleb? Is he coming back?" Her eyes searched his.

He looked at the ground, shaking his head. "I don't know, Grace. I wish I did. All I know is he was hurt pretty bad when he left. It speaks volumes to a man when the woman he loves is considering marrying someone else." He looked at her sternly.

Grace rubbed at her forehead, pinching it beneath her fingers. "I already told you what that was about. It was about Anna. I was never actually going to marry Chris. I don't love him. You know that." Her tone was sharp.

"Yes, you told me. But Grace," he held her gaze, "you haven't told Noah."

"How can I?" she bellowed, her voice ringing with a mix of irritation and desperation. "He hasn't called me since he left! And every time I try to call him, his phone is off!"

Caleb smiled sympathetically. "I can't give you all the answers. I've said what I can. You're going to have to figure the rest out on your own." And with that, he walked away.

* * *

All too quickly, Caleb's visit home came to an end. He returned to New Mexico, and life on the ranch resumed its' normal pace. As the weeks ticked by, Grace found little comfort in what had become her daily routine – getting the girls up and ready for school, helping her dad and

Eli with morning chores, helping cook and clean up from breakfast, helping keep up with laundry and cleaning around the house, picking Abby up before lunch on the days she attended preschool, and whatever other tasks she could tend to around the ranch or in the house to keep herself occupied.

She still hadn't heard from or spoken to Noah, and she'd all but ceased with her efforts to contact him. Every time her calls went straight to voicemail, and every time she found herself ending the call, never leaving a message. More than once, she'd sat down thinking it would be simpler to just write him a letter telling him all she was thinking and feeling. But her letters always ended up wadded up in the trash can before she finished them.

As winter gave way to spring, the days became longer as the sun began to heat the earth. Although Texas winters were nothing like Grace had experienced while living in other parts of the country, this winter had seemed to drag on forever, cloudy and cold for what seemed like days on end. She welcomed the warmth and birth of new life around her as birds began to sing and flowers began to bloom. And while she was feeling some relief from the cloud of gloom that had settled over her since December, it still lingered.

She was lost in thought one morning, sipping her coffee on the back patio, when her mother joined her. "Beautiful day, isn't it?" Jane remarked.

Grace smiled but said nothing. She wasn't feeling particularly conversational. She was trying to sort out where to go from here and what her next steps in life should be.

"I think I'll run to town in a little while and pick up some things for the garden. Would you like to come along?" her mother asked.

She thought for a moment, taking a few sips from the mug in her hand. "Sure, why not. Maybe I'll pick up some job applications and see what's out there."

Jane eyed her curiously. "If that's what you really want," she said. "But you know there's plenty of work around here you can help with. And we both know you don't need the income."

"It's not about the money," she replied tersely. "I just feel like I need to do something different, like I need a change." Her foot seemed to have a mind of its own, tapping rapidly against the wooden boards beneath her, jostling the mug she was holding.

"Grace," Jane said caringly, taking the mug from her hand as she did, "please talk to me. You haven't been yourself in months. What's going on?"

She ran a hand through her thick, wavy hair before leaning forward, resting her chin on her upward bent knee. She let out a long, forlorn sigh. "Please don't make me say it out loud. You and I both know you already know exactly what this is about," she said, eyeing her mother.

Jane sighed. "Talk to him, Grace."

Grace stood and paced the patio. Her sigh became a low growl. "Why does everyone keep saying that?" she bellowed. "I've been trying since December!"

Jane also stood. "Because I love you, I'm going to be honest with you, Grace." Her tone was firm, holding just a hint of annoyance. "You say you've been trying since December, but I don't believe you really have."

Grace stopped pacing and turned to face her mother, eyes blazing and jaw tight. She opened her mouth to protest, but Jane raised a hand to stop her from speaking. "Just listen. If you really wanted to talk to him, you would have made that happen by now. You could have left him a message to call you. You could have asked to talk to him one of the times he's called to check in and update us about Sol. You could have driven to Beeville yourself several times by now. If you expect me to stand here and feel sorry for you, you've got another thing coming."

Grace didn't know what to say. She was in shock. She couldn't remember the last time her mother had spoken so sternly to her. Her mind was blank, unable to formulate a response.

Jane softened both her expression and her tone, gently placing a hand on her daughter's arm. "I think you've spent these last few months feeling sorry for yourself. And being scared. You are stronger than this, Grace Elaine! You've proven that time and time again. Why are you having such a hard time now?" Her mother's eyes shone with compassion.

She shook her head. "I don't know. I don't know why this is so hard. I guess because I *am* scared," she admitted. "I'm scared to tell Noah the truth. And I'm scared I'll lose him if things don't work out. But that may not matter. I may already have lost him." She hung her head, disappointed in herself. "He hasn't once tried to contact me since he left."

"Grace, when he left his father had just been in a terrible accident, and you were still in New York. He knew about Chris proposing to you, and he left before any of us knew what your answer was going to be. I think it hurt him more than words can say to know you were considering saying yes. I don't think he wanted to hang around and find out. I think he was just as scared as you're feeling now."

Her mother's words pierced like an arrow. She hadn't fully considered how the whole situation with Chris might have made Noah feel. Sure, Caleb brought it up to her, but he hadn't spelled it out the way Jane Buckner just had.

"I don't know where to go from here, Mom. So much time has passed. I'm not even sure he wants to talk to me anymore."

Her mother smiled tenderly. "Love is not something that just goes away in a matter of a few weeks or even months. Not if it's real. That is something the Lord Himself gifts to us. It's meant to be a blessing. A blessing you're making far more complicated than it has to be. Have you been praying about what to do?"

Grace nodded her head. "I've prayed so much I'm sure God is tired of hearing about it by now!" she answered, rolling her eyes.

Jane grinned, offering a slight chuckle. "The Lord never tires of hearing from us," she said reassuringly, "especially when one of His children is having a difficult time."

She smiled at her mother. "Thanks, Mom. Thanks for listening, and thanks for being honest with me. I needed that."

"You're welcome, sweetie. I'm just glad we finally had this talk. Now, can I offer one more suggestion?"

Grace nodded. "Sure. What is it?"

"Why don't you try writing Noah a letter and see how that goes? Maybe that would be a good place to start."

Grace sighed heavily, almost growling again. "I've tried, trust me," she replied. "It always ends up wadded up in the trash."

Jane smiled. "Why don't you give it one more shot? Maybe this time will be different," she said, encouraging her daughter. "Why don't you work on it now while everything is fresh in your mind?"

Grace stared forlornly at her mother. How could she tell her no? How could she explain she doubted the words would come any easier? It was probably best to just be obedient and do what was being asked of her. If nothing else, at least she could tell her mother she tried.

CHAPTER 16

"There's a call for you, Momma." Grace set down the feed bucket she was filling as Anna skipped down the barn hallway toward her, cellphone in hand.

"Thank you, baby," she said, taking the phone from her. "Who is it?" Her pulse quickened with the thought it could be Noah. But when she looked at the number on the screen, she knew it wasn't.

"I don't know. Some lady from a bank or something."

Grace creased her brow. *A bank?* She put the phone to her ear. "Hello, this is Grace Thompson."

"Hello, Mrs. Thompson. This is Jennifer Stevens from Community State Bank in Hailey. How are you today?"

"Fine," she answered.

"If you don't mind, could you please answer a few simple questions to verify your identity before we continue?"

"Yes, but what's this about?" she inquired.

"I'll be glad to discuss that with you as soon as you answer these few questions for me. First, what is your maiden name?"

Grace answered, albeit with hesitation. "Buckner."

"In what city did you attend high school?"

"Marble Falls, Texas."

"And last question, Mrs. Thompson. What is the name of your oldest child?"

"Annabelle. Now can you please tell me what this is all about?" She knew her tone rung with impatience.

"Absolutely, ma'am. As I said before, I am calling from Community State Bank in Hailey. Let me begin by first offering my sincere condolences for the passing of your husband."

Grace could feel her unease growing as a nervousness settled in the pit of her stomach. "Thank you. But why are you contacting me? I don't remember my husband having any type of account with your bank. Did I overlook something? I'm sorry if I did."

"No ma'am, absolutely not. You are correct. He did not have any type of banking account with us, but we do have a safe deposit box here in his name. My deepest apologies for not notifying you sooner, but it was only recently we learned of his passing."

Grace furrowed her brow. "What's in it?" she asked.

"I'm sorry ma'am, but I cannot answer that. We do have a key here at the bank, but the box cannot be opened unless someone whose name is on the authorized list provides proof of ID and signs for the box."

Grace was confused. "Okay, I understand that. But what does this have to do with me?"

"Mrs. Thompson, since your husband has passed, you are now the only person authorized to open the box. I'm sorry for the inconvenience, but we need you to come and retrieve whatever is inside so the account can be finalized and closed."

Grace felt her mouth drop open as her pulse quickened. The unsettled feeling in the pit of her stomach had now grown into a churning tremor. Until this very moment, she had no intention of ever returning to Hailey again.

"How soon do I need to come?" she questioned, her voice shaky.

"As soon as possible, ma'am. Again, I'm sorry for the inconvenience, but we really need to get this taken care of in a timely manner considering it has been several months since your husband's passing. And again, my condolences for your loss."

Grace took a deep breath to calm her nerves. "I appreciate you contacting me. I live in Texas now. I'll have to book a flight for later this week if that's okay."

"Yes ma'am. Please be advised we do close our lobby at noon on Fridays, but we are available Monday through Thursday from eight to four. Our lobby is closed entirely on Saturdays and Sundays. Please bring a valid photo ID with you when you come."

"Okay. Thank you."

"Again, my name is Jennifer Stevens. Thank you for talking with me today. Please let me know if you have any questions. We look forward to your arrival. Enjoy the rest of your day. Goodbye."

Grace clicked off her phone, the shock of the situation resonating through her. *I have to fly to Idaho. I have to go back to Hailey.* Bile rose in her throat.

"Momma, is everything okay?"

She turned to see Anna watching her closely, her sweet little face riddled with concern. She'd completely forgotten she was standing there. She knelt in front of her, attempting to comfort her with a smile. "Yes, baby, of course. That was a nice lady from a bank in Hailey letting me know there are some things there I need to come get."

Anna furrowed her brow. "Why do you have to go? Can't they just mail it?"

"I wish they could, but that's not how it works. They have to make sure it's really me they are giving the things to, or they could get in trouble."

She looked at her mother, concern still clouding her expression. "I don't want you to go."

"I know, sweetie," she said, stroking her daughter's hair, "but this is just one of those grownup things I have to take care of. Please don't worry," she said, kissing her forehead. "I should only be gone for a day."

"Who's going where for the day?"

Grace turned to see her mother coming toward them. She rose to her feet as Jane halted in front of her. "I just found out I have to fly to Idaho. Jared has a safe deposit box I didn't know about."

"Hmm. I thought we took care of everything with the banks up there?"

"We did, with the ones we knew about. But this is a different bank, Community State Bank. I didn't think to check with them since I never found any paperwork with their name on it."

Jane looked just as hesitant as Grace was feeling. "When are you going?"

"They want me to come as soon as possible. The lady was very apologetic, but she said it needs to be taken care of."

Jane's expression remained strained. "Well, I guess we'd better book a flight and get this done and over with. I'll go with you."

"I appreciate that, Mom. I really do. But I need you here with the girls. I don't think I'll be gone more than a day. It shouldn't take long at the bank. If I fly out early in the morning, hopefully I can fly back home later the same day."

Her mother didn't look all that certain. "Well, okay. I guess. If you're sure?"

"I am. It will be fine. This should be a simple trip, and I'll be back home before you even have a chance to miss me," she said, smiling as confidently as she could muster to reassure both her daughter and her mother. But on the inside, her own stomach was in knots.

* * *

Grace pulled her rental car to a stop outside of Community State Bank. She hadn't stopped feeling anxious since she'd received the call two days ago saying Jared had a safe deposit box that required her attention. She put the car in Park and took a deep breath to calm her nerves. She couldn't possibly imagine what awaited her inside.

She was just about to step out of the driver's side door when her phone rang. "I'm here, Mom. Just pulled in," she said, answering the questions she already knew her mother was going to ask.

"Okay, honey. I just wanted to check. Call me as soon as you're finished at the bank."

"I will, don't worry. This shouldn't take long."

"Okay, talk to you soon. Love you."

"I love you, too. Bye."

Grace ended the call and stepped outside. The chill of the air nearly took her breath away. It certainly didn't feel like spring had sprung here just yet. She quickly stuffed her phone in her pocket and zipped up her heavy winter coat. She was thankful she'd checked the weather before catching her flight so she was dressed appropriately for the conditions.

Once inside, she found the nearest available person and inquired after Jennifer Stevens. "My name is Grace Thompson, and I received a call from her two days ago about a safe deposit box in my late husband's name."

"Yes, ma'am. Thank you for coming. Right this way. Ms. Stevens has been expecting you."

The kind, middle-aged woman led her to a small office. A much younger, blonde woman was sitting behind the desk. "Ms. Stevens, this is Mrs. Thompson."

The young woman rose from her desk, extending her hand. "Thank you so much for coming Mrs. Thompson. This shouldn't take long at all. If you'll follow me, we'll get this all taken care of."

Grace followed her to the opposite side of the bank into a room containing a small, round table and a few chairs. "Please, have a seat," Ms. Stevens directed. "If you can take out your photo ID for me, I'll be glad to retrieve the box for you."

Grace handed over her driver's license, and the young woman left the room. When she returned, she was carrying a rectangular, black box. She placed it on the table. "Here's your ID," she said, "and here's the key to the box. I'll step out, and you just let me know when you're finished." She smiled, exiting the room and closing the door behind her.

Grace could feel her heart pounding against her ribcage as she stared at the box in front of her. Why this small, metal box was so intimidating she couldn't wrap her head around. She held her breath as she cautiously placed the key in the lock and turned. The lid popped open, revealing a manila envelope. She carefully took it out, examining it. No markings or stamps whatsoever were printed on the outside, and whatever was on the inside felt thick and fat.

She slowly peeled back the flap of the envelope, carefully tearing away the glue holding it shut. When she held it open, her heart nearly stopped. Multiple stacks of one-hundred-dollar bills were piled inside, each stack bound with a rubber band. She quickly closed the envelope as her pulse pounded in her ears. She suddenly felt nauseous, her nerves sending her stomach into a wild roil. Her mind raced. Part of her wanted to tell the bank to keep the money. She had no idea where it came from or what it was for. But she imagined that wasn't an option. She was certain they weren't legally allowed to do such a thing. Furthermore, the thought of even telling anyone what was in the envelope made her that much more nervous.

Grace stood and gathered the envelope, doing her best to reseal it with whatever glue remained as her hands shook. As soon as she opened the door, Ms. Stevens walked over. She didn't seem to notice the nervousness Grace was certain she wasn't hiding very well.

"Thank you again, Mrs. Thompson, for coming. I'm sorry this is difficult for you. Let me offer my condolences for your loss one last time."

That's it, Grace thought. *She thinks I'm upset about losing my husband. She doesn't suspect anything.*

Ms. Stevens smiled warmly and placed a single sheet of paper on the table. "If you could, just sign right here," she said, pointing to the line where Grace's signature was required. "You're signing to verify you have possession of the contents of the box and that you no longer wish to maintain this account."

Grace quickly scribbled her name as Ms. Stevens thanked her yet again. Then, taking the envelope, she made her way to her rental car as hastily as she could without drawing attention to herself.

Once inside the safety of her vehicle, away from prying eyes or listening ears, she pulled her phone from her pocket and called her mother. Jane answered on the first ring, and Grace could hardly contain herself. "Mom, you are never going to believe this!" she exclaimed in a hushed whisper.

"What is it, Grace?" she responded.

"There was an envelope in the box, and..." Her words trailed off as her driver's side door slowly opened. Her breathing stopped. Panic seized her as her throat constricted with fear. Alarm and disbelief coursed through her to the very core, jolting her like a bolt of electricity. "No... No... It can't be..." She spoke barely above a whisper. But on the inside, she was screaming, her heart nearly pounding out of her chest.

"Grace? Grace? What's going on? Grace!" Her mother's voice grew louder through the speaker of her phone. She slowly let it slip from her fingers, a hand firmly grasping it and disconnecting her call. She was frozen in her spot, eyes wide in horror, not believing what she was seeing.

"Hello, Grace."

She sucked in sharply at the familiar sound of the voice, gulping for air as her entire body began to tremble. Towering over her, blocking any chance of escape, was Jared.

* * *

Noah sat down at the table with his father. Sol was rubbing his shoulder with one hand. "How are you feeling?" Noah questioned. "You worked hard today, not resting much."

"I feel better than expected," Sol replied. "My muscles are sore, but that is from resting too much for so many weeks. It feels *gut* to be working again. I am thankful *Gott* has heard our prayers." He smiled broadly.

"Me, too, *Daed*. I'm glad you're doing better than the doctors anticipated."

"Doctors do not always know what will happen. That is ultimately up to Him," Sol said, motioning heavenward.

Noah smiled. He offered a silent prayer of thanks for his father's speedy recovery. No one expected Sol to be working full days this soon after his accident. It was almost exactly twelve weeks to the day. Surprising them all even more was the fact that he had started working partial days as early as eight weeks from the date of his accident. Sol always said with God, anything is possible!

Katie Ann joined the two men. "Noah, there is a letter for you from Jane," she said, laying it on the table in front of him.

He creased his brow. While he had spoken with Jane several times over the phone since the night of the accident, they had not exchanged any letters. He picked it up and broke the seal, pulling two sheets of paper from the envelope. One sheet was clean and crisp while the other was wrinkled with small tears around the edges. The crisp, clean letter was clearly marked to get his attention. *READ FIRST* was scrawled across one of the folded sides in Jane's handwriting. Opening it up, he began to read:

Dear Noah,

I hope this letter finds you well and your father's recovery progressing. Our entire family continues to lift him up in our prayers. We know the Lord is our healer and speak that daily over Sol. Please tell Katie Ann I pray for her daily as well. Taking care of a sick or injured man is not for the faint of heart! I'm sure she will understand what I mean!

The true purpose of this letter, however, is not about your father. I am writing this because Grace has not had the courage to do so herself. I know she will likely be angry with me when she finds out what I've done, but sometimes a mother knows best. You see, the other letter I've enclosed with this one is one of many Grace has started to write to

. 261 .

you but ends up throwing away. I retrieved this particular letter without her knowledge or consent. Yes, I know that sort of behavior is frowned upon, and you can scold me if you like. But in this instance, I am doing what I can to set you two on the right track. Just read the letter. I'm sure you'll figure it out from there.

Love and Prayers,

Jane

Noah laid Jane's letter aside and stared at the folded, crinkly piece of paper lying in front of him. Why was Grace writing letters to him and throwing them in the trash? He hadn't spoken to her or heard from her since before Christmas, and his pulse quickened as he carefully opened the torn, wrinkled note. As his eyes scanned over it, it was definitely her handwriting. He quickly began to devour her words.

Noah,

I'm not sure how to begin this letter. Truth be told, I've lost count of how many letters I've started to write to you. The words just never seem right. So, bear with me as I attempt to tell you all that's on my mind and in my heart.

These past few months without you here at the ranch have been lonely to say the least. I don't think I realized how much I would miss you until you were gone. Of course, there are many things I've realized since you left, but please know I do miss you more than words can possibly say. I've called you several times but couldn't bring myself to leave a message. I'm sorry for that. For so long, I kept telling myself if you wanted to talk to me, you would call. You would make the first move. But that was just me being stubborn. And protecting myself I suppose.

That's what I've come to realize without you here. I've been scared

to open my heart to you, scared I would end up losing you somehow.
You've been my best friend for so long, and my heart aches at the
thought of you not being in my life. But maybe that's exactly what has
happened because I didn't want to be honest with myself or you.

So, here it is, the whole point of this letter. Noah, I am in love
with you. And now that I'm being honest, I've known that for a very
long time. I've just been scared. I don't know where we go from here or
how you feel anymore, but at least you know where I stand. I love you,
Noah. I always have and always will.

Yours Affectionately,
Grace

Noah's heart practically leapt from his chest! He read and reread
her letter, specifically hovering over the words confessing her love.
She loves me. She loves me! He quickly rose from his seat, his heart
flooding with newfound hope.

"Ach, mei sohn, what is happening?" his mother asked, grinning at
him. "I have not seen you look this happy in many weeks." His parents
both eyed him curiously.

"This letter, the second letter," he said, pointing to it emphatically,
"it's from Grace!" A wide smile split his face. He didn't care one bit if
he was acting like a goofy teenage kid.

Sol chuckled. "Did I not tell you it is good to talk to her?"

Noah nodded in agreement. "You have no idea how good!" he
exclaimed. "I have to call her!"

He raced up the stairs and retrieved his phone from the bedroom.
He pushed the button and waited for it to power up. It seemed like it
took forever to fully power on. He was just about to select Grace's name
from his favorites' list when several messages and a voicemail notifi-

cation flashed across the screen. He scanned them quickly. They were almost all from Caleb. It was strange to have so many text messages from him, and most of them said the same thing over and over again. *Call me as soon as you get this!*

When he clicked on his voicemail inbox, sure enough, his only voicemails were from Caleb as well. Apprehension coiled in the pit of his stomach. As he put the phone to his ear various scenarios were playing in his mind, but nothing could have prepared him for the words he heard from his longtime friend.

"Grace is missing."

* * *

Grace sat on the cold, metal chair in the corner of the dimly lit motel room. The air filling the room smelled stale and musty. Jared had the curtains drawn shut but kept repeatedly peeking out the window. It seemed he was searching for something or someone. Or maybe someone was searching for him. She wasn't sure.

They had driven for nearly four hours before he finally stopped, pulling into an old, dingy roadside motel. He hadn't spoken much at all during their drive, and he seemed extremely nervous and on edge, not something that was typical for him. Of course, she also wasn't sure what would be considered typical behavior for a man who was supposedly dead.

Moving from the window, he sat down on the edge of the bed. He turned his attention to her, a strange smirk lurking at the corners of his lips. She shuddered, fear and dread pulsing through her. Her brain was still attempting to process what was happening. Part of her was denying this was even possible while another part of her was quietly screaming she should run. Yet no part of her body seemed willing to move.

"I guess this is quite a shock for you." He finally spoke in a hushed tone, the strange smirk still playing on his lips. "Have you missed me?" He leaned forward, lightly touching her leg as he did.

Grace just stared at him, her mind shifting into overdrive. While she didn't dare take her eyes off him, she felt the overwhelming need to scan the room for anything she could use as a weapon for self-defense if it came to that. She shifted slightly in her chair. "Don't touch me." Her voice was shaky at best.

He sat up straight, jeering as he did. "Don't you have anything to say?" he mused, taunting her. "Any questions you want to ask your *dead* husband?" His eyes glinted wildly.

She continued to stare at him, her mind still racing. She knew beyond the shadow of a doubt she couldn't trust him. She wasn't sure what to do. She had never been more scared in all her life. Yet from somewhere within, a voice was guiding her, telling her she was stronger than this, not to let the fear win.

She spoke quietly, maintaining eye contact. "How? How are you here?"

He snickered. "Well, *darling*, if you have enough money, everything and everyone has a price."

Her brow creased as her jaw tightened. "I saw your body at the hospital. You were dead."

Yet again he scoffed at her. "No, my dear, you saw *a* body." His eyes flashed as a sly grin formed on his lips. He leaned closer again. "That man wasn't me."

Grace sucked in sharply, terror overtaking her. She gaped at him, shaking her head in disbelief. "No... No," she repeated. "Who... Who was it? Who did I bury?" She fought to hold back her tears. She couldn't explain what she was feeling if she tried, knowing she'd buried a man in her husband's grave who wasn't her husband at all.

Jared straightened, rising to his feet. "You buried the man they sent to kill me," he answered, pausing as he moved closer, standing only inches from her. "*And* my family." His expression grew tense, angry, as his fists clenched shut. His jaw constricted as his muscles tightened. He looked away, almost as if looking into the past.

Grace shuddered again, recoiling as her heart raced, dread filling her to the very core. She'd witnessed similar reactions from him during their marriage, and it usually never ended well for her. Her eyes searched the immediate vicinity for anything she could grab to protect herself.

He turned his attention back to her, seeming to notice her recoiled posture and the panic that flooded her face. He unclenched his fists and returned to his seat on the side of the bed. His jaw loosened, and his expression softened. For a brief moment, as he gazed at her, his eyes held what could only be described as defeat, and if she wasn't mistaken, remorse. He rested his elbows on his knees and ran both hands through his hair, keeping his face down.

Grace relaxed ever so slightly, her eyes wide as she stared at him. In the matter of a few seconds, he had gone from being the monster she remembered to looking like a wounded, beaten man. This was not the Jared she knew at all. This was a version of him she had never seen during their marriage, even after his outbursts would leave her crying on the floor, reeling in agony.

She quickly scrolled through her memories, attempting to remember a time she might have witnessed even the smallest amount of compassion from him. That's when it suddenly dawned on her. What if this is how he always reacted after his anger was spent, how he always felt when he could see the fear in her eyes? How could she possibly know? Anytime he lashed out at her, as soon as he was done inflicting damage, he would leave the room. He never once stayed, and he never once gave her a backwards glance. She had always assumed he was so angry he couldn't stand to look at her, but what if she'd had it wrong all these years? What if he didn't stay because he couldn't stand himself, couldn't stand to look at what he'd done to her? She gasped as tears filled her eyes. For some unexplainable reason, grief seized her heart.

The sound of her gasp drew his attention, and he raised his head. His expression remained soft, his eyes sad. "I didn't want to kill him, Grace. I didn't plan it. But when he came for me, he told me you and the girls were next when he finished with me. He smiled when he said it, like he would enjoy it. I snapped." His eyes blazed again. "I did what I had to. I staged the accident using his body, and then I disappeared."

She continued staring at him in disbelief. "How? Why? I don't understand."

He ran his hands through his hair again. "All you need to know is I did business with some men I shouldn't have, and I made a lot of money at their expense. They found out and weren't too happy about it."

She shook her head, furrowing her brow as she tried to absorb all he was telling her. "What about the hospital? The body? How did you get away with that?"

"Like I said, if you have enough money, you can buy just about anyone and anything. I paid off a lot of people to keep quiet. And since the body was burned, it made it that much easier to get away with. All I had to do was plant my wallet and my wedding ring on him and that was that."

She had so many questions she wanted to ask but was finding it difficult to comprehend everything he was revealing to her. It was all too much to take in. Then she remembered the safe deposit box and the money. She turned her eyes to the manila envelope laying on the table. "How did you know I was going to be at the bank?" She eyed him with scrutiny.

"I'm the one who made sure the bank found out I was dead. Well, *supposedly* dead. I need that money. And I couldn't exactly walk in and ask for it myself."

"How did you know I'd come for it? And when I'd be there?"

He grinned. "Because Grace, you've always been responsible. If they told you to come take care of it, I knew you would do it."

"But how did you know I'd be there today?"

"I didn't." He shot her a cunning grin. "I guess you could say I've been staking out that bank for about a week now, ever since I provided the information of my *passing*."

"Okay, fine then," she said. "You've got your money. Now let me go."

His eyes flashed wildly again, his softened expression morphing into something entirely different, something that made her shudder. "Now honey, I can't exactly do that can I? You know I'm alive. I can't just let you go. Besides, those unhappy fellows who wanted me dead also know I'm not so dead after all!" The deranged way he chuckled sent chills racing up her spine.

Grace found herself recoiling away from him, pushing her back against the chair. She stared at him wide-eyed, her heart pounding against her ribcage. "Are you... are you going to kill me?" she managed to ask, her voice trembling.

Yet again, his expression flipped like a light switch. He looked hurt, maybe angry. "Grace, I know I... I 've done..." He looked away, clenching his jaw shut. "I would never do that." When he returned his eyes to hers, there was that same look of defeat mixed with remorse she'd seen only moments earlier.

Keeping her guard up, she continued to scrutinize him with apprehension. She couldn't figure him out. His reactions were all over the place. She found herself questioning his sanity. "What are you going to do?" she finally asked, her voice a little less shaky than before.

"Try to stay alive," he answered, his expression turning grim and his eyes cold. "Come on, we need to go." And with that, he grabbed the manila envelope in one hand and her wrist in the other, pulling her to her feet and toward the door.

CHAPTER 17

Noah threw his truck into park, practically bailing out of the door before coming to a complete stop. He made it to the Buckner Ranch in record time. As soon as he heard Caleb's message, he wasted no time jumping in his truck and taking off. He returned Caleb's call once he was on the road. Caleb himself was headed toward home to be with his family, and he filled Noah in on as much as he knew.

Noah burst through the back door. Elaine and Beth were sitting at the kitchen table with Jane while Andrew and Eli hovered nearby. Jake was pacing nervously.

Jane rose when she saw him. He hurried to her side, wrapping his arms around her. "Any news?" he asked.

"No," she sobbed. "Nothing."

"We haven't heard anything since they found her cellphone in the parking lot at the bank," Beth added.

"Why did she go alone?" Noah asked. "Someone should have gone with her."

"I tried," Jane responded, her pitch shrill. "She said no. She said it would be quick and easy, and she would be fine." She began to cry even harder.

Noah looked around. "Where are the girls?"

"With Hannah," Eli answered. "She has them upstairs trying to keep them distracted playing with the twins."

"Do they know?"

Eli nodded his head, his expression glum.

"I'm sure they will feel better knowing you're here," Jane said. "I know they've missed you."

Noah took a deep breath and headed upstairs. As soon as Anna saw him, she threw herself into his arms, tears streaming down her face. She clung to him, her arms locking around his neck. He knelt to the floor, holding her tightly. He loosened one arm and held it open for Abby. She, too, ran to him, falling into his embrace. Balancing himself on his knees, he held the girls close, clinging to them as if his life depended on it. Seeing their worry and heartache only magnified his own. He silently prayed for the Lord's hand of protection and intervention as he himself felt helpless.

Anna, finally releasing her grasp of him, took a step back and wiped her eyes. "Will they find Momma?" Her voice was filled with uncertainty.

Noah did his best to keep his own emotions in check as he answered. "Yes, I believe they will. I've been praying nonstop for her."

"Me, too," Abby chimed in. "I know Jesus will bring Mommy home."

Noah smiled at the beautiful, innocent faith of this sweet, little girl. He wiped the tears from her cheeks and kissed her forehead.

"Noah?" He turned when Anna said his name. "Can you find Momma? Can you bring her home?"

Her innocent request ripped at his heart. He wanted nothing more than to do that exact thing. How could he tell her no? He sighed. "How about this, you stay here with Aunt Hannah and the twins while I go downstairs and talk to Grandma Jane and Grandpa Jake? Okay?"

Hannah called the girls to her, and Noah headed back downstairs.

"What are the police saying? What's the plan?" he inquired as he rounded the corner into the kitchen.

Jane was seated at the table again, dabbing at her eyes with a tissue. "They said they would let us know as soon as they know anything," she replied.

"So, we're supposed to just sit here and wait?" he questioned, his tone sharp with impatience.

No one answered. Jane began to cry again as Beth attempted to comfort her. Elaine sat with folded hands, praying quietly, and Jake continued to pace. Andrew and Eli stood expressionless.

"I can fly up there," Noah said. "I can help search for her."

Jane sniffled. "The police said they are doing everything they can. Until they locate her rental car, we don't even know where to look."

Before he could say anymore, Caleb walked through the door. "Have they found her yet?"

Jane rose and hugged her son. "No," she answered, shaking her head.

"It'll be okay, Mom," he soothed, "They'll find her. We have to keep praying."

Noah suddenly felt like the room was closing in around him. He rushed out the door onto the patio, pacing back and forth a few times before dropping to his knees. He raised his head when he felt a hand on his shoulder. Caleb was standing beside him. He looked at his friend. "I should have told her, Caleb. I should have told her how much I love her."

Caleb knelt beside him. "I believe you'll still get that chance," he said reassuringly. "Let's pray."

* * *

Ding. The low fuel light came on. Grace looked at Jared. They'd been driving for around two hours now, and she had no idea of their location. Jared was mostly avoiding main highways, and she was completely unfamiliar with any of the roadways they were traveling on or the small towns they were passing through. Maybe if they stopped for gas, she could find something that would give her some sort of indication as to where they were. She wasn't even sure they were in Idaho anymore.

Ding. There it was again. Jared still didn't flinch or seem to notice. She hesitated to speak, not sure which version of him was present with her at the moment. He hadn't spoken to her in over an hour.

Swallowing the lump in her throat, she spoke. "Are you going to stop for gas?"

Her voice seemed to draw him from his trance. He looked at the fuel gage and muttered a curse under his breath, clearly annoyed. "I guess I don't have a choice."

Swallowing once more and taking a deep breath for courage, she spoke again. "Where are we?"

She immediately regretted it.

He turned his head, glowering in her direction. "Don't ask that again, you hear me?"

She sank back into her seat, shifting her weight to scoot as close to the passenger side door as possible. She was becoming more and more certain Jared was teetering on the edge of a complete mental breakdown.

It wasn't long before they pulled in at a small, roadside gas station. It looked as old, dingy, and dirty as the motel they were at only a few hours earlier.

Jared scanned the parking lot before turning to her. "Do not get out of this car. If I have to come after you, it will not be fun for you. I promise." His eyes blazed as he pointed a finger in her face. "Got it?"

Grace nodded, not saying a word. She wasn't about to push her luck, especially not knowing where she was or anything about her surroundings. The day was slipping away, and the temperature was dropping as the sun began to sink on the horizon. Even if she success- fully escaped, if she found no one to help her, she would freeze to death before morning.

Jared returned from paying for the gas. He started the car and didn't drive far before stopping again. He was pulling into yet another crummy motel.

Grace found her voice again. "Why are we stopping here?"

This time he sneered when he answered, a wild look in his eyes. "We're staying the night."

A chill snaked its' way up her spine. The absolute last thing on this earth she wanted to do was spend the night in the same motel room as him, but she knew she had no choice. When he returned with a room key, she obediently followed him inside.

He tossed a plastic bag on the bed. It spilled open, revealing chips, sodas, and some peanuts. "Here. I got this at the gas station. It was all they had. Eat something."

She shook her head no. Even if she managed to eat a few bites, she had no doubts her stomach would make quick work of rejecting whatever she swallowed.

"Fine, don't eat." He took a bag of chips and soda from the bag before moving toward the window to scan the parking lot one last time. He locked the deadbolt on the door and scooted the table over in front of it. Turning back to her, he instructed, "Don't even think about trying to leave. I'll hear you move this table if you do, and I already told you it won't go well for you if I have to chase you." He then moved to the phone, disconnecting the cord from the wall before cutting it in two with a knife.

Grace felt her pulse quicken as she stared at him. A lump was forming in her throat again, but she swallowed it down. "I have to use the bathroom."

Jared eyed her with suspicion as he placed another handful of chips in his mouth. He walked to the bathroom, checking it over before motioning for her to go in. Just as she was about to close the door, he put his hand up to stop it. "The door stays open," he said, his glare burning into her.

She quickly used the restroom, splashed some cold water on her face, and exited the bathroom. Jared was stretched out on the bed, his eyes closed. She walked quietly to a chair and sat down.

Without opening his eyes, he addressed her. "Come to bed. We're leaving at daybreak."

When she didn't move or respond, he turned and leered at her. "Come lay down, Grace. I won't bite. I promise." When she still didn't move or respond, his eyes narrowed as a scowl crept across his face. "Get over here, Grace. I'm not asking."

Swallowing the bile rising in her throat, she rose from her chair and sat on the edge of the bed. She slowly lifted her legs and lay back, every muscle in her body tensed and trembling. Jared turned toward her, propping himself up with one elbow. He gazed at her in uncomfortable silence, his scowl morphing into a look that made her blood run cold. She was all too familiar with what that look meant. Fear, raw and paralyzing, seized her as his fingers traced a line down her throat and across her collarbone. Her heartbeat pounded a deafening cadence in her ears.

Suddenly, he jerked his hand away, almost as if her skin had burned him. He gazed at her a moment longer, his eyes still boring into her, but he lay back and turned away from her. "Get some sleep."

Grace breathed deeply, relief flooding her entire body. Her heart slowly began to resume its' normal pace. She lay in silence next to Jared for what seemed like hours. She wanted to stay awake and alert, but her body was beginning to give in to the exhaustion she was feeling. She was dozing in and out of sleep when she felt his arm reach across her middle, scooting himself closer to her. He didn't say a word, and his eyes remained closed. He appeared to be sleeping. He'd been murmuring off and on during the night, and he continued to do so now, his words not fully audible. She lay completely still, frozen in her spot, unsure whether he was really sleeping.

Then, plain as day, his utterances became clear. "I'm sorry, Grace. I'm sorry I hurt you. I'm sorry for everything. I'm sorry. I'm sorry..." His words trailed off, and when she turned to look at his face, he was sound asleep.

An unexpected ache swelled in her chest. Despite all he'd done to her in the past and all he was doing to her now, she knew he was a product of his childhood. A product of never dealing with the abuse he'd suffered at the hands of his father. A product of never seeking healing or forgiveness. A product of one wrong choice after another. If only he would have allowed Jesus into his heart, his entire life could have taken a completely different direction. As she lay there next to him, her kidnapper, she did something most people would never expect. She prayed for him.

* * *

"Wake up. It's time to go."Grace blinked her eyes a few times, slowly sitting up as she did. Jared was standing beside the bed, peering out the window. Light was just barely beginning to filter in. She rose to her feet and walked to the bathroom, not even attempting to close the door this time.

"Come on, let's go," he called after her.

He sounded more nervous than he was last night, agitated. She quickly finished and joined him, pulling on her coat as he retrieved the manila envelope from beside the bed.

Following him out the door, they moved hurriedly toward the rental car. Grace could sense something wasn't right. Jared was scanning their surroundings, tensing when he saw a man moving toward them. Stopping in his tracks, he pushed Grace behind him. When she glanced around his shoulder, she saw the gun pointed directly at them.

* * *

Noah entered the kitchen to the sound of glass shattering. Jane was standing at the sink, broken shards of glass scattered across the floor. She was pale as a ghost. Noah froze in his spot, looking from her to Caleb. "What's going on?"

"Help me get Mom to the table." Caleb's voice sounded strained, his expression grim.

Noah willingly took one of Jane's arms, helping maneuver her around the broken glass to a chair at the table. By the time they got her seated, she was sobbing uncontrollably. Noah felt his own anxiety level bordering new heights as his pulse quickened. "Someone tell me what's going on," he demanded.

Just as Caleb was about to answer, Jake walked in. Seeing the broken glass, he immediately went to his wife. "What's wrong?

What's happened?" he asked, concern deepening the lines around his mouth and between his brows.

Noah was about to lose it if someone didn't tell him something quick! "Caleb, what's going on? Is it Grace?" His heart was trying to beat its' way out of his chest.

Caleb nodded. "Yes, they found her rental car."

"What? When?" he exclaimed.

"A little less than an hour ago. They found it at a roadside motel near Bondurant, Wyoming, not far from Jackson Hole."

Noah stared at Caleb, his brow creased. "Wyoming? What is she doing in Wyoming?"

"I don't know," he said, lowering his eyes. "They didn't find her, just her car. But there's more." He looked from Jake to Noah, his expression an odd mix of emotions Noah couldn't read. "They fingerprinted a soda can they found in the cup holder. The prints don't belong to Grace."

Noah continued to stare at him, his pulse pounding wildly in his ears. He was afraid to ask but did so anyway. "Do they know who?"

Caleb slowly nodded, his forehead creased with worry. "Jared."

Noah sucked in sharply, dropping into a chair near him. He felt like someone had kicked him in the gut.

Jake, too, sat down next to his wife, shaking his head in disbelief. "I don't understand," he said to his son. "Jared is dead."

"The police don't think so," Caleb answered. "Apparently the FBI had been investigating him for fraud and money laundering. They believe he was in business with some very dangerous men. They think he faked his death."

"And now he's got Grace!" Jane bellowed, crying out.

Noah stood from his seat, his mind racing. He started pacing back and forth across the kitchen, avoiding the glass. "What are they going to do? How are they going to find her?"

Caleb shook his head, shrugging his shoulders. "I don't know. They said they would broaden their search around the area where the car was found, but they don't know how they're traveling now. The car was found at a motel, but Jared and Grace were not there. The manager said a man fitting Jared's description paid cash for a room last night, but he never saw him after he checked in. He didn't check out this morning, but the room was empty."

"What about Grace? Did he see her?" Noah was bordering on desperation for answers.

Caleb shook his head, looking disheartened. "No, he didn't see her. And the cameras facing the parking lot don't work," he said, gritting his teeth.

Jake asked the one question Noah was thinking but couldn't bring himself to voice out loud. "Caleb, tell us the truth," he said, his tone serious. "Do they think she's still alive?"

Jane wailed at the question, and Noah struggled not to vomit the bile rising in his throat. His stomach lurched and churned wildly.

Thankfully, Caleb nodded his head. "Yes, they haven't found any indication she's been harmed. They checked the car and motel room for blood and bodily fluids but found nothing."

Bodily fluids. Noah again fought the urge to vomit as his stomach lurched yet again. He tried not to think about scenarios involving bodily fluids. "What do we do now?" he asked. "I can't keep waiting around like this, doing nothing!"

Caleb grasped him firmly on the shoulder. "I know," he said. "That's why you and I are flying to Wyoming."

* * *

Grace stumbled through the heavy snow, the cold stinging her hands and face. Jared was doing his best to help her, supporting some of her weight as they trudged over the snow covered, rocky terrain. It felt like they'd been walking for miles, and her feet were frozen. No one had said anything since they stepped out of the SUV. They'd been forced out of the vehicle at gunpoint, no choice but to traipse off into the wilderness.

Jared had asked the man where he was taking them. He'd even tried to get him to let Grace go. The man, however, scoffed, telling Jared to be quiet or he would put a bullet in him right there in the backseat of the vehicle. His laugh was sinister when he said he didn't really want to do that because it would permanently damage his leather seats. Then snickering again, he said they would find out soon enough where they were going.

Grace was far too terrified to speak at all. She didn't really need to ask where they were going because she already knew beyond the shadow of a doubt this man was going to kill them and dispose of their bodies. Her body quaked with each breath she took. It felt as if the despair engulfing her might extinguish her last breath at any moment. All she could do was think of her girls and how she would never see them again. She hoped and prayed they would always know and remember her love for them. And Noah. If only she'd told him how much she loved him. At least he would know. But instead, it seemed she was taking it to her grave.

"Right here looks good," the man said, halting them in their tracks. He walked to the edge of a steep drop off and peered over. "Yep, this should do just fine," he said, sneering. He motioned with the gun for them to move closer to the edge. "You see, I figure if I shoot you two right here, you'll just fall on off into that ravine down there. I won't have to touch your bodies and risk getting blood on my good clothes," he sniggered, "and no one will find you until all this snow melts. Win, win don't you say?" He winked as a foul grin turned up at the corners of his mouth.

Jared spoke up. "You have the money, and you have me. Let her go," he said, motioning to Grace. "She has no part in this."

The man wagged his gun back and forth as he clicked his tongue. "No, no, no," he said mockingly, "No witnesses. Those were my orders. And what can I say," he said, shrugging his shoulders, "I'm a man of my word." His lips curled as he continued to sneer at them. "Now, if that's all, let's go ahead and get this over with." He raised the gun, pointing it at Grace, a strange look of pleasure flashing in his eyes. "I think I'll shoot her first so you can watch her die."

Grace held her breath, turning her face to Jared. He met her stare, a look in his eyes she'd never seen before. Was it fear? Was it dread? He silently mouthed, "I'm sorry, Grace." And with that, he lunged in front of her just as the man pulled the trigger.

The bullet struck his right side, causing him to recoil at the force. He grasped his side, blood covering his shirt and hands. Then, looking at the man, he lunged for him. The gun went off multiple times, riddling his body with bullets. But somehow, despite his wounds, he managed to grab the man around the neck and drag him over the edge. Grace watched helplessly as both men fell from the cliff and out of sight into the snow-covered ravine below.

She collapsed to her knees, overcome by it all. She gasped for air as she cried, the cold, wet snow penetrating her jeans and stinging her ungloved hands. She sucked in several breaths and attempted to stand, but her right leg almost buckled under her. When she looked down the snow was stained red, and her pant leg was drenched in blood. She suddenly felt a burning sensation in her upper thigh. *I've been shot.*

Adrenaline took over as her brain and body shifted into survival mode. She quickly removed her belt, wrapping it around her leg just above the entry wound and tightening it as much as she could. It didn't help that her fingers felt frozen and didn't want to bend. Then, mustering all her strength, she retraced the footprints in the snow as she started toward the road. She prayed she would make it back to the SUV before she either bled to death or hypothermia set in.

By the time Grace stepped through the clearing and the vehicle was in sight, she was practically dragging her leg, the pain almost unbearable. As she pulled on the driver's side handle, the door opened. And sure enough, as she felt for the keys with frozen fingers, they were there, in the ignition and ready. She turned the key and the vehicle roared to life. She quickly fumbled with the heat and buckled her seatbelt.

As she started down the mountain backroad from the direction they had come, she could feel the dizziness setting in. She struggled to focus on the road, her vision blurring. She was growing more and more lightheaded, everything closing in around her, turning dark. She fought to keep her eyes open, but it was no use. She'd lost too much blood and was losing consciousness. Everything went black.

* * *

Noah hadn't left Grace's bedside since he and Caleb arrived at the hospital. No more had they stepped off the plane and their phones were buzzing with messages. Grace had been found! She was taken to the hospital and was in ICU. They rushed straight from the airport to the hospital, anxious to see her and find out more about her condition.

Once there, they quickly learned the doctors and nurses would only talk to family and would only allow family to visit. Thankfully, with Caleb being her brother, there was no issue for him. Noah, however, found himself on the outside looking in, thinking there was no way he would be allowed to see her. But thanks to Caleb's quick thinking, their problem was solved. As soon as the nurses questioned who Noah was, Caleb immediately responded, "This is her fiancé." No one questioned him anymore after that, and he hoped more than anything he would get the opportunity to make that statement true.

As he sat watching her sleep, tubes and hoses stretching from her to the multiple machines surrounding her bed, he felt overwhelmed and more than a little frightened. But in his fear, he prayed. God had answered their prayers for Grace to be found alive, and Noah had no reason to believe he would stop answering their prayers now.

Caleb slowly slid the door open, stepping inside around the curtain. The bright light temporarily stung Noah's eyes. The nurses were keeping the room dark for Grace. They said it would help her brain and body rest so she could heal.

"What did you find out?" he asked Caleb.

"I've been outside talking to the police, the FBI, *and* the doctor," he answered. "This is one complicated situation," he said, shaking his head. "The police said Grace was found inside a wrecked SUV on a mountain backroad not far from here. He said it's a miracle she was found at all. That road stays pretty deserted this time of year, but some people out snowmobiling came across her and called 911."

Noah offered his silent thanks to God for sending those people to find her. He knew beyond the shadow of a doubt that was the

Lord's hand at work in all of this. "What else?" he asked. "What about Jared?"

Caleb shook his head, shrugging his shoulders. "They don't know where he is. Grace was the only one in the SUV, and she was driving when it wrecked. The FBI agents haven't been able to find out any other information because she's been unconscious since they brought her in." He looked at his sister, his expression pained.

Noah furrowed his brow. "Did the SUV belong to Jared?"

"No, they said it's registered to a man named Jack Pelosi. They wouldn't share any information about him other than his name is well known to them, and he is a person of interest in all of this."

Noah shook his head. "I still can't believe this is happening. It seems like a bad dream." He looked at Grace again. "Do they know what caused the wreck?"

"Yes, blood loss." He motioned to her right leg. "That gunshot wound in her upper thigh probably sent her into shock. She lost a lot of blood before they found her. The doctor said she likely blacked out. But he also said the EMTs found a belt tightened around her leg just above the wound. They said it probably saved her life. She would have died without it."

Noah rubbed his forehead. Gunshot wounds and blood loss were things he knew about from his time in the military, but those weren't things he ever expected to deal with at home, especially not with Grace. He watched her motionless body, listening to the repetitive beeping of the machines. Even though she wasn't responding to his touch, he was holding her hand just the same. "I wish she would open her eyes," he said, his voice barely above a whisper.

Caleb put his hand on Noah's shoulder. "We need to give her body time to rest. She's been through a lot. They gave her a blood transfu-

sion, and she also has a concussion from the wreck along with hypothermia from exposure to the cold. The doctor said any of those could
be what's keeping her knocked out." Caleb paused and sighed heavily.
When Noah turned to him, he was gazing at his sister with watery eyes.
"We just need to keep praying. If this goes on for too long, the doctor
said she could slip into a coma."

* * *

Grace wandered down the narrow path, an array of colors spread before
her as fragrant blooms lined both sides of the walkway. A cool breeze
wafted across her face, tousling her hair. She closed her eyes, taking in
a long, slow breath. The air smelled sweet, like lavender and roses. It
reminded her of her mother's flower garden, and she smiled.

Above her, an expansive archway was draped with plentiful vines
of wisteria, clusters of pink and violet dangling just above her head.
Brilliant rays of light shone through narrow openings, warming her
skin. She smiled. This place was beautiful, peaceful. A feeling of contentment wrapped around her and warmed her from the inside out.

As she continued down the path, the archway came to an end,
revealing an open field of soft, green grass rippling in the breeze. She
stepped onto the spongy ground, letting her bare toes sink into the cool,
lush grass. She closed her eyes once again, sighing deeply. She felt at
peace here.

The sound of laughter drew her attention. Two little girls danced
and twirled about in the open field, giggling as they reached to catch
soft, pink flower petals floating through the air. When they saw her,
they smiled and waved, giggling some more before skipping over a hill
and out of sight. Her heart swelled. These were not just any little girls.

These were her girls. She quickly moved after them, the long, wavy grass tickling her feet and ankles.

As she rounded the top of the hill, a shimmering lake came into view, glistening like crystal in the summer sun. It had the appearance of etched glass as rays of light cascaded across the water. A gentle breeze danced at the water's surface causing tiny, iridescent peaks to rise and fall.

More giggling drew her attention. Just to her right, her girls were skipping up the stairs of a wooden gazebo situated at the water's edge. A path of lilacs and honeysuckle paved the way, and more grapelike clusters of wisteria dangled from the rounded ceiling. Following the path, she paused as she reached the top step of the gazebo, watching as her girls stood beside a man standing in the center. He was gazing serenely out across the water, and he was holding something in his arms. She leaned to the side, peering around him just enough to see. It was a baby. A beautiful, baby boy. She looked to her girls again, feeling confused. Who was this man?

She continued watching, not making a sound. Anna stood leaning against the man's side, sweetly kissing the baby's cheek, while little Abby held tightly to his opposite hand. Turning and smiling at her mother, she tugged on his arm. "Daddy, Mommy's here," she said quietly. Grace held her breath as the man turned his face to hers.

CHAPTER 18

G race slowly opened her eyes, blinking several times to clear the fog. Everything was blurry, and she felt indescribably dizzy. As she attempted to look around, trying to focus, a wave of nausea washed over her. *Don't throw up. Don't throw up.* She fought to gain control. She reached to rub her forehead, a throbbing sensation pounding away near her temples, but her arm caught. She tugged again, creating a stinging sensation in the top of her hand. Out of alarm, feeling disoriented and confused, she pulled harder. But something stopped her. Someone grabbed her wrist, pulling her arm down. Panic set in as she fought to move, fought to see. *Where am I? What's happening?* She was screaming on the inside, but her words made no sound.

"Grace. Grace. It's okay. Grace."

Someone was saying her name. She blinked several more times, her body tense, her heart pounding. She tried to focus on the direction the voice was coming from, turning her head to the left. She immediately regretted it. The nausea overtook her, and she couldn't stop it. She threw up. She lay back, dizzy and sick to her stomach. The throbbing in her temples now felt like someone was using her head as a bass drum.

Someone took hold of her arm again. But this time, she didn't have the strength to fight. She kept her eyes closed, trying to keep the nausea at bay. She took several slow breaths, trying to will her body to cooperate.

"Don't worry. That should help her relax."

The voice speaking was unfamiliar. She was trying to make sense of what was happening, but her mind was growing foggy again. She tried to open her eyes, tried to blink, but her eyelids felt like someone had attached ten-pound weights to them. She tried to fight it, tried to stay awake, but it was impossible. She couldn't stop the sleep that was now forcing itself upon her.

* * *

Noah and Jane stared helplessly at Grace. She was pale, sweating, and covered in vomit. Her nurse had administered a medication of some sort through her IV to calm her and was now injecting a second vial of something. "What is that?" Jane questioned.

"This should help control the nausea," the nurse answered. "Hopefully she won't feel quite so sick when she wakes up." She smiled reassuringly at them. "Don't worry. This is all normal considering the trauma her body has endured. And now that she's calm, if you'll give us just a minute, we'll get her cleaned up." She ushered them out the door.

Once in the hallway, Noah leaned against the wall, scrubbing both hands down his face. He had hardly slept or ate in almost a week. His mind and body felt weak and exhausted. He was trying to stay strong, but it was tearing him up inside. And just when Grace was finally waking up, an answer to their prayers, she had to be sedated.

Jane touched his shoulder. "You really need to eat something and get some rest. None of us are any good to Grace if we aren't taking care of ourselves."

He knew she was right. He was pushing his body beyond the breaking point, and something had to give. He looked at his watch. "How long will the sedative last?"

Jane offered a slight smile, her eyes filled with understanding. "She will probably be asleep for at least a few hours, maybe longer. Now is a good time for you to get some food in your belly and take a little nap."

Noah nodded in agreement, following her to the waiting room. When they walked in, Jake and Caleb rose to their feet. "Any changes?" Jake was quick to ask.

Jane offered another slight smile. "Well, she opened her eyes a little and seemed to be waking up, but they had to sedate her. She was disoriented and pulling on her IV. She was trying to move around and ended up throwing up all over herself. They asked us to step out so they could clean her up."

Noah plopped down in a chair, resting his head in his hands. Caleb walked over, nudging his foot with his shoe. "Come on brother, you need to eat. You look rough. I'll go with you."

Noah raised his head, sighing heavily. "That's what your mom said, too."

Caleb chuckled. "Then you better listen! Come on, Grace would not be happy if she knew you were going without food *and* sleep. You need to take care of yourself so you're strong enough to take care of her when she does wake up."

Dragging himself out of the chair, he followed Caleb to the hospital cafeteria. "I just want to grab something quick and get back up there."

"Sure, whatever you want. I just want to get some sort of sustenance in you." Caleb eyed him uncertainly. "You think you can stay awake long enough to eat?"

Noah honestly wasn't sure. His body was getting weaker and weaker. "I don't know," he answered. "I hope so."

In the hospital cafeteria the two men settled on their choices, paid for their food, and took it back with them to the ICU waiting room. Noah sat down in a recliner and opened his sandwich. The wrapper said it was chicken salad, and it had the texture of chicken salad, but it was tasteless. He wasn't sure if it was the chicken salad itself or if it was him. Regardless, he scarfed it down in no time, realizing how hungry he really was once he swallowed the first bite. Setting the empty wrapper aside, he kicked up his feet and put his head back. Maybe he would rest his eyes for just a few minutes...

"Noah, Noah, she's awake!"

Jane's voice startled him from his sleep. Temporarily forgetting where he was, he leapt from the chair, stumbling over the footrest of the recliner as he did. His heart was racing, beating wildly in his ears. Apparently, he'd done a little more than just rest his eyes.

"What? When? How long has she been awake?" He tried to look at his watch, but his eyes wouldn't focus.

"Just a few minutes," she responded, beaming at him. "Caleb is with her now. Jake and I came out so you can go in."

Noah thought his heart might explode with gratitude. *Thank you, Lord! Thank you! Thank you! Thank you!*

* * *

Grace held onto her brother's hand, not wanting to take her eyes off him. It felt so good to see his face, to know she was safe and had survived. This time when she woke, she didn't feel nearly as disoriented as she had the first time. Her head was still pounding, but the dizziness and nausea were drastically less, lingering only slightly in the background. Waking up to see her family surrounding her, hearing their voices, left her feeling thankful beyond words. She wasn't sure any greater feeling in this world existed. Only seeing her girls could make this moment any sweeter. She understood, however, why everyone thought it was best for them to wait in Texas. She didn't really want Anna or Abby to see her like this anyway.

Just then the door slid open, and Noah stepped inside. As soon as she saw him, tears began to cloud her vision. She had been wrong when she thought nothing could make this day, this moment, any sweeter. Just the sight of him stole her breath.

Caleb released her hand and rose from where he was seated beside her. He smiled and turned to exit the room, clapping Noah on the shoulder as he passed by.

Noah moved to her bedside, his eyes searching hers. Silent tears were spilling as he softly caressed her cheek. She closed her eyes, leaning into his touch. Then grasping his hand with hers, she pulled him closer, clinging tightly as she wrapped her arms around him. Her IV pulled slightly in her hand, but she didn't care. Noah was here, and she was never letting him go again.

* * *

Grace was released from the hospital one week after regaining consciousness. Considering all she'd been through, she was grateful her stay wasn't extended any longer. Her doctor said she was doing extremely well, and he saw no reason to keep her. She could continue her recovery from the comfort of home.

The FBI and police who were working her case also gave the green light for her to head back to Texas. She had given them all the information she could, and they would contact her if they needed anything further. Before leaving, they shared with her they had successfully located the bodies of the two men in the canyon based on the information she provided. Her heart ached anytime she thought of Jared and how he had sacrificed himself to save her. The man had done many cruel and terrible things to her, but in that moment, when she needed him most, he stepped up in a way she never imagined. For her, he became the miracle she was praying for to survive.

The happiness she felt being back home with her girls and her family was a feeling she couldn't put into words. And Noah. She couldn't even begin to describe the love she felt for him. During her time in the hospital, she had apologized repeatedly for not being honest with him and for letting fear get the best of her. Facing death and coming out alive had a way of putting things into perspective. Grace had learned firsthand that life is too short to let fear hold you back from sharing your heart, and it gave her the courage she needed to tell Noah she loved him.

Noah had responded with a kiss that spoke of his love and of their future, touching the deepest depths of her heart. Then he said the words she already knew were true, "I love you, Grace. I always have." And she believed him with every fiber of her being.

Noah also admitted his own responsibility in creating the separation that had plagued their relationship, telling her he never should have walked away like he did. He apologized for being too stubborn to contact her after he left. They both agreed they shared fault in the situation, vowing to never let anything come between them again. And now, with open honesty and their future before them, their friendship was transforming into something beautiful, something Grace had always dreamed of.

She wasn't even upset when she found out the part her mother had played, mailing the letter to him. In fact, it touched her heart knowing her mother wasn't willing to simply stand by and let them both allow fear and stubbornness to come between them. While Jane Buckner had always given her children plenty of freedom to make their own choices, *and* mistakes, Grace was thankful for her intervention this time.

* * *

Grace was enjoying her favorite morning routine, sipping coffee on the back patio, when Noah approached. She turned from the railing she rested against, a smile playing on her lips. Her heart gave a flutter at the sight of him. Those heart-stopping blue eyes were locked on her, stealing her breath and sending heat spiraling through her veins.

"How about we start the day off with a ride?" he asked, grinning down at her. "Is your leg up to it?"

She instinctively touched her right leg, feeling the scar left behind from where a stray bullet had penetrated her upper thigh. "I think so. It doesn't bother me nearly as much it did. It just *looks* awful," she said, rolling her eyes.

Noah sidled in close, slipping his arms around her waist. "Doesn't make a bit of difference to me," he said, pulling her against him. "I love you just the same, bullet holes or no bullet holes." His roguish grin sent his pulse skittering as he leaned in for a kiss.

She playfully slapped his chest as she pretended to push him away, rolling her eyes again. "Ha, ha, very funny," she said dryly.

Noah chuckled. "Come on, I've got the horses saddled." He stole another kiss before taking her hand, intertwining her fingers with his. He tugged her along beside him, grinning the whole way.

As they entered the long hallway of the stall barn, Grace looked at Noah, pinching her brow. Something was different about him this morning. She couldn't quite put her finger on it, but something was different about the way he was looking at her. A broad grin framed his handsome face and his eyes sparkled, an ocean of blue she could get lost in. She felt her heart flutter yet again.

At the far end of the hallway, two horses stood ready and waiting. A beautiful bouquet of red roses was resting atop one of the saddles, and Grace smiled warmly, nipping her lip. Reaching to take the flowers, she inhaled deeply, delighting in the sweetness of their fragrance. When she turned, Noah was kneeling in front of her, resting his weight on one knee. Her eyes rounded as she drew a hand to her mouth.

"Grace, I've always loved you and always will. I know what it's like to live without you, and I don't ever want to experience that again. I'd be the happiest man alive if you'd do me the honor of being my wife." His eyes never left hers as he opened a small, mahogany box revealing a stunning, pear-shaped diamond ring. "Will you marry me?"

She took in a breath, nodding her head as soft tears blanketed her cheeks. "Yes! Yes, Noah! A thousand times, yes!"

He took her left hand, placing the ring on her finger. The dim lighting of the barn intermingled with the early morning sun as it cascaded across the diamond. Shimmering rays of light danced from her finger. As she looked from the ring to the man she would spend the rest of her life with, she knew beyond the shadow of a doubt she was exactly where God intended her to be.

Standing to his feet, Noah took her in his arms, lifting her from the ground and pulling her close. A giggle tripped from her lips as she wrapped her arms around his neck. A ribbon of warmth snaked its' way up her spine, flooding her with utter contentment.

Noah carefully returned her feet to the ground before gently cradling her face in his hands. "I love you, Grace." As he drew his lips to hers, she was anticipating his kiss, returning it with fervor. The chains that had held her back were no more. Where fear had once reigned, only love remained.

EPILOGUE
TWO YEARS LATER...

Noah put the truck in park, grinning broadly as he did. He was practically bursting with excitement, and it was written all across his face. Grace smiled at him. She couldn't help but share in the anticipation he was feeling. This was a day they'd all been looking forward to for a few weeks now, especially him.

As she stepped from the passenger side door, her girls were already unbuckled and standing patiently to the side. They both were grinning from ear to ear, fidgeting with eagerness. Grace smiled at them as she maneuvered to the backseat, gently unbuckling her sleeping newborn. As she lifted him from his car seat, Noah was right there, ready to cradle him in his arms. She willingly handed him over, receiving a tender kiss from her husband as she did.

After retrieving the diaper bag and closing the door, she turned to her husband and children. Noah had their son gently cradled in the crook of his arm with Anna and Abby standing on either side of him. Anna softly kissed her brother's cheek while Abby clung tightly to Noah's free hand. Turning to her mother, she smiled sweetly and said, "Come on, Momma, let's go see Daddy's family."

Grace smiled warmly. She had thought often of the vision the Lord had given her while she lay unconscious in the hospital in Wyoming. The chain of events that had put her there very well could have taken her life, but by His grace, it was the start of a new beginning. She believed that dream was the Lord's way of guiding her, telling her to trust her heart and to trust Him. And now here she stood, that vision coming to fruition right before her eyes.

She joined her family just as the back door opened. Sol and Katie Ann stepped outside. Their own excitement was evident by the broad smiles etching their faces. Noah stepped forward, beaming with pride. "*Daed, Mamm,* meet your grandson, Solomon Jacob."

Katie Ann clutched a hand to her chest as her forehead pinched in elation. "*Ach,* Noah, he is a beautiful *boppli*!" she exclaimed, reaching to take her grandson in her arms.

Sol, moving to stand next to his son, firmly clasped his shoulder, nodding his head in approval. Even though he may never voice it aloud, Grace knew he was deeply touched by their decision to name their son after him. She smiled warmly as her heart overflowed. And lifting her eyes to heaven, she offered the Lord a silent prayer of thanksgiving, thanking Him for showing her His abundant grace.

Made in the USA
Monee, IL
28 June 2025

20154040R00184